LONG SHADOW

VEILED INTENTIONS
BOOK 2

ELLE KEATON

ONE

NIALL

Niall jabbed the Down button viciously with his index finger.

The sailing to Piedras left in two hours, and he was damn well going to be on it. He was done with Seattle; he didn't belong here anymore.

Getting home, no matter how fuzzy the idea of home was, was more important to him than meeting with the perky real estate agent again, more important than handing over the keys to his condo—he'd drop them in the mail—more important than making sure all his moving boxes were properly labeled. Niall couldn't stand another day with those four walls closing in on him. The city had trapped him, with its cement walls and gleaming office buildings; the entire time he'd been away from Piedras he'd paced back and forth like a captive animal in its tiny cage. He missed his dog, he missed his crappy motel room, and it was possible he missed Sheriff Mat Dempsey, but *that* he wasn't ready to admit.

The display above the elevator doors indicated the car had moved up one floor and then stopped.

"Jesus Christ." Unwilling to wait a second longer, Niall took the stairs to the lobby two at a time, letting gravity carry him downward. His heavy footsteps created a cacophony in the empty stairwell.

Most of his belongings were in storage now. Niall had been surprised to discover that, except for his furniture, his life fit in an eight-by-five storage unit with room to spare. The furniture he'd left behind for the agent, telling him to donate it once the sale went through. Niall didn't care about it, and it likely wouldn't fit when he rebuilt his cabin.

He hit the ground floor landing with a crashing *boom* and burst out into the tiny lobby, very nearly running into the delivery driver standing there.

"Shit. Sorry," Niall said.

He went to swerve around the younger man, trying to regain his escape velocity.

"Any chance you know Niall Hamarsson?" the man asked.

Niall jolted to a stop, twisting around to stare at the driver.

"That's me," he replied. What were the chances?

A small box was tucked under the driver's arm. "I have a delivery, if you wouldn't mind signing for it."

After digging his wallet out to show ID, Niall scrawled his signature next to the X, and the driver handed him the box. "Thank you," Niall said automatically.

The driver grinned at him and turned away, pushing through the lobby doors and leaving Niall staring after him. Shaking his head he glanced at the box, but the return address—downtown Seattle, by the zip code—showed no name. He didn't have time to deal with the contents right now.

Snapping back to his objective—*escape*—Niall headed to the parking garage, where his car was parked in the loading zone, a suitcase of clothing and a few boxes of belongings jammed inside it. He slid behind the wheel, tossing the package on the passenger seat along with the stack of mail that had been jammed into his mailbox, and started the engine. If traffic wasn't completely fucked, he'd make the next ferry. If it was, he'd be spending hours in his car waiting for the one after that.

Niall drove as fast as he could without catching the attention of the highway patrol. The Subaru's elderly stereo system belted out Nirvana's *Nevermind* on repeat. He'd been a young teen when Nirvana was big, but Cobain's lyrics still appealed to the wounded, animalistic, *angry* side of him.

Outside Mount Vernon, an RV pulled out in front of him. Swearing, he swerved into the slow lane to avoid hitting it. A horn blared from behind him, and the box slid off the passenger seat into the footwell. The first lines of "Come as You Are," raspy and painful, sounded from the speakers. Niall took a deep breath and slowed his speed. He didn't need to get in an accident now, not when he was almost there. Almost home.

But it wasn't until he was at the top of the hill heading down toward the ticket booth and saw the ferry pulling in to the dock that he was able to stop pounding the heel of his hand on the steering wheel in impatience. And it wasn't until he'd been directed onto the ferry deck, the big engines rumbling underneath him, that he was able to breathe again.

Upstairs in the passenger area, the change of season from winter to spring was evident in the number of families heading to the islands for the weekend. Children ran back and forth, excitedly peering out the floor-to-ceiling windows or begging their parents to go on the outside deck. Niall claimed an empty booth where he could spread out and watch the water and islands pass by.

In the past he'd never thought he would get tired of the city. Now he'd been away from Piedras for a little over a week and thought he was going to suffocate from the buildings, the cars, the people, and his tiny condo on the twelfth floor. Years ago, after high school, he'd been on a mission to get away from the islands and the small-minded people there. Staying on Piedras had not been part of his life plan. No, he was going to be the best damn cop he could be, the best *homicide* cop. He was going to give others what he and his grandparents never had—he was going to bring closure to families.

To some extent, he had. Niall had had a very high solve rate. But it came with a cost, one he couldn't afford anymore. The cold cases haunted him. The guilt when victims' families called, emailed, or even visited him in person to ask if there was anything new, if there was… anything. When the answer was no, Niall's thoughts always returned to his own mother and how her disappearance had gone unnoticed for weeks and was still unsolved. Would never be solved.

Ana was a ghost looking over his shoulder, demanding closure, telling him he hadn't tried hard enough, wasn't dedicated enough, wasn't good enough. Numbers didn't matter; her specter was louder. On the opposite shoulder lurked a devil who whispered that Ana Hamarsson hadn't disappeared, she'd just run away from her son and the responsibilities of parenthood. For the most part, Niall managed to ignore the malevolent demon. And while he'd never tried to find her, he had little doubt she was dead.

A fuzzy-headed blond child toddled by at full speed, a similarly fuzzy-headed man hurrying to catch them from behind. The child shrieked with laughter at being able to outrun their parent. As they closed in on the booth Niall occupied, the child stumbled and would've smacked headfirst into the table if Niall hadn't reached out and grabbed one arm.

The child giggled, unaware they had barely avoided tragedy.

"Thank you! She's deceptively fast. Hopefully after this, she'll fall asleep," the father said.

"No problem."

Niall went back to staring out the window, but the dark

waters outside had no answers for him. As lousy a mother as Ana Hamarsson had been, she didn't deserve to disappear without a trace. In the late 1980s, the Green River Killer had still been trolling Seattle and its suburbs for vulnerable women, and Ana had definitely fallen into that category, but her murder was not among those the killer eventually confessed to. Niall suspected she'd gotten into a killer's car willingly though, and that had been that.

Sometimes Niall hoped she'd just run away to a better life, but as an adult he knew how impossible that would have been for her, an addict whose overwhelming drive was finding her next fix. He sighed, wanting to think about anything but his mother, but for some reason he couldn't shake Ana tonight. She'd disappeared sometime in late fall or early winter, leaving Niall behind with her druggie friends. But no one knew exactly how long she had been gone, only that she'd left her young son behind, hidden in a closet for days. He supposed he was lucky that one of her less-terrible friends dropped him off near a police station instead of pushing him off a pier or selling him to someone for drugs.

All Niall remembered was walking for what seemed like a long time and being hungry but too afraid to say anything. Then he'd been told to sit on a bench and not to move or the bogeyman would get him, and the person with him had left. He'd sat there for hours, needing to use the bathroom, too petrified to do anything—even cry—until someone realized he was alone and alerted the police. Niall wished he could remember the officer's name. She'd knelt in front of him and asked him why he was there, if he was okay. Niall had had to think about it, but he'd been told not to move, not that he couldn't talk to people. He'd liked her shiny badge.

Finally, the ferry bumped against the pilings of Hidden Harbor, dragging him from his memories. Niall made his way down to his car, glad to be back on the island. He'd missed it: the island, his dog.

And the damn sheriff.

As uncomfortable as he'd been in the city, Niall was shocked at the intense relief he felt at the sight of the island. Not at all like when he'd come back in February, fleeing his old life with no plan in mind, only knowing he couldn't go on as he had been. This time Piedras felt a lot like home, and not just because of whatever was going on between him and Mat Dempsey. Now Niall felt a mix of hope and something like... optimism... about the future.

Niall pulled into the Orca Motel parking lot and turned off the engine. Even the sight of the shabby motel, built in the seventies or early eighties, didn't dampen his spirits. It took a couple trips to bring in and unload the boxes he'd brought with him, then he stacked them along one wall. There were only five of them, but they seemed to take up a lot of space in the small room. The boxes contained the few things he honestly cared about: photo albums that had belonged to his grandparents, his favorite books, service awards from SPD.

On the last trip to the car, he remembered the package he'd received earlier that day and grabbed it and the mail. Inside, he tossed it on the desk and sat down on the edge of the bed. He was suspicious of the parcel and didn't want to open it. Whatever it held could wait until morning—or longer.

TWO
MAT

"Jesus Christ," Mat muttered as he climbed out of his cruiser.

Orange-red flames licked the sides of the old wooden building, dancing up into the night sky. Matt could feel the heat from where he stood, well back from the building. It was—had been—a hay barn originally, a picturesque building tourists often stopped to take photos of during the summer months.

There'd been a spate of fires across the island, including the one at the Hamarsson place, the last one before today's. Most of them had been set in empty or abandoned buildings. By Mat's count, this was the fourth since January. At first, Mat had thought the perpetrators were teenagers and he hadn't lumped those other fires in the same category with Niall's cabin burning. But now he was concerned the island had an arsonist.

The pump engine had arrived before him. Mat was always impressed by how quickly and efficiently the volunteers got themselves set up. Water was already pouring onto the flames, the firefighters' silhouettes delineated by the scintillating glow, a mesmerizing dance of men and elements.

This time it was one of Merle Wainwright's outbuildings turning to ash. Mat didn't know for certain it was the work of the same person, but soon enough they'd have state investigators out seeing if they could establish a pattern, and Mat wouldn't be surprised if they decided all the fires were related somehow. This seemed like more than vandalism, more than the car prowls that also had been on the uptick in recent months.

"Did you have anything inside?" Mat asked Merle.

"No, it was empty. Me and the missus were thinking about remodeling it, making it into one of those places people will stay for a lot of money. 'Stay in a real barn' kind of thing. But we hadn't got around to it."

"Well, I'm sorry." Mat looked up toward the Wainwrights' residence. He could see a lone figure, Wainwright's wife, standing on the front porch.

"Give my regards to Joella. Flynn will be by in the next few days to go over everything with you."

Wainwright shrugged, his shoulders slumped in defeat as he watched the flames winning the battle.

Eyes searching the group of firefighters, Mat spotted Devon Flynn barking out orders to his crew. Devon was the recently promoted—and paid—fire chief for the island's mostly volunteer department. He had to be concerned about the fires. Mat strode over to talk to him, staying out of the way of the hose and the team operating it.

"What do you think?" Mat asked.

"I think we have a problem," Devon answered grimly.

"Me too. This is the last thing we need right now, some sicko setting fire to the island."

"It's bad for everyone."

Mat knew what Devon meant. A firebug was bad for the island economy as well as a danger to the residents. They needed to figure out who was behind the fires before tourist season—and before the rains stopped. Never in his life had Mat hoped the wet weather would last just a little while longer.

"Thanks for coming to the funeral," Mat said, recalling the last time he'd seen Devon.

Not quite a month ago, Mat had watched as his older brother's coffin was lowered into the ground. He and his sisters had stood with his mother, holding her up while she cried. Mat hadn't cried. He felt guilty about that, but he was also angry with Sean.

After the shady stuff his brother had been up to before he'd been killed, Mat wouldn't have been surprised if no one had come to see him laid to rest, but most of the island residents had come to say their farewells and offer Mat and his family condolences.

"That's what friends are for."

"Well, it's appreciated. I'll let you get back to work. Unless you need me to stay?"

Mat was tired. It had been a long week—*month, year*—and he was feeling worn down. He had a brief fantasy where everyone on Piedras behaved long enough that he was able to catch up on his sleep. Then he laughed because it would never happen.

Devon looked sideways at him. Mat shook his head. "Nothing."

"Get out of here. I'll send you the report. We can meet in the morning?"

Mat agreed, knowing a few hours' sleep would help his thinking.

On his way back down Merle's long driveway, Mat kept his eyes out for anyone who looked out of place, someone who didn't belong. What would that look like on an island the size of Piedras? Most of the population was probably lined up along the side of the road rubbernecking. If it was one of them—and likely it was—it was going to be difficult for Mat or Devon to catch them until they made a mistake. Hopefully, it wouldn't be a mistake that cost lives.

It was nearly ten at night. There were fewer rubberneckers than he'd expected and, scanning the crowd, Mat saw all of them were neighbors, living close enough that they could be worried. He stopped and got out of the cruiser.

"Everything is under control. You can all head home and let Chief Flynn finish up here."

There was some grumbling but most of the bystanders wandered back to their cars or their homes. Only a few of the stubborn remained, and as long as they didn't interfere with the firefighters, Mat couldn't force them to go home. Still, he'd sit here for a while to make sure none of them caused any trouble.

A loud one-sided conversation woke Mat the next morning. For a moment he was disoriented, but then the voice resolved into his mother's; she was on the phone arguing, again, with Mat's youngest sister, Fiona.

Rolling over onto his back, Mat pinched the bridge of his nose, reaching for patience he didn't feel at that moment—especially before any kind of caffeine. He hadn't gotten home until after midnight, and he'd had trouble falling asleep, images of the Wainwrights' burning barn playing on repeat in his head.

He loved his family; he did not love family drama. His role had always been the peacemaker, the fixer, but he didn't know if he could fix the relationship between Fiona and his mother.

After Sean's funeral service, his two sisters had fallen into a screaming match about their brother. Mat had agreed with Ella— not that he'd said as much, not until Fiona had outright asked him. Weeks later, the ripples from the fallout were still flowing outward. The Dempsey family was falling apart, and there was nothing Mat could do about it.

Mat hadn't sugarcoated the truth: Sean had been up to no good, and no good had gotten him killed. When he'd told her that, Fiona had stormed to her room and stayed there until the next day, when she'd made a dramatic departure. Why she refused to believe the evidence when it was clear as glass, Mat didn't know.

"Sean always told me you never liked him, never backed him up." Fiona's enormous suitcase had thumped down the staircase one step at a time, punctuating each word she spat out. "I told him he was wrong, but it seems he wasn't."

"Fi." Mat had wanted to at least try to reason with her. Not that it had ever worked before.

"Don't call me that. I hate that nickname."

At the bottom of the stairs, she'd righted her suitcase and continued rolling it toward the front door.

Mat had tried again. "Fiona, among other things, Sean was trying to coerce island residents to sell their property at a loss so he could buy it and make a profit off of it. He was in way over his head. He was also involved in Chastity Reynolds's death. Am I upset that he was murdered? Of course. Sean was my brother too. You're right that we didn't always see eye to eye, but I'm not happy he's dead."

Ella and their mom had listened to the exchange from the kitchen doorway, Ella's expression one of repressed fury, his mom's resigned. While Fiona was growing up, she'd often clashed with their mother, and the death of Sean Dempsey Sr. when Fiona was nineteen had not brought them closer together.

When a car had pulled up outside, Fiona had announced, "My taxi is here. Enjoy your lives without me."

Jesus Christ. If he hadn't suspected his mom would smack him, Mat would've laughed at that. Fiona always did have a flair for the theatric.

"Let me help you with your bag." He'd crossed the room to pick up her enormous suitcase.

"No, thank you." Wrenching open the front door, Fiona had dragged her bag outside and down the front steps, the *bang, bang, bang* echoing across the property. The waiting driver popped his trunk, and Fiona didn't argue with him when he climbed out to help her with her luggage.

With her suitcase stowed safely in the trunk, Fiona had climbed into the back of the taxi and slammed the door behind her. They all had watched the driver back his car around and head down the driveway to the main road.

Fiona's dramatic departure had been a month ago. Since then, Mat and Alyson had been working on picking up the pieces Sean had left behind.

After a few minutes of wishing he was asleep but having to acknowledge he was fully awake, Mat dragged himself out of bed, pulled a sweatshirt on, and left his room. There was no reason to stay in bed, and now that—judging by the quiet—his mom was apparently off the phone, she'd probably like someone to talk to other than Niall Hamarsson's dog. Ella and her daughter, Riley, had also left, having flown back to Houston after Sean's funeral.

The dog in question met him at the bottom of the stairs. He'd been staying with Mat and Alyson while Niall took care of business in Seattle. Understandably, Niall hadn't wanted him underfoot while he got his condo ready to sell, but Fenrir had done nothing but mope for the first few days.

"Hey, Mom," Mat said as he wandered into the kitchen.

"Good morning, sweetie. You were out late last night."

Mat rolled his eyes. Thirty-seven years old and his mother still called him sweetie. "Fire at the Wainwright place."

"Oh, no!"

"Not the house. One of their barns. It was empty."

"Well, thank goodness for small miracles, but I bet Merle and Joella are upset. I seem to remember they had plans for that barn."

Mat nodded, moving past her to reach the coffee pot. He reached into the cabinet for his favorite mug and filled it, then sipped and leaned back against the counter. "Merle told me they'd been thinking about completely renovating it."

Alyson nodded. "That's what Joella had been saying. I think they'd been to the bank for financing already. With tourism growing, it only makes sense, and people did like that place."

The structure had been a pretty one, a traditional shade of red with white trim, and the Wainwrights had paid an artist to add several elaborate Dutch-style protective circles along each side.

"It's a shame. I have to admit I'm concerned about these fires." He took another sip of his coffee, the warmth of it comforting as it slid into his stomach.

"I would be too," Alyson said. "Everyone is."

Fenrir nudged her hand and then looked imploringly toward the kitchen door. Alyson obliged, opening the door and letting him outside into the backyard.

"After you moved to California, there was an arson here—do you remember? Your dad caught the man, though. One of the Delacombes burned down his hotel in Hidden Harbor to collect insurance money."

"A hotel is a bit bigger than some garages and an empty barn."

"I'm just saying it's not the first time. Maybe somebody remembered and thought they'd be the ones to get away with it."

"Mom, this is not an episode of *Bones*. Who was it?" Mat knew the hotel had burned and been rebuilt, but he hadn't known it was arson. There'd been a time when he hadn't come home for years and had purposely not paid attention to island news.

"Shay Delacombe's father. Useless man. Claribel's brother's son, David. Except remember how he started pronouncing it *Dahveed*? Believe me, that wasn't what Alice and Donald named him. If you're going to change your name, change your damn name."

Somehow, Mat thought his mom was talking about something else entirely, but he wasn't sure he wanted to know what. There was a thump against the kitchen door. Alyson reached over and opened it again to let Fenrir back inside. As she did so, a knock sounded at the front door.

"Oh, that must be Niall."

"What?" Mat said, following his mom out of the kitchen to the front room.

"Did I forget to tell you? He texted last night that he was back. That's actually all he said, 'I'm back,' but I can't imagine anyone else stopping by this morning."

Alyson opened the front door to reveal Niall Hamarsson, his fist raised to knock again.

"Oh, good morning," Alyson said.

Mat swallowed and forced himself to act normal. Niall was much like a skittish animal—a mistreated one, or maybe just wild. Mat knew he had to let Niall carve the path in their relationship, but it was difficult when the man moved at glacial speed. Niall's light-green gaze caught Mat's own, and Mat thought he saw a glimmer of heat and humor before Niall's attention turned toward his dog.

"Did you behave yourself?" Niall asked.

That Fenrir was pleased to see his person was abundantly clear, and—not for the first time—Mat found himself jealous of the dog. This time it was his mother's amused gaze that caught his.

"Want a cup of coffee?" Mat offered.

Mat wasn't sure which Niall liked more, his dog or a good cup of coffee. He swore to himself—for the tenth or twentieth time—that he would let Niall lead this dance they were on. He wouldn't force anything between them. But, damn, it was difficult.

THREE
NIALL

"I'm sorry, Mr. Hamarsson." Long, slightly greasy, brown hair swung down in front of the motel clerk's Lennon-style glasses. The glasses slid down his nose a quarter inch, and he nudged them upward with one finger before rushing on. "Your, um, dog...?" The canine in question sat politely next to Niall, ears cocked, appearing to listen attentively to the young man behind the counter. Ricky paused again and cleared his throat, then kept speaking, proving he had some balls.

"The dog is just too big. I can tell by looking at him that he weighs over thirty pounds, and that's the weight limit for pets at the Orca. Thirty pounds. With the busy season getting closer, we, I was, um, told... we can't have him here anymore. He might scare other guests."

It was impossible for Niall to misunderstand what Nervous Ricky was telling him: he was (very politely) being evicted from the Orca Motel. Fenrir stared up at Niall, his golden eyes knowing and a tad judgey. Trust a wolfhound of sketchy origin to be the wise one between the two of them. Niall could almost hear the words "I told you so."

Funny, Fenrir's voice sounded a lot like Sheriff Mat Dempsey's.

"Can I at least have a little time to figure something out? I'm sure you heard—my place burned down, so it's not like I have somewhere to stay." Niall was going to use the pity card for as long as possible.

Guilt flared, and Niall shoved it aside. Yes, he could stay somewhere else; he was just avoiding the Dempsey homestead. Mat Dempsey and his mother had both offered Niall a place in their home, and offered it again when he'd picked up Fenrir the other day. But Niall needed space, at least that's what he told himself, and Mat seemed to take up all Niall's space whenever he was around.

He glanced out the front window—it was pissing down rain again—to the parking lot where no cars were parked except his. He stifled the urge to lean over the desk Ricky used as protection and scare the kid just a little. It wouldn't be difficult; the kid was already about to pee himself. But, Niall reminded himself, it wasn't Ricky's fault. Fenrir gave him the look again. Damn dog.

"I'll check out the bulletin board at the Hook. With any luck, there will be something there," Niall said instead.

Ricky nodded enthusiastically. "There's one at Chester's in Killegen's Point and the laundromat too."

"Right, thanks."

He and Fenrir headed back out into the rain and down the hill. The ferry terminal was at the bottom, empty, as the morning ferry had already come and gone. Inside the Hook, a popular greasy spoon in Hidden Harbor, there was a bulletin board hanging near the front entrance. Island residents posted all sorts of things: "Free Chickens," "Bob's Yard Service," "Babysitting by Susie." There were no posts offering housing to ex-homicide detectives and their canine shadows. Niall sighed. He had nothing to keep him busy right now. He might as well drive out to Killegen's Point.

. . .

As Niall approached Chester's Grocery-Mart, a camper appeared abruptly out of the mist. He jerked the steering wheel to the right and barely avoided hitting it, but he managed to stay on the road. He only got a glimpse of the vehicle—battered, dingy white and beige, faded orange stripe along the side—before it disappeared again. What was it with RVs trying to kill him?

Muttering about crappy drivers and nearly being run down by a camper from the set of *Escape to Witch Mountain*, Niall pulled into the empty parking lot, yanking on the parking brake hard enough that his battered Subaru jerked to a complete stop, throwing him against the seat belt.

"Dammit." He banged his palm against the steering wheel in irritation. This was the third or fourth time he'd spotted the camper since he'd been back on Piedras, and it pinged all his internal warning signals. "Sorry," he said to Fenrir, who'd slid to the edge of the back seat.

Niall peered out his side window and back down the road, but a spring fog had descended, seemingly held in place by towering evergreens and the island's rocky crags. Even if he had X-ray vision—not the superpower he'd dreamed of as a kid anyway, that had been invisibility—Niall wouldn't have been able to see the RV now through the mist.

"Dammit," he growled again, irritated he'd missed the license plate.

Between Ricky's bombshell and Mat Dempsey, who was being kind and patient and playing it very cool with Niall, Niall was in a generally cranky humor. Mat didn't deserve to be the butt of his current frame of mind, his temper was his own fault. He'd unwittingly let Mat get under his skin and now Mat's presence, in the same safe space Fenrir was allocated to, chafed. As much as Niall tried, he couldn't stop himself thinking about the sexy sheriff.

After turning off the engine and stuffing his keys into his coat pocket, Niall glanced into the rearview mirror, where amber eyes regarded him with silent reproach.

Niall groaned. "I'm sorry. I can't take you into the grocery store. Sage likes you, but you are not a service animal."

Niall's adopted wolfhound released a soft *humph*, twisting and curling around into a ball in the back seat. The car rocked back and forth as he moved until his back was decidedly directed toward Niall.

"I'll leave the window open," Niall offered by way of apology.

Fenrir chose not to answer, and Niall shook his head. He really needed to get out more if he was expecting the dog to reply. It was as pointless as wanting Mat Dempsey—as if Niall was suddenly going to be the kind of man Mat needed in his life. Mat *thought* he wanted Niall, but he didn't really *know* Niall, did he? Hunching his shoulders against the damp, Niall stomped across the asphalt, attempting to crush the traitorous thought that, maybe, he *could* be the man for Mat.

Chester's was the main grocery store on Piedras Island, the one locals frequented instead of the more expensive store in Hidden Harbor with the fancy organic this and brand-name that. Chester's stocked Western Family brand, and if the produce they sold was organic it was because it had always been grown that way. If he was going to find a place for himself and Fenrir, it would likely be advertised here.

Niall planned to check out the bulletin board first, but then decided he might as well pick up a few groceries, a cup of coffee, and maybe one of Chester's legendary cinnamon rolls while he was at it. Probably he should get coffee first and read the board second.

Sage was at the cash register. "Good morning, Niall," she called.

Sage was one of the only people on the island who completely ignored his moods, cheerfully greeting him no matter what state he arrived in at Chester's. He kind of admired her for it.

"Morning, Sage." Niall kept moving toward the waiting coffee, a beacon of caffeinated hope he could hold in his hand.

The bulletin board was fixed to the wall beyond the coffee station. A quick scan of the tattered flyers and index cards tacked there informed Niall he was going to have to consider other options. He'd check out the laundromat's board, but at this point he figured it was a losing bet.

As he strolled through the produce section sipping his coffee, his thoughts floated back to the mysterious camper. He hadn't gotten a clear view of the driver, only an indistinct dark profile he thought was male. He'd noticed the camper parked at Chester's a few times, but it had always been gone by the time he was done shopping. And he'd spotted it around the island over the past few weeks—never twice in the same spot—but he'd never seen the occupants.

It was an older-model RV, twenty years or more, and small, the kind with a cab at the front connected to the back so passengers could move about. It was about fifteen feet long—short compared to the monsters produced these days. The exterior was banged up and rusty, and a section of the siding had peeled away from the body.

Niall didn't like it, not one bit. He couldn't put his finger on exactly why, but the camper had his cop instincts paying attention.

"Who drives the RV?" he asked Sage once he'd gathered up the items he wanted, including a second cup of coffee.

Sage cocked her head at him. "What RV?"

Niall realized Sage might not know what cars customers drove. Regulars, perhaps, but not seasonals. So at least her question confirmed his suspicion that the driver was not a local.

"An older RV camper I saw on my way in. I thought maybe the owner had been shopping."

Sage shook her head as she ran Niall's items across the scanner. "Not that I know of. It's been a slow morning—no one except Fred from across the street has been in. But it's still early, and there's a few other places in Killegen's Point. The laundromat is open twenty-four hours, maybe they were there?"

"Maybe."

He paid, thanked Sage, and made his way back out to his car. The rain had lightened up a little while he was inside, hinting at another decent day. Fenrir sat up as Niall approached, wagging his tail in greeting. Apparently, Niall had been forgiven.

Before leaving Killegen's Point, he checked out the laundromat's board, finding nothing suitable for a cranky ex-cop and his trusty wolfhound.

The road Niall was following now was not the main artery between Killegen's Point and Hidden Harbor. It was a narrow, almost one-lane road that cut across from Killegen's Point to the easternmost point of the island. Niall drove slowly along it, passing a yellow No Outlet warning sign. Most likely, the only drivers he would come upon here would be locals. As thoroughly as he scanned both sides of the road, he didn't see any sign of the camper. But there were plenty of driveways it could've driven down, plenty of spots densely covered with brush or trees it could have slipped behind. Plenty of places for an RV to hide.

Niall slowed to a stop as he neared the end of the road. Beyond it, the land dropped into a sheer bluff that overlooked the straits between Piedras and the mainland. Without consciously thinking about it, he parked along the shoulder and climbed out. Fenrir let out an impatient bark from inside, and Niall let him out too, knowing he wouldn't go far. Fenrir was low maintenance. Niall chuckled—that was not a concept he would apply to himself.

Pausing at the guardrail, his hands jammed into the pockets of his jacket for protection from the cold. He stood at the end of the road for a few minutes watching the fog begin to melt away, slow at first and then faster, until he could see all the way across the water to the mainland crouching in the distance. Niall took a deep breath of the salt-laden air, filling his lungs, then released it. As he stared out at the dark silhouette of land, something unnameable inside himself loosened a bit further, something *clicked* into place. Piedras felt *right*.

Niall didn't feel like an old-timer, but he did have a history on the island; he existed here as more than a bitter homicide cop. Some islanders—like Mat Dempsey—even seemed to want him there. Most of the residents seemed to accept Niall's presence, at least, and the few who whispered behind his back... well, that's the way things had always been.

And, he thought as he breathed in and out again, more than likely the camper was no big deal. He was making a mountain out of a molehill—something his grandmother used to say quite often. There was likely a perfectly good, *lawful* reason the owner was driving around the island and only using facilities when they were less likely to run into other inhabitants.

The cop in him protested. Niall tried to ignore it.

His thoughts drifted further afield as the fog continued to fade, to the sexy and very available Sheriff Dempsey. Mat seemed to see right into Niall's soul and never once flinched—he actually thought he liked Niall. Mat was something Niall had never had in his life, or not often, anyway. Mat represented family, safety, commitment. Given everything Mat had done since Niall had come back to Piedras, it should have been easy for Niall to trust him. But he couldn't find the off switch for the little voice inside that pinged a warning every time he and Mat got close.

It was, however, proving challenging to stop thinking about him.

Fenrir trotted over and sat on his haunches, leaning against Niall's leg.

"I know, I make everything difficult. You think I haven't heard it before?" He scratched the top of Fenrir's head, listening to the waves crashing far below them. "You're right, I should just be able to let everything go. Mat deserves more than me, though. He deserves more than a man who's ready to bolt at the slightest bump in the night."

Fenrir thumped his tail against the damp ground.

"You're not supposed to agree with me," Niall groused. "You're supposed to argue that Mat is a good man, he's solid, he's even in law enforcement, he knows my history—which should be a deterrent—and it doesn't seem to make a difference to him. And, oddly enough, he seems to want to be with me even when I'm an ass—which is often. The thing is, I don't know what the fuck I am doing."

Fenrir's tail thumped again.

"Smart-ass."

Niall shivered as the wind picked up, its cold fingers burrowing inside his parka and underneath his sweater, giving him goose bumps. He loaded Fenrir into the car, turned it around, and began to head back. On the way back to Killegen's Point, he couldn't help but peer along each driveway as he passed by, but he saw nothing.

FOUR

MAT

Wednesday morning, Mat narrowed his eyes at a pink box sitting on his desk. There were doughnuts inside that box, and they were fresh. Their gooey, sticky deliciousness wafted from the box to where he'd paused three feet away. He wanted one, but it had been a long, cold winter, and the effects of not getting nearly as much exercise as he should were making themselves known. It was harder to get rid of the extra pounds nowadays, but he doubted his ability to hold out against the treats for long after the past few days.

Niall Hamarsson was on his mind too, a different kind of weight, although Mat tried not to think about him. At least, not too much. Not more than once or twice a day, in between trying to keep everything under control on the island. Between teenage vandals, petty theft, car prowls, a break-in at the senior center, and now arson, his brain still found time to obsess about Niall.

Peeling off his Piedras County Sheriff's Office jacket, Mat slung it over the back of his chair and sat down. The chair creaked loudly; Mat hoped today wasn't the day it chose to collapse. Another reason not to have a doughnut, right? After a brief hesitation, half expecting he'd find himself on the floor any second, Mat carefully scooted forward and tapped his keyboard.

His computer wheezed and hiccupped, the screen flashing before turning black again. He had a kind of contest going on in his head: which would crap out first, the chair or the desktop? A few seconds later the screen flashed again and stayed on this time, beginning to load the department's home page. He breathed a sigh of relief. Having to put in a request for a new system was the last thing he wanted right now—although he was going to as soon as the county higher-ups were finished with the reorganization. The irony that the fancy computer system in his patrol car was newer and faster than the one on his desk not lost on him.

While his desktop slowly loaded, Mat caved to the call of the doughnuts, pulling the pink box closer. He wasn't fooling anyone, least of all himself. The damn doughnuts were a siren he couldn't resist.

On Saturday, Devon Flynn had called to say he'd discovered an empty plastic gas can within fifty feet of the Wainwright barn. How it had survived the heat of the blaze was anyone's guess, but he'd brought it to the station. Mat had spent the better part of the day processing it, but there were no fingerprints he was able to find. Maybe whoever had discarded it wore gloves, maybe the plastic didn't take fingerprints. It was difficult to know. For now, he'd carefully wrapped and stored the can in the station evidence locker while trying to justify the expense of sending it off to one of the state labs for a more thorough examination.

His team did not have the training and his department did not have the funds for processes like cyanoacrylate fuming, which would probably turn up fingerprints from the factory the can was made in. It wasn't often Mat missed the San Francisco PD, but right now he'd sacrifice one of those doughnuts for a more experienced team of deputies and more funding.

Slowly, like Indiana Jones lifting the lid of the crate holding the Holy Grail, Mat raised the top of the doughnut box and breathed deep, filling his lungs with the heavy scent of sugary fried goodness. The container held a baker's dozen of everything scrumptious from a new bakery that had opened on Spring Street, dangerously close to the station. Mat reached in and grabbed one. He was just stuffing the last bite of a glazed old-fashioned into his mouth when his personal cell phone buzzed from inside one of the pockets of his jacket.

Fumbling to wipe his fingers and swallow the last of the doughnut at the same time, Mat barely managed to retrieve his phone before it stopped ringing. He wished he'd thought to pour himself coffee to wash his treat down with. Doughnuts were meant to be enjoyed, not bolted down.

"Lo," he said around the doughnut.

"Hey, Matty." The voice was that of his sister Ella.

"What's up, El?"

"Um, is this a good time to talk? I know you're at the station, but I wanted to talk to you when Mom wasn't around. You've been so busy I haven't been able to catch you at home."

Something in her voice had Mat sitting up and taking notice. "Of course. Let me find somewhere a little more private."

No one else was in yet, but a private phone conversation would guarantee someone arriving soon. It struck him as odd that no one except Birdy and himself had checked in—he knew she was behind the donuts—but he'd figure out why that was after talking to Ella. Mat made his way through the bullpen to a rarely used side exit that opened out to a breezeway between the station and the older brick building that had once housed the *Island Times*. The bitter March wind cut viciously through his thin cotton shirt, and goose bumps formed on his arms. He'd left his coat hanging on his chair, but he wasn't going back inside to grab it. Leaving the door propped slightly open with a rock, Mat moved a few feet away from the entrance, his back to the wind.

"Okay, what's up?"

"I'm leaving Richard. I'm hoping to come home—we—me and

Riley, I mean." Ella rushed out the words as if she'd practiced them, her tone firm.

"Are you okay? What's going on? Talk to me." Mat forced himself to keep his voice calm.

"Richard and I are over. It's been over for a while now, but I didn't want to admit to myself—admit that I failed. The only good thing left is Riley."

The sheriff in Mat had to ask, "Has he been… hurting you? Or Riley?" Because if Richard had laid a hand on Mat's sister or his niece, Mat was going to take him apart piece by piece and dip him in a vat of fresh lemon juice.

"No." Ella drew in a shuddering breath. "No, not that way. He's—he's having an affair. Thank god, because otherwise he'd blame this on me. But I don't have anything. I was scared to take more than what we need to fly home again. Richard controls most of our money. Not all, but most."

"He is a complete shit, and I never liked him." That was the truth. Richard was one of those people who claimed other people's successes as his own and somehow got away with it. But Ella had loved Richard, so Mat had tried his best.

"Mat, please. I know you're right, but—this is really hard for me. I just want to make sure you're okay with a six-year-old and your sister moving back into the house."

"Jesus, Ella, of course. Why would you have to ask me that? It's more than okay. I want you guys there. I miss you and I love Riley. We'll get through this, okay?"

He didn't speak for a few minutes because Ella burst into tears at his words, the receiver crackling and popping as she sniffled. Mat waited while she calmed herself down and wondered how long she'd been carrying the weight of her marriage around, how long she'd been worrying and thinking and *wanting* to leave Richard but not knowing if she could, if her family would support her.

"I've got your back, Ella. Mom and I both do."

"I'm so ashamed," Ella whispered. "And I haven't told Mom yet because, with the funeral and the thing with Fiona, it seemed selfish to announce I wanted to come home and hoped to stay while I get my life together. I feel like such a failure. I wanted to talk to you first, big brother."

"Ella, you're not a failure. Leaving takes guts. I promise you we'll get through this, together, as a family. Do you want me to talk to Mom?"

"No." Ella hiccupped and sniffed. "No, I'll… I'll talk to her. I'll call her in a bit."

Thinking back, Mat realized Riley had been unusually quiet during their visit. Since he'd been working eighteen hours a day, the difference from her normal chatty self had flown under his radar. Now that he knew the truth, he was lucky his grip didn't snap the phone in half. It was difficult to keep his anger from bleeding into his tone of voice, but that was the last thing Ella needed.

"You know you're welcome to stay for as long as you want—forever, even. It will be great to have you back, Mom's been planning stuff for Riley to do this summer, she won't mind moving the schedule up," Mat assured her. "Plus, Riley's an awesome kid, and I kinda like you too," he teased.

Mat didn't add that he'd already been worried about his mom—he wasn't sure how she was dealing with her oldest son's death. Maybe it would be good for her to have Riley and Ella around to fuss over.

"Okay. God, Mat, I feel better just talking to you. I've been so stressed out. I'm going to buy our plane tickets now."

"Wait." Mat reached for his wallet and pulled out his credit card. "Let me do this for you." He read off his credit card number. "Save your money for, you know, lawyers and stuff."

Mat berated himself for not realizing something other than Sean's death was bothering Ella. They'd been close as kids. Sean had always been too good for his younger siblings, off doing his own thing, and Fiona was the surprise baby, with too many years between Ella and Fiona for them to even be in school together.

"I'll pay you back."

"I don't want you to pay me back. I want you to be happy and safe."

"I'm going to call Mom now. She's going to want to talk for a while. She'll probably make cookies."

Alyson Dempsey always made cookies when one of her kids needed comforting. There were going to be dozens of them. He was in so much trouble. Cookies were almost as impossible as doughnuts. "Help me. She's already baking enough for the entire island. Hurry back so I'm not forced to eat them all."

"Okay. I love you, big brother." With a watery chuckle Ella clicked off, but not before Mat heard one last sniffle.

Shoving his wallet and phone back into his pocket, Mat took a deep breath, filling his lungs with oxygen and holding it a moment before releasing it. He wasn't cold any longer; he was molten hot, fury burning through his veins. He took another breath, trying to get a handle on his anger, trying to dampen it but feeling one burst of flame away from losing it completely.

Mat did more deep breathing exercises and some shoulder rolls to calm himself down before he went back inside. In the bullpen, Deputy Flynn had appeared from wherever she'd been and was sitting at her desk, concentrating on her screen. She glanced up as Mat strode toward his desk. Something about her expression had him slowing his steps while his heart rate picked up.

He narrowed his eyes at her. "What?"

She grimaced. "Patrick called out, sir."

"What do you mean, 'called out'?"

"Apparently he has the flu, sir."

"Birdy, what have I said about calling me sir?"

"You've asked me not to, sir." There was a wicked gleam in

her eye, and Mat knew he wasn't going to win the argument today—or likely ever.

"What about Holstrom? Can he swap days?"

"Hmmm. It seems Deputy Holstrom picked something up from his wife, who was sick last week. He thinks his son brought germs home from day care and says he hasn't felt this bad since he joined his fraternity in college."

Wasn't that just great. His mood worsened. He wished there was something he could do about it other than eat doughnuts. "So, half my force is sick. Can we move anyone from Orcas?"

"From what I understand, this flu is quite contagious. Deputy Jones called in sick last night. There was a message this morning."

Mat groaned. This meant he and Birdy would have to take calls from all the islands, deciding between them which needed a response and which could wait. With someone running around playing arsonist, this was the last thing he needed.

"Did no one but me get a flu shot this year?" he demanded, knowing he'd sent a memo out to all staff. Did he send them to dead air? Did no one read his emails?

"I did, sir."

"Well, I guess I'm lucky you pay attention. We get to cover while the others recover. What about Duane?"

Duane Cooper was the entirety of Piedras County's marine emergency response team. While he technically only responded to marine incidents, those were limited this time of year, and he was also a qualified deputy.

Uncertainty flashed across Birdy's face. "I've been meaning to bring something up with you, but with everything going on, I didn't want to burden you."

"Can I make myself some coffee before hearing whatever *additional* bad news you have to tell me?"

The damn glazed doughnut felt like a rock in his stomach. It was going to be a long few days for the two of them, and the most Mat could hope was that neither he nor Birdy came down with the flu as well. And there were no random crime sprees, no more arson, no car prowls, just a nice quiet few days until they were back to full staff.

Why did he think that wasn't going to happen?

Birdy nodded and Mat veered into the tiny break room. Opening one of the cabinet doors, he pulled the bag with his special roast off the top shelf. The rich aroma of the beans went a long way toward soothing his frayed temper. The steps of grinding, measuring, and pouring water into the coffee maker were routine, and Mat found it somewhat soothing.

As soon as there was enough coffee in the carafe, Mat poured himself a cup, the liquid black and dark as his mood. Gripping the mug, he made his way back to the main room, where Birdy waited. The mound of paperwork on his desk seemed to have doubled since last week. Whatever happened to going paperless? *Not ever going to happen in police work* was the answer, Mat knew. All paperless meant was that now they had actual paperwork and also had to enter everything into the department's database. Shoving the paper and files aside as much as possible, Mat set his coffee down and *carefully* plopped into his chair, noticing the box of doughnuts had moved to one of the empty desks. Probably a good thing.

"Spill."

Birdy opened a desk drawer to pull out a beige file folder and held it in front of her chest, the lightweight cardboard crumpled in her grip.

"You asked me to reconcile the budgets and get all the departments organized, especially with the reorganization."

Right, because the island council got it in their heads that a reorganization of the sheriff's department needed to happen. To Mat it meant they were gearing up to cut the budget. Likely he'd have less money and more to be in charge of. The council had been making noises about the move for several years, but Mat had managed to head them off—until now.

"No offense, sir, but there's a lot of paperwork kind of everywhere."

When Mat had returned to the island and been elected sheriff following his father's death, he'd simply kept the same managerial system Sean Dempsey Sr. had. He's reasoned that what had worked for his father surely would work for him. But that had been ten years ago, and now it was obvious the entirety of the Sheriff's Office needed updating.

The department needed to be better organized, more streamlined—more everything. When the island council asked questions, he wanted to be able to answer immediately—and, he decided right then, he was going to ask for an entire new computer system for the department, screw waiting for the right moment.

"Okay, what'd you find?"

"Some accounts don't reconcile. Not exactly. I mean, it could just be my error."

Right. The chance of it being Birdy's error was about one in a thousand.

"The files Duane sent over are kind of skimpy. Funny thing is, it's not that he spends too much, it's that he spends too little. He never uses his entire budget, and"—she leaned forward, confident in her data—"he doesn't exactly have the biggest budget in the organization. I visited East Bay, where the boat is moored, and the small office there where he keeps his log. Things just seem weird."

"Clarify." Absentmindedly, Mat took a big sip of his coffee, and the liquid burned its way down his esophagus. As he wheezed and tears leaked from the corners of his eyes, Birdy continued, a human steamroller.

"There's a new boat out there, an expensive one with fancy forward-scanning sonar, moored next to the rescue vessel. The office has nice things inside too—a new desktop computer and stuff. I mean, *maybe* he's spiffing it up for himself—and Sharleen, since they share the space—out of his own money, but I don't see how he could afford it."

Mat frowned. "Could the boat be someone else's? The police boat isn't the only one moored out there." East Bay Marina provided moorage for a lot of locals' vessels.

"I asked Sharleen, and she said it's Duane's."

"Fuck me." Mat sat back, and his chair protested with an ominous squeak.

Birdy grabbed a glass jar from her desk and waved it under Mat's nose. Scowling, he stood and pulled his wallet out of his back pocket. After extracting a five-dollar bill, he dropped it into the swear jar.

Mat had inherited Duane from his father. He'd been associated with the sheriff's office for at least twenty years, and Mat liked having an older, experienced team member. But he'd also given Duane a lot of leeway.

Where was Duane getting that kind of money? He sat down again and leaned forward, resting his elbows on his thighs. It was possible this could be easily explained and turn out to mean nothing, but for the life of him he couldn't think how.

"Keep this between you and me for now. We can't look into it for the next few days anyway with everyone out sick. I'll dig further if I have time, maybe go down and check it out myself—pop in for a little visit."

Birdy handed him the file folder. "What I found is in here. Maybe there's a good explanation?"

Mat scooted his chair back around so he could open the bottom drawer of his desk. Carefully, he shoved the folder underneath the multitude of training manuals. "I'll look it over tonight."

. . .

Mat spent the rest of his morning wishing he had two or three deputies as motivated and smart as Birdy. And hoping that Duane had a good explanation for the new boat and the way he'd handled the funds the county had awarded him. Mat divided up the schedule between them. Mat would be on call for that night and Birdy would take the next, and so on through the week. Between them they would make sure the island was safe… and, fingers crossed, neither of them would come down with anything. And hopefully Radden and Holstrom would be back to work soon.

It wasn't until later, after Birdy had left for the day, that Mat thought about Niall Hamarsson. He blamed his exhaustion for making it easier for thoughts of the other man to slip through his defenses. Since the evening on the beach—a lifetime ago, it seemed—Niall had been downright elusive. The past week he'd been away tidying up loose ends, but before that he'd been impossible to pin down. When Mat had mentioned something to his mom about feeling frustrated, she'd given him a long talk about letting Niall come to him, that Niall needed to find his own way and Mat had to be patient.

Fuck being patient.

And yet he had been, hadn't he? When Niall showed up Saturday morning to reclaim Fenrir, Mat had pretended he wasn't drinking in the sight of him. Instead, he'd calmly collected Fenrir's belongings and let Niall leave again.

He wasn't sure how many times he'd be able to do that.

His thoughts drifted back to the day of Sean's funeral. Mat had been greeting mourners with his mom and sisters, waiting for the service to begin, when some odd sixth sense tuned to Mat's exclusive Niall Hamarsson channel had alerted him to the other man's arrival. He'd literally *felt* the atmosphere change when Niall stepped through the front doors of the funeral home. Niall had dressed up, wearing "island formal": clean jeans, leather loafers, a white button-down shirt topped off with a dark brown wool blazer. A person would have to be completely oblivious not to recognize that Niall was a dangerous package, a wolf in sheep's clothing. A wolf Mat wanted.

Ella, ever watchful, had asked him if something was wrong. Mat hadn't been able to reply for a moment, his gaze locked on Niall as he moved through the crowd.

Her eyes had followed his own. "Oh, who is that?"

"Hmmm? Oh, Niall Hamarsson."

"Niall Hamarsson?" Ella raised her dark eyebrows. "My, hasn't he turned out well."

Niall looked good, his broad shoulders barely contained by the blazer, his thighs testing the tensile strength of denim and drawing the eyes of anyone with a pulse. Surely Mat was going to hell for reacting to Niall like this at his own brother's memorial.

Ella had elbowed him in the side. "Don't start drooling. I don't have extra tissues."

Mat looked down at his younger sister, narrowing his eyes.

"What?" She put on an innocent look. "You think I don't know which way you swing?" She snorted. "I had to tell all my girlfriends in high school you were in love with your German pen pal to get them to leave you alone. Don't you think it's time you told all of us?"

Mat had been saved from replying to Ella's little bombshell. Niall had stopped walking for a moment, his gaze searching the throng until Mat raised his hand and got his attention. The mass of funeral goers moved aside, allowing Niall to pass. Once he reached Mat and his family, Niall greeted the women first.

"My condolences."

"Thank you, Niall, that means a lot," Alyson replied. Instead of shaking Niall's hand, she had stood up on her tiptoes and wrapped her arms around his shoulders. Mat had barely managed to suppress a smile at the slightly stricken expression that had flitted across Niall's face.

"Thanks for coming," Mat said when Niall reached him.

Their eyes met, and, for Mat anyway, time seemed to stop. The crowd of mourners around them disappeared, and Mat's world narrowed to the faded agate green of Niall's eyes. An ember of smoldering heat flared deep in Niall's regard; he hadn't forgotten the kiss at the beach any more than Mat had.

The station's front door rattled in the frame, startling him. Mat would've ignored it, but the sound came again. Just what he needed, a drunk or a prankster trying to break into the station when they thought everyone was gone for the day.

Scowling, Mat pushed away from his desk, trying to see over the partition into the reception area, but Birdy had set it up so people walking by on the street couldn't see all the way inside. The door rattled a third time.

"The hell."

Mat wound his way through the desks past the partition and into the lobby, then peered out through the glass doors. It took a moment for the shadowy figure on the other side to resolve into someone Mat recognized.

Niall Hamarsson was waiting to be let in, almost as if Mat had summoned him.

FIVE

NIALL

Niall waited with his hands jammed into the pockets of his jeans. He already regretted deciding to stop at the station when he'd spotted Mat's cruiser in the parking lot. Mat stared out the doors a moment before unlocking the station door and opening it wide enough for him to slip inside. The building was dimly lit. It was after ten p.m., and Mat was probably the only person there. And who was Niall kidding? Even he'd known it would only be a matter of time before the pull toward Mat Dempsey proved too strong to resist. Mat was a planet; Niall was merely a moon being pulled into his orbit.

"Evening," Mat grunted as Niall brushed past him.

Mat probably wondered what the hell Niall was doing at the station this late at night. Niall wondered too, especially since he'd been avoiding him of late, but Mat was too polite to come out and say so.

"Hey," he said lamely.

"Where's your shadow?" Mat asked.

"What?" He frowned before realization dawned. "Oh, a funny man. Fenrir's in the car."

And quite the look Niall had been on the receiving end of for that. Fenrir had had enough of being left in the car.

"Go get him. No one else is here to care."

A minute later Niall was back with Fenrir, who greeted Mat enthusiastically, going so far as to grin for him. Niall had never known a dog to do that before, but there was no doubt in his mind; Fenrir could smile.

After relocking the front doors, Mat led them through to his workstation. There were manila files and stacks of paper covering most of his desktop.

"Working late?"

Because it was always great to state the obvious.

Mat raised a dark eyebrow as he sat down, motioning for Niall to take the chair at the next desk. Fenrir slumped down between them with a whump.

Mat must've decided to take pity on Niall. When he spoke, he merely answered Niall's foolish question.

"Most of my deputies are out sick. They missed, or more likely ignored, the memo about the required flu shot. Me and Birdy are splitting the shifts for a couple days until we're back to full power. Well, as much as we ever are around here."

"The flu, that's tough."

An awkward silence fell between them. Niall didn't know what to say or why he'd stopped by, other than the gravitational pull of Mat himself. Mat seemed to bring out an emotionally reckless side Niall didn't know he had. Should he confess he'd spotted Mat's cruiser in the parking lot while he drove along Spring Street on his way back to the Orca after a boring meal at the local diner? That he hadn't wanted to go back to his room, that the instant he'd seen Dempsey's car he hadn't wanted to be alone?

As much as he'd tried to ignore his feelings, Niall was drawn to the other man. Not moth to flame—it was the other way around, a different sort of metaphor. Niall was a black hole while

Mat was a carefree soul with no idea the damage Niall caused. Not on purpose, never on purpose. Niall didn't mean to hurt people, but somehow people around him ended up getting hurt anyway. And when that happened, they left. Disappeared. Whatever.

The silence dragged on several beats too long. Niall searched for something to say that wasn't pathetic. Maybe he should tell Mat about his upcoming eviction?

"Has anyone reported an RV, a camper-style one, parking on their property?"

The second the words fell out of his mouth, he knew they were all wrong. Niall wanted to rope them back in and ask how Mat was doing. Was his mom doing okay after the funeral? And his sisters?

This was the first time Niall had allowed himself to seek out Mat since he'd come back from Seattle, and really since Sean's funeral. Why he'd thought Sean's funeral would be a safe place for him to lay eyes on Mat, he had no idea. On the other hand, it would've been extremely bad form not to make an appearance. Seeing Mat hit Niall somewhere around his solar plexus, a weird sort of fight-or-flight instinct, except he wanted to run or throw himself at Mat like the damn dog and beg him to take him home.

Mat was staring at him with what Niall recognized as astonishment. Niall wondered what he was thinking, certainly not some nonsense about an RV. It was possible he was irritated. Niall could relate to that.

"An RV," Mat said slowly.

Niall nodded. "An older model. I've seen it around a bit."

"You know, seeing a camper around 'a bit' is not a reason to call out a BOLO on it."

Niall leaned back; his chair squeaked loudly. Fenrir raised his head and looked around before putting his chin back on his paws.

"Dempsey—Mat—I know, there's just something bugging me

about it. Nothing I can put my finger on, but..." He trailed to a stop, sitting forward again, the chair protesting again.

Mat eyed him with what Niall thought was amusement in his gaze.

"Sorry. It's the chair, not you. I swapped it out earlier when I got tired of worrying I was about to end up on the floor."

"As a cop, I've had to trust my gut," Niall continued, ignoring Mat's comment about the chair but also hoping he wouldn't end up on the nasty gray carpet, "and my gut says there's something funny about this vehicle. It's been on the island at least a month —I saw it when I first came back. I've seen it at Chester's a few times, driving around too, but only in the early mornings, never any other time, and I can't figure out where it's staying. It's not at either campground. I've checked."

"You're telling me you've been keeping an eye on some mysterious camper, basically stalking it, because you only see it in the morning?" Mat stared at the ceiling for a minute, searching for patience, Niall thought. He took a deep breath in through his nose before continuing. "Niall, we have a lot of residents on the island, in all of Piedras County actually, who are barely hanging on financially. They live precariously, paycheck to paycheck or on assistance checks. Maybe it's one of them. Who knows? Maybe one of the Reynoldses was kicked out of his girlfriend's place and is using the camper as a place to live. It's not a crime to live in a camper."

"I didn't say it was a crime, I just think it's out of the ordinary. I don't know how to explain it any better."

"Is that really why you stopped by? To lodge a complaint about a camper?"

No. He'd stopped because going any longer without seeing or talking to Mat was unacceptable. Maybe they could be friends. Maybe Niall could make that work.

"Yes."

Mat seemed to come to some sort of decision, leaning back in his chair with his ankle over one knee. Niall was not going to check out his crotch or how his broad chest filled out the sheriff's uniform.

"You didn't stop by to say hello? If nothing else, Niall, I do want to be your friend." He waggled his eyebrows. "Don't misunderstand, that's not all I'm hoping for, but if friendship is all you can give me right now… I can wait. I'm a patient man."

Ironic, really, that Mat would bring up friendship—making Niall aware *he* didn't want to be friends. Not the way Mat meant, anyway. But he didn't know how to get to what he wanted.

The night when Mat had come to find Niall on his beach, not allowing Niall to wallow in self-pity, instead *talking* and forcing Niall to shut him up the only way he knew how—by kissing him —flashed through his mind. Mat's strong, muscled body against his, his warmth, his willingness to let Niall take what he needed while still remaining protective of him, the scrape of their whiskers in the dark.

Niall forced himself to look at the other man. Mat was watching him. His dark eyes brimmed with heady promise. He tipped his chair backward, appearing casual, but his body was tense. He obviously expected to be shut down, expected Niall to disappear—as he had between their time at the beach and Sean's memorial.

Niall had felt so naked, exposed. No man had ever done that to him before.

His temper rose irrationally, and it wasn't directed at Mat but toward himself. What did he want? What *was* he doing? Why, at nearly forty, was he still unable to articulate his feelings, to map out his own wants and needs? And why did he think he could navigate something with Mat Dempsey, of all people?

Mat broke the spell, inching forward and placing a hand on Niall's thigh. His touch practically burned a hole through Niall's jeans. Niall shut his eyes. That was too much like standing on the edge of a cliff so he quickly opened them again.

Mat smiled, but it was slightly crooked, wry rather than amused.

"I came out to my mom and Ella."

Niall blinked. Not that he'd known what Mat was going to say, but those words snapped him out of whatever rabbit hole he'd been heading down.

"What now? How'd that go?" he rasped out before clearing his throat.

Mat rolled his eyes, leaning away from Niall again. His hand fell away, leaving a cold spot. "It was fine. Embarrassing, but fine. Ella, of course, already knew. She's the one who kind of forced my hand... and I suspect my mom already knew too, but she played it well, telling me she loved me for who I am, all the right words."

"That's... that's nice."

"It was nice. I hadn't known I was carrying the truth about my sexuality around like a burden. It's been a relief to not feel like I'm hiding something."

Niall nodded. He'd never been in the closet, never had the luxury of anonymity, although who knew about it hadn't mattered to him since junior high. And once he'd finished his final growth spurt, very few people challenged him about his sexuality... or anything else.

"My mom asked if you were the reason I chose to say something now."

Niall's gaze snapped back to Mat's. An emotion he wouldn't give a name to shot through his chest, leaving him breathless. Okay, fine: hope. It was fucking hope.

"Don't worry, I told her it was none of her business. What you and I do, or don't do, has nothing to do with my mother."

"Alyson is a force to be reckoned with," Niall commented.

They both chuckled because it was true. Alyson Dempsey was a woman who made her own strong way in the world. Niall could appreciate her.

Mat stood from his chair, looking down at Niall. "I'm not trying to chase you away, but I have paperwork to look over, and you distract me."

Niall nodded, standing too, the movement bringing them only inches apart. This close he could smell the aftershave or soap Mat favored. It was woodsy with a hint of cinnamon, and his beard was growing in, giving his cheeks a dark cast while accentuating the smile lines at the corners of his eyes.

An inch farther and Niall was quickly brushing his lips across Mat's, nearly drowning in the impulse to take more but retreating because he'd forgotten to breathe. His heart was pounding like he'd run a marathon. Mat looked stunned, which made Niall feel a little pleased and less like he was the only one who had no idea what he was doing.

"Come on, dog," Niall said roughly as he made his way back to the front door.

Fenrir padded along next to him, Mat's footfalls quiet against the thin carpet behind them.

Coming around them, Matt unlocked the door and pushed it open so Niall and Fenrir could slide out into the night.

"I'll keep an eye out for that camper," Mat said.

Niall turned to meet his clear gaze. There was no mockery lurking in it, just the truth: Mat took Niall's concern seriously.

"Thanks."

He sketched out a farewell and made his way out to his car. For once it wasn't raining, although the streets were still wet.

The draw between them was powerful. Had it always been there? Had he been attracted to Mat back when they were in school together? Niall had put so much of his childhood behind him, locked it in a mental box, that he wasn't sure if he could remember. Or if he wanted to. Maybe it was better to keep those memories where they were, tucked away inside his head.

. . .

His brain had other ideas; Mat starred in his dreams that night. Mat back when he and Niall were scrawny teens in high school. Mat trying to protect Niall even though Niall was older and bigger. Niall knew he was dreaming, but still he kept trying to tell Mat he wasn't worth it, he'd never be worth protecting. He was too damaged, broken beyond repair.

"I'm not trying to *fix* you," dream Mat replied. "You have to do that yourself."

The dream shifted to the present in that jarring way dreams do. They were at the beach, and Mat was kissing him—or Niall was kissing Mat, it hardly mattered. Their bodies pressed against each other so that Niall couldn't tell where he ended and Mat began. The sticky tanginess of the salt air surrounded them, wrapping them in a protective cocoon.

Niall jerked awake, his heart pounding uncomfortably, his bare skin hot and overly sensitive, the scratchy motel blanket snagging on his nipples. It took him a long time to get back to sleep.

SIX

MAT

Mat stood next to the glass doors for a few minutes, watching Niall's car pull out of the parking lot, turn right, and head up the hill toward the Orca Motel, his brake lights reflecting blurry red against the damp pavement. Lifting his hand, Mat touched his mouth where Niall's lips had brushed against his own. He *hadn't* imagined the kiss, as quick as it had been. It had been real and made something a lot like optimism bloom in his chest.

"Huh."

Back at his desk, Mat returned to poring over the paperwork Birdy had given him earlier that day—or maybe it was yesterday by that point. The data was there, and she was right: the numbers did not add up satisfactorily. But before he acted, Mat wanted to know if Duane could explain himself. Could he account for where money was coming from for the fancy watercraft and the expensive equipment Birdy had seen in his office? Maybe he had inherited money or made good on an investment? There could be a perfectly reasonable answer.

"This sucks," Mat grumbled as he flipped through the pages.

It was his own damn fault, letting Duane continue to run

things the same way Mat's father had let him. Mat should've come in and demanded an audit right away and made sure everything in marine was on the up-and-up even though marine rescue didn't run under the same authority as the sheriff's department. It was kind of a satellite, with Duane giving yearly updates to the island council.

Nearly a decade ago, Mat had been reeling from his father's death and shocked he'd been elected to follow in Sean Sr.'s footsteps. Asking for more change had seemed… wrong, like rocking the boat. So he hadn't, and things had continued as they were with marine rescue only having minor oversight. Until now, when the council wanted to expand the sheriff's responsibilities.

The printed words and spreadsheet numbers began shifting in and out of focus. Mat rubbed his watery eyes with the heel of his hand.

"Damn. It's time to go home."

Mat slapped the folder shut. Instead of putting it back in the bottom drawer, he tucked it into his messenger bag. This wasn't something he wanted floating around the office for anyone to find —not that there was anyone but Birdy and him over the next few days. He sincerely hoped Duane had an explanation for all of this.

"Yes, sir, if a call comes in, we will page you," the young man at dispatch assured him. Mat crossed his fingers that the rest of the night would continue to be uneventful.

The road home was dark and empty of other vehicles. Mat drove with only the cruiser's headlights illuminating his way. The camper Niall had mentioned came to mind—it was better than dwelling on the asshat Ella was married to or the fact that he was running the sheriff's office with a skeleton crew.

Mat wasn't going to discount Niall's cop instincts. If he thought something was odd, Mat would keep an eye out, and he'd mention it to Birdy too. As he drove, he found himself automatically checking pullouts and driveways for the mysterious RV but didn't see anything remotely suspicious—and what would he see at two-thirty in the morning, anyway?

He approached Niall's driveway. At the end of it lay the ruins of Jo and Od Hamarsson's cabin, waiting to be rebuilt. He slowed, tempted for a moment to stop; he'd enjoyed sitting on Niall's beach and watching the stars. Something about being small compared to the expanse of sky above was freeing. This late there would be less light pollution and, with no cloud cover, the stars would be bright.

A yawn snuck up on him, so big his jaw cracked. Blinking and shaking his head, Mat continued driving. Minutes later he was crawling into his comfy bed, his clothing neatly slung over the back of the wooden chair in his room. He'd find a time to watch the stars when Niall was there, and maybe one of these days Niall would crawl into bed with him too. Although maybe not at Mat's mother's house.

When he woke the next morning, only a few hours later, it was to the sound of his mother knocking on the bedroom door.

"Sorry, hon. I wanted to let you know Ella and Riley will be here later today. Ella managed to get a flight to Bellingham, and I'm leaving to pick them up."

Mat sat up, rubbing the sleep from his eyes. As much as he loved his sister and niece, their arrival was going to make for a full and busy house. "Okay. I'm probably going to be working late. I'll check in if I can."

He fell back against the pillows, the day already winding itself out in his head.

. . .

Later that morning, the weathered gray boards of the East Bay Marina quay creaked under Mat's weight as he strode toward the end. Boats of all types were moored here; they rocked with the current and wind, ropes and rigging clanging against masts, the sound carrying out across the water. It was a sound Mat had grown up with, one that always signaled *home* to him. He didn't think he could ever live away from the water. That was one of the reasons he'd chosen to move to San Francisco so many years ago.

Unlike the Hidden Harbor Marina, which catered almost exclusively to the wealthy tourist crowd, East Bay was dingy and worn, a working marina with an attached boatyard. The thirty or so boats moored out here, including the Piedras County Marine Rescue craft, were not hobby boats. They were owned by residents—folks who lived aboard and people who made their living with their vessels. As Mat drew closer to the end of the pier where the PCMR boat was moored, the acidic feeling in the pit of his stomach worsened. Could be too much coffee, but he didn't think so.

A sleek, intimidating Boston Whaler was tucked snug as a bug in between the county's nicked-up thirty-year-old patrol boat and a thirty-five-foot wooden sailboat someone was restoring. Nothing on the newer boat indicated it belonged to Duane, but Birdy had discovered—buried deep in the ownership paperwork —a reference to a company that had ties to Piedras County, so he was going to have to dig further. Mat didn't know anything about WoodlandStar LLC, and only a post office box in Anacortes was listed as the address. An LLC was a lot of effort just to hide the ownership of an expensive watercraft. He wondered what else was hiding behind the company's name.

The boat bobbed and tugged against the ropes binding it to the dock, practically begging to be taken out and driven fast with the throttle wide open. It was a marine patrol team's dream. The three thirty-five-horsepower engines mounted on the back ran over six thousand dollars each, he knew. Wouldn't that be nice in the summer months when jackoffs seemed to be everywhere. And it was beautiful. Mat wasn't much into power boats himself, but this was a gorgeous example.

"Nice boat, isn't it?"

Mat managed not to jump out of his skin, but it was close. He'd been so focused on the boat he hadn't heard footsteps behind him.

Looking over his shoulder, Mat watched as Sharleen Dixon drew closer. The dock moved slightly with the water's current and her added weight.

Sharleen looked like she always did, the rough-draft version of an English professor. Mat thought she was in her early fifties. Her faded red hair was wild from the wind, escaping Sharleen's efforts to keep it out of her face. She wore wrinkled khakis and a button-down shirt under a thick fleece vest, completing the outfit with a pair of thick black rubber boots that had seen better days. Mat noticed Sharleen's ancient pickup truck now parked next to his cruiser. He shifted his attention back to the Whaler.

"Whose is it? I haven't seen it out here before," he asked.

Sharleen shrugged, staring at the boat. "I'm not sure. You'd have to ask Duane. He brought it here a month or so ago, could be longer. It's been a while, anyway."

"Do you know anything about WoodlandStar LLC?"

She glanced at him, frowning, something in her expression sharp. "No. Never heard of it."

"When Birdy was out here the other day, you told her the boat was Duane's."

"I meant I assumed it's Duane's," she replied. "He never told me."

Mat thought that was kind of odd. All the boat owners he knew were chatty about their boats, wanting to compare specs with everyone in listening distance.

And how would Duane afford such a boat? As far as Mat knew, a significant chunk of Duane's income went to alimony, as his wife of twenty-some years had divorced him a few years after Mat moved back to Piedras.

"Duane's busy these days," Mat said, steering the conversation away from the boat. He wondered how well Sharleen knew Duane, if they were friends or if they merely shared the marina office.

Sharleen nodded. "You know how slow it is in the winter, but we're all starting to gear up. Gotta get the boats ready for summer."

"This was a tough winter for sure."

They chatted aimlessly as they turned to walk back toward land, the kind of catching up acquaintances do when they haven't seen each other in a while: the weather, if the summer would bring lots of tourists, how each other's moms were. They reached the end of the dock, and Mat looked up to see Duane driving in just as he was saying goodbye to Sharleen.

"Here he is. You can ask him about the boat yourself. See you later," Sharleen called out as she headed to the small shared office tucked to one side of the dock.

Mat waited while Duane climbed out of his truck, which was bigger and newer than Sharleen's. Where was the money for his lifestyle coming from? Duane hitched up his baggy work pants before slamming his door shut and striding over to where Mat waited. He was a grizzled man, years of exposure to the elements and a lack of sunscreen had created a kind of caricature of a fisherman. His hair had once been blond, but over the years it had thinned and faded to the sort of gray hair blonds often get when they are older. Even his bushy mustache was washed out.

"Duane." Mat shook Duane's extended hand. "How's everything going? I haven't seen you in a while."

"Good, busy. Getting ready for spring."

"Nice, nice."

Mat looked out over the marina. Sharleen's shadow moved about on the other side of her office windows—making coffee, maybe. A seagull squatted on one of the pilings, waiting for fish or taking a nap, and two crows fought over a piece of something unidentifiable. The ever-present breeze picked up a little, making the boats rock harder and causing the sailboats' rigging to bang against their masts again, a sort of marine orchestra echoing out over the small bay. Duane began walking toward the boatyard office. Mat followed him, wanting to talk a little more.

"I stopped by to see how you're doing and if you need any help getting the paperwork together for the reorg. Deputy Flynn can stop by and give you a hand if you need."

They stopped walking when they reached the office. A sign tacked next to the weathered wooden door said "Dockmaster/Marine Response."

Duane waved a hand. "I've got it under control, boss."

The way he said *boss* grated on Mat's nerves. Sure, Duane was acting casual, and his body language didn't scream *criminal*, but something was off. Birdy had been right to bring her suspicions to Mat's attention.

"All right then," Mat said agreeably. "I'll let you get to work. Deputy Flynn's available to you if you change your mind. The council hasn't set a firm date yet, but I imagine all this will happen before summer."

"I won't let you down, boss."

If Duane was trying to piss Mat off, it was working.

Mat strode across the gravel parking lot toward his cruiser, an uncomfortable prickle between his shoulder blades. It took everything he had not to look over his shoulder and see what Duane was doing, but he kept walking, not wanting to put Duane on alert any more than his visit already had. Opening the cruiser door, Mat turned and sketched out a wave; Duane stood where he'd left him, his stare decidedly hostile.

As he maneuvered the cruiser out of the parking lot and began driving toward the main road, it suddenly occurred to him that one of the only residents he hadn't seen at his brother's service was Duane. A surprise, as Duane and his father had been close friends as well as working together. Surely he would've come to say his goodbyes to his old friend's son.

Mat had a bad feeling about all of this. He couldn't put a finger on exactly what it was, but he'd get to the bottom of it.

Niall and Fenrir slipped in through the side door of the Orca after their rainy, very-early-morning walk. Niall was hoping Ricky and the rest of the management would forget they were staying there if they never saw them—as long as he paid his bill on time, right? Niall toed off his wet boots and left them next to the door before unzipping his coat.

"Wait here," he ordered Fenrir.

From the bathroom he snatched a towel he'd bought for this very purpose and brought it back out to dry off the dog. Fenrir waited until Niall had almost reached him before shaking, sending droplets of water everywhere. At least Niall still had his jacket on.

"Really?" Niall asked, wiping him down anyway and hanging the towel back up in the bathroom along with his jacket. "Are you *trying* to get us evicted?"

The box he'd received the day he left Seattle caught his eye. It sat on the desk next to another piece of mail Niall was avoiding. He'd managed to ignore them both for several days, putting them out of his mind and pretending they didn't exist. But it was only six thirty in the morning, he'd already had what passed for coffee and walked the dog, he'd checked his email—nothing from the insurance agency or anyone else important— and he didn't watch much TV unless he was tired, so now he had nothing else to pass the time.

Picking up the package, Niall perched on the edge of the bed, holding it in his hands for a moment. Whatever was inside was light. He shook it but didn't hear much other than the rustle of paper. Turning it over, he ran his thumb underneath the packing tape and ripped it off. Setting it beside him on the bed, he carefully lifted up the flaps of the box.

The contents were wrapped in paper, the kind a person would use for packing dishes or delicate items. The paper protected a standard-sized envelope and a plastic sandwich bag containing two film canisters. Niall reached for the envelope and took a breath to slow his racing pulse. Nothing in his experience led him to believe that anonymously delivered photographs were a good thing.

The envelope wasn't sealed. Whoever had sent him the box had merely used it to keep the photographs tucked inside from floating around the box. Carefully, Niall pulled the photos out of the envelope.

In the top photo, a girl was looking up toward the photographer from a rope swing hanging over a river or creek. She gripped the rope with both hands and was kicking her feet out; water gleamed darkly beneath her. He'd never seen the image before, but he was certain the girl was Ana Hamarsson—his mother. Niall didn't recognize the location, but she was grinning, her expression joyful and teasing. He turned it over; "1978" was scrawled in pencil on the back.

In the second snapshot, Ana peeked out of a frost-covered camping tent, only her head visible. Again, she was smiling brightly, nothing in her face indicating her future. And again, "1978" was written on the back.

With utmost care, Niall eased the third and last photo out of the envelope. This one showed Ana from the back, her head turned so she was looking over her shoulder at the invisible photographer, a shy smile on her face. She wore nothing but underwear, and her long, thick blonde hair hung down her bare back in a single braid past her narrow waist. On the other side of the photo was written, "1979."

Niall felt dizzy, and he realized he'd forgotten to breathe. Looking at these pictures of Ana, seeing her a way he'd never before been able to imagine her: *happy*. His grandparents had always told him that she had been troubled in high school, and maybe she had been, but her demons didn't show themselves here.

He reached for the bag with its rolls of film and lifted it out, the plastic-and-metal canisters a heavy weight in the palm of his hand. Tucked into the side of the box was a note.

Niall, I thought you might want these pictures. They aren't mine, they belonged to my father, David. I found them in his belongings not long ago. The film I found along with the photos, I thought you should have it and develop it if possible. It seems possible we're half-brothers. Although I imagine I'm the last person you'd like to be related to, I'd be willing to be tested if that's what you decide.

I'll leave the ball in your court.

Shay Delacombe

Niall had to read the words several times in order to understand what they meant. Shay Delacombe had sent these... and they could be half brothers? The fuck. Niall didn't know what to think. He didn't recall if he'd ever known Shay's father, who from the sound of the note was no longer alive.

Niall hated Shay Delacombe, right?

He supposed he mostly hated the fact that he was a defense lawyer. And he'd been partially responsible for getting the case against Jeremy Vaughn tossed out—Niall was still mad as hell about that. Niall had been on the receiving end of one of his cross-examinations, once. Shay tore apart crap evidence like it was wet tissue paper, which Niall admitted was why he was paid the big bucks. But Shay had also successfully defended a few clients—like Vaughn—who Niall knew were guilty. Shay Delacombe excelled at what he did for a living, no one could deny that.

With trembling fingers, he collected the pictures and shoved them back into the envelope. He didn't know what to do. He wanted to destroy the pictures, they made him irrationally angry. It was much easier for him to think of his mother as a terrible person who had abandoned him than as a human who been a girl, a happy teen, *someone else*. He also wanted to pull them out again and let himself see that Ana had been happy once; she'd laughed and possibly loved.

Because he couldn't help himself, Niall moved over to the desk and opened his laptop. As soon as the browser loaded, he typed in "David Delacombe, Piedras Island." The first photo that popped up was not flattering. Delacombe had been booked for setting fire to the boutique hotel he'd owned in Hidden Harbor. Niall peered at it, trying to see if there was an obvious resemblance between them.

Delacombe was dark, with olive skin and dark hair like Niall's, but beyond that Niall didn't see a likeness. Niall searched Shay, pulling up his law firm's website and finding a photo of him with some other suited men standing by a conference table. Shay looked like his father, although a little more delicate, a little finer. All three of them shared coloring and height, though since Od Hamarsson had been over six feet tall, Niall had always assumed his height came from his grandfather.

Niall didn't remember—or maybe had never known—that Delacombe was behind the fire at the Dockman. He wondered how Shay had been affected by his father's actions. He might even have been in law school when it happened. Shay was three or four years older than Niall, which would mean David had been fucking around on his wife and son—if what Shay suggested was the truth.

He sat back in the chair, its squeak reassuring him that he wasn't experiencing a mental break. The box was real, as were the photos, and the note from Delacombe. What if they were related, half brothers, brothers? Would it make things easier or more complicated? Did he even want to know? The part of him that had spent years in fight mode bristled at the thought of Delacombe being family, but another part was curious. And, frankly, it was better than being related to any of the Reynoldses or—a truly horrifying thought hit him—*the Dempseys*.

The other envelope was easy after the contents of the box. At least he knew what was inside, even if he didn't want to deal with it. It was oversized and bulky, the return address indicating it had been sent by the City of Seattle Human Resources Department, specifically from the division handling the Seattle PD.

He shook his head; this waffling about shit was not normal for him. Niall was the man who dealt with issues and stressful situations unflinchingly, staring them in their literal (and figurative) faces with his eyes wide open: death, taxes, clowns. Jesus, he really was losing his grip.

Still, he hesitated, his fingers motionless, the envelope unopened.

This was fucking ridiculous. He didn't turn emo over envelopes; the old Niall ripped them open, dealt with the contents, and moved on. Old Niall didn't have the time to hesitate. If he could open the box, he could open this fucking envelope.

Tearing open the flap open with a jagged motion, he pulled the sheaf of papers out and tossed the envelope back onto the desk. He quickly scanned the pages. Retirement choices galore, COBRA insurance coverage, et cetera. The damn envelope was full of questions, and he had to pick his answers.

In the past when Niall had considered his future, which

hadn't been often, he'd always thought he would die in the line of duty. He'd never believed he might retire and have time, nearly another entire *lifetime*, to choose another career if he wanted. *To possibly find a partner*, a seductive little voice whispered. His fortieth birthday was coming up quick, and maybe he wouldn't live another forty years, but it sure seemed a lot more likely now.

"Want to go for another walk?" Niall asked the dog.

Fenrir's ears perked, indicating his opinion of the paperwork versus heading outside for a pee and a nice stroll.

"Okay, fine. Sounds better to me too." He tossed the paperwork back onto the desk next to the envelope it had arrived in.

He needed to think, and he did it better when he was outside.

Grabbing Fenrir's leash again, Niall snapped it onto his collar before shrugging into his rain parka. Fenrir never minded walks, even multiple ones within the same hour. The cloud cover wasn't heavy today. There might even be sunshine later, but in the Pacific Northwest it was always better to be prepared. At the last second, he grabbed his cell phone and car keys, stashing them in one of his coat pockets.

Outside, Niall discovered the morning was promising, the moody clouds chased away by the first hints of warmish sunshine. Fenrir tugged gently on the leash, directing them toward Hidden Harbor's waterfront. He liked to sniff around the tiny, rocky public beach next to the ferry dock. It wasn't as good as the beach on Niall's property, and Fenrir was supposed to remain on his leash, but in a pinch Fenrir approved of it.

As Niall ambled down the hill behind Fenrir, a movement in his peripheral vision caught his attention. Turning, he glimpsed the orange-striped beige camper turning onto the street in front of the high school.

He stopped in his tracks. Fenrir jerked against the leash and turned his head to give Niall a "WTF" look.

"Shit." The RV continued on, vanishing from Niall's line of sight.

There was nothing he could do, no way for him to follow it. His car was several blocks away in the motel parking lot. By the time he reached it, the camper would have disappeared. Again.

"Goddammit."

Fenrir tugged again, not caring about the camper at all. Releasing a frustrated sigh, Niall allowed him to walk them to the ferry dock. Once there, Niall dug out his phone and texted Mat.

Saw RV just now heading west toward Killegens.

He pressed Send and waited impatiently for Mat's reply.

EIGHT

MAT

"Uncle Mat? *Pssst*… Uncle Mat!"

Riley's voice yanked Mat from a dreamless sleep.

Slowly, his brain turned on. His sister and niece had arrived the evening before while he was still at the station. Everyone had been asleep by the time he'd made it home.

"Riley, sweetie, what's the matter? Are you okay? Is something wrong?" He tried to force the sleep fog away, rubbing his eyes to try and get the sleep out of them. His niece waited impatiently next to his bed, not quite jumping up and down, but she was close to liftoff.

"Your phone was buzzing." Riley made a buzzing sound so Mat wouldn't misunderstand what she meant.

Mat groaned. He'd been exhausted—he was still exhausted—and instead of bringing his phone upstairs with him, he'd forgotten it on the set of shelves just inside the front door. Way to be a responsible sheriff. Sitting up, he pushed the covers aside and swung his legs out of bed.

"I like your jammies," Riley commented.

Mat looked down at himself. He was wearing the flannel

lounge pants Ella had given him for Christmas. They had tiny robots, spaceships, and aliens decorating them.

"Thanks, kid." Mat reached out and ruffled her hair.

"Uncle Maaat!" Riley shrieked, dancing backward. "Don't mess up my hair!"

He pointed to his head. "You can mess up my hair."

"You have boy hair, and it's short."

Mat smiled at her words. "Look, kiddo, I need to check my phone, okay? Thanks for letting me know it was buzzing."

"I brought it to you." Riley pulled her left hand from behind her back, showing him the phone she had clutched in her fist.

"Thanks, sweetie."

Mat took the phone and swiped the screen to check what he'd missed. The first thing that registered was that it was only seven thirty in the morning. No wonder he felt like he had a hangover. Secondly, no calls had come through. The notification was a text from Niall.

"Who's Nail?" Riley asked, her head cocked to one side.

"It's Niall, honey, and it's complicated. Go find Grandma or your mom. I need to get ready to go to work."

As quickly as possible, Mat showered and dressed in his uniform. Then he stopped in the kitchen to fill his to-go cup with coffee.

"Somebody was up bright and early today," Mat said to his sister, who was sitting at the kitchen table with a cup of coffee and an e-reader in front of her.

Ella smiled. "Someone wanted to see her uncle even though Grandma and I both told her you were sleeping."

"I need to get to the station anyway, and Riley is a much nicer alarm clock than my usual one. Where is she now?"

"Mom's helping her with her bath. I needed just a second to myself after the flight and everything yesterday. Let's not talk about that right now though. Mom said you've been busy."

Mat pulled his fancy stainless steel to-go cup out of the dish drainer. "It's been ridiculous. Maybe it's because people have been cooped up all winter, I don't know, but it can stop anytime." He poured coffee into his cup and twisted the lid on tightly. It held just enough to get him to the station.

As he passed his sister at the table, he bent down and hugged her. "I'm glad you two are here."

"I'm sure your tune will change if she keeps waking you up," she grumbled, leaning against him for a second. "Go be sheriff before she gets back down here, or you'll never escape."

Mat chuckled. He didn't mind Riley waking him up in the morning. His niece was one of his favorite people—and, he mentally corrected, technically it was Niall who was responsible for waking Mat up. *And*, if Mat was being really honest, he didn't mind Niall texting at any time of day or night, although he would prefer if they communicated in person and not about some random camper Niall was fixated on.

As he drove back in to Hidden Harbor, a thought occurred to Mat that both thrilled and saddened him.

NINE

NIALL

Five minutes passed with no response from Mat. Niall spent the time alternating between checking his phone and pacing up and down the tiny beach. Looking out across the choppy gray water, he spotted the ferry making its way to the dock, growing larger as it drew closer. A few islanders were lined up to load on. Most were in cars, but there were some pedestrians waiting as well. Niall recognized Stu Dennis, an old-timer who was likely on his way to meet up with his "girl" in Anacortes. Stu nodded toward him and raised a hand in greeting, and Niall nodded back.

He checked his phone again. Several dots were running back and forth across the bottom of the screen. *Finally.* It seemed to take forever for Mat to respond. Then the dots at the bottom of the screen stopped moving, but there was still nothing. Impatiently, Niall started to text Mat again, when a response appeared.

On my way to the station now.

Niall watched the ferry dock and disgorge its meager load of early passengers before the waiting cars and pedestrians loaded on. Then he and Fenrir walked to the station.

. . .

"Really?" Mat asked in an exasperated tone once he'd opened the cruiser door and climbed out.

"What?"

Niall and Fenrir had been waiting next to a rockery planted with rhododendrons that looked as if they were thinking about blooming soon.

Mat shook his head. Before replying, he reached inside and grabbed a messenger bag from his back seat, looping it over his shoulder. "Seriously? *'What'*?" Mat repeated, squinting at Niall as if Niall was missing something important. He also looked slightly amused, which Niall had no explanation for.

"What?" What was Mat so worked up about?

Mat stopped moving, closed his eyes for a moment, and reached up to pinch the bridge of his nose. Niall had noticed Mat did that when he was feeling irritated or frustrated. "You're obsessing about this RV, enough so that you... you text me at seven thirty in the morning?"

"Well, yeah. I *told* you I only saw it in the mornings, and I texted you when I saw it again."

He did not understand what Mat's issue was.

Mat shook his head and started walking again, passing Niall and Fenrir, who fell in step behind him. Mat let them inside. "Might as well bring in the dog, no one else is here."

At his desk, he slung the messenger bag over the back of his chair before taking his jacket off and tossing it across the chair as well.

"Make yourself comfortable." He gestured at the same chair Niall had sat in on Wednesday. "Do you need a cup of coffee? I need another one."

Niall eyed the chair with suspicion before carefully sitting down. "Coffee sounds great. Thanks." Fenrir plopped to the carpet with a grunt.

A few minutes later, Mat returned from the station break room carrying two steaming mugs of coffee. One had the words

Property of Area 51 stenciled on it. The mug he handed Niall read, *K9 Handler: Go ahead and run, my partner loves fast food.* Niall chuckled. He'd never seen that one before.

Niall watched Mat make himself comfortable at his desk and take a sip of coffee, and wondered what he was missing.

After a minute or two of pressing buttons on his desktop, moving his chair around, and pushing paperwork around, Mat turned his chair to face Niall. "Hear me out, okay?"

Niall narrowed his eyes but nodded, waiting.

"I eventually came around when you offered to assist with the Reynolds case. Fresh from Seattle, you'd injured yourself, you had time on your hands—hand." Mat laughed at his own terrible joke. "It's hard to stop being a cop. Even when I'm at home, I'm a cop. You're the same way—we're hardwired to be aware of our surroundings, to notice things that are maybe out of place."

Mat stopped speaking to take another big sip of coffee. After setting the mug back down on his desk, he continued.

"The department is shorthanded right now. I didn't get out of here last night until after midnight and we've got somebody setting fire to empty garages and buildings. Thankfully nothing happened last night, but Devon thinks it's just a matter of time before they strike again."

Niall grimaced, nodding. He'd heard about the big fire last weekend.

Mat steamrolled on. "The department already fields regular calls from a few of the older residents. Sandy Johnson, for example. She lives alone, out past Marshal Soper, and calls about once a week to report a suspicious noise. I, *we*, don't need you adding to the list. No one else has reported this RV. No one. I haven't seen it, Birdy hasn't said anything, and—okay, so the other two deputies might not notice right away, but—you get my point?"

Niall got it. He was half embarrassed for texting Mat and obviously waking him up and half furious because he *knew* there was something up with that vehicle.

"I think I mentioned before there are a handful of residents who've hit hard times. I haven't checked around, but maybe someone's lost their job? We have drug problems on the island too, just like so many small communities—meth is here, and it's not going away. I don't have enough deputies to investigate all the calls we receive."

Mat's words brought up memories of his own history, when his mother had flitted from friend to friend or dealer to dealer. Sometimes they'd lived in apartments or single rooms, but as her drug habit worsened, so did their living situations. At one point they'd squatted in a rotting camper with several other users. Because he'd been small, Niall had been forced to sleep on the grimy black floor underneath a tiny table—someone else slept on the table above him. He thought it hadn't been long after that time that Ana had disappeared forever, leaving Niall at the mercy of her so-called friends.

Mat spoke again. "And that was my sheriff TED Talk, thank you for coming. The next is from me, Mat. Not Sheriff Dempsey, just Mat."

Niall eyed him warily.

"I liked that you texted me. I liked it a lot." He settled himself more comfortably in his chair, taking another sip of his coffee. Niall waited for him to continue talking, but he didn't.

"That's it? You liked it?"

"Yep."

"You are..." Niall shook his head.

"Great? Wonderful? Patient and perceptive? I'm very patient, this is true."

Ignoring Mat's words for the moment, Niall said, "I finally got my separation paperwork." To be honest, he didn't think Mat was very patient, but maybe this wasn't the time to point that out. He considered telling Mat about the box and Shay Delacombe but decided he needed to think about that a little longer.

Mat's dark eyebrows lifted toward his hairline. He nodded, his expression sympathetic. "Oh, yeah? I bet that feels weird."

"I never thought I'd be in this situation."

"What do you mean?" Mat asked.

"Honestly?"

Mat nodded.

"I never thought I'd live this long. I assumed some perp would get to me. It's not like cops generally have long life spans." Niall tried to pick his words carefully. He'd been to plenty of service funerals, although he hadn't attended the one for Mat's father; it had been too soon after his own grandmother's death, and he hadn't felt like his presence would be missed... but maybe he'd been wrong about that.

"That's one of the reasons I came back home, you know," Mat said.

"I thought you moved back because your father died."

"I did, but also being a small-town sheriff seemed a lot safer than working in San Francisco. Before Dad died, I was investigating a slew of gang killings and ended up getting death threats of my own."

Niall cocked his head to the side. "Did you, do you, feel like you gave up?"

That was one of Niall's worries, that he was giving up. Being a coward, leaving unsolved cases out there, victims with no justice and families with no closure. He hadn't known about Mat's run-in with gangs, and he was suddenly very glad Mat had decided to move back to Piedras.

"It was a struggle at first, I'll admit," Mat said slowly. "The island is small, but I feel like I have a real impact here. I'm not just fighting and not seeing anything change for the better. At the same time, I'm more visible and can't have anonymous downtime."

"I feel like I'm letting people down," Niall admitted, the

words practically burning his tongue as he uttered them out loud for the first time.

"You're not." Mat leaned forward into Niall's space. "Have you ever thought about consulting? With your experience and record, I bet a lot of departments would be willing to pay for your expertise. Departments like mine that don't have enough in the budget to hire an expert permanently but might need help with a tough case."

"You've said repeatedly you don't want my help."

"Ah, now, don't go twisting my words. You know very well there's a difference between consulting and stopping by every time a change in the weather spooks you. And I don't mean my office exclusively. I mean departments across the state, or even the country."

Niall did know what Mat meant, but it didn't make him feel any less like he was abandoning victims and their families. "There is something up with that RV."

"I believe you."

A simple statement that meant everything to Niall. He blinked, almost at a loss for words. "You do?"

"I do, but until something happens, we can't do anything about it."

Niall nodded. He knew that, of course, but having Mat say he believed him was more important to Niall than he'd realized.

"Sooo," Mat drew out the word, "Birdy's on duty tonight, and even though someone got me out of bed far too early, do you want to grab dinner later? I'd offer my place, but my sister Ella and her daughter are back and staying with us—there's some family stuff going on I haven't told you about—and with them *and* my mom it's probably a bit much right off the bat. They have no idea how to mind their own business. Lulu's is open." He waggled his eyebrows, waiting for Niall's response.

Lulu's. Niall had forgotten about the old-timer café located out near the airstrip. It was a locals-only kind of place, even less of a tourist spot than the Hook in Hidden Harbor, which got the occasional visiting hipster as well as the old-timers.

"Is Lulu still alive?" Niall asked. The owner had seemed ancient when he was a kid.

"And kicking," Mat confirmed.

"Okay." Why not? Maybe it would be a good thing. Maybe he and Mat could work on this friendship thing. Maybe Niall could do this after all.

"Yeah?" A broad smile stretched across Mat's handsome face.

"Yeah. Don't make a big freaking deal about it. It's just dinner."

Mat leaned closer. "Maybe, but it's dinner with you."

TEN

MAT

Mat arrived at Lulu's before Niall. That wasn't a shock, seeing he was over half an hour early. Nerves had him leaving the station as soon as he could. Asking Niall to dinner had been risky, but Mat had had a realization—or what he hoped was a realization—that morning, and he'd decided the risk was worth it. There was an invisible wall surrounding Niall, and it was Mat who was going to have to breach it. Niall didn't know the way out. Mat needed to act a bit more like Fenrir, just sneak around those barriers and make himself comfortable.

The diner was situated in what was likely an old modular-style home, a double- or triple- wide painted a bright shade of purple. Inside there was dark 1970s wood paneling plastered with terrible oil and watercolor paintings. All the art was for sale and had been as long as Mat could remember. Some of it he recalled being there back when he was a small boy.

He snagged a corner booth. It was too big, really, for only the two of them, but it would afford them a little privacy—unless Niall wanted to eat in the bar, where it was even darker. On a Friday, the bar would be busy, and likely they'd run into a regular Mat had ticketed at some point. That was definitely a problem with being sheriff: there was no place other than his house that wasn't public space.

"Menu?" a female voice asked, startling Mat from his thoughts. He looked up and nodded, recognizing the server. "Evening, Sheriff," she added.

He held up two fingers and Gracie left, returning seconds later with thick plastic menus and plunking down two glasses of ice water.

"I'll be back." Gracie disappeared through the swinging doors into the kitchen.

There were only a couple other tables occupied tonight: a couple Mat recognized who had recently moved to the island and Stan Elberman, an old-timer who decidedly ignored Mat. He'd been giving Mat the cold shoulder ever since Mat interrupted Stan's impromptu hunting party last month.

Mat's fingers thrummed against the tabletop. He was nervous. Up until this second he'd been focused on the fact that Niall had agreed to meet him, and now Mat realized he, Mat Dempsey, Piedras County Sheriff, was having dinner with another man—in public. And he was nervous.

Well, if Niall showed up.

He'd show up.

And when he did, Mat would basically out himself to everyone in the restaurant. He was ready, he reassured himself.

"Can I bring you something to drink while you wait?"

It was temping to order a double vodka, but he settled on a nonalcoholic lager instead.

He was sipping his drink, trying to pretend he wasn't feeling anxious, when the door opened and Niall stepped inside. Mat stopped breathing for a moment. Niall looked *good*, wearing a similar outfit to the one he'd worn to Sean's funeral—jeans, white shirt, and wool blazer.

Good enough to eat and also all wrong. Niall wasn't built for street clothes. He was a throwback, a Viking who should have a thick pelt of fox fur hanging off one shoulder and a bearded ax gripped in his hand. A skeggøx—Mat had gleaned the name from surreptitious research as a teen, and he *may* have refreshed his memory more recently. Niall took up a lot of space in Mat's head. He took another sip of his beer, not tasting it, and watched Niall as he approached the table. He wasn't the only one; everyone else's attention was drawn to Niall as well. He even had the attention of the cook on the other side of the kitchen pass-through.

Mat knew what appealed to him about Niall, but what drew others' attention? A six-foot-four olive-skinned man with dark hair that curled at the ends and was long enough to brush against the collar of his shirt. Niall was a big man, but he wasn't bulky; he was lean and muscled from years of exercise or maybe just a high metabolism. Unlike Mat's, Niall's body hadn't gotten the memo about impending middle age.

"Have a seat," Mat offered gallantly when Niall reached the table.

With a small nod, Niall lowered himself onto the bench opposite Mat and picked up one of the menus. "What's good these days?"

Mat opened his menu. "Depends."

"Depends on what?"

"If you plan on working out later."

Silence.

Mat shut his eyes for a second, cursing his mouth, his face heating. When he opened them, Niall's amused agate gaze was locked onto his.

Mat huffed out a laugh. "I mean, the country-fried steak is great, but it has about a million calories. I sit around a lot; a guy my age has got to watch what he eats. I usually get a burger, no mayo, and a side salad."

"Because mayo is also full of calories?"

Mat grimaced. "No, because mayonnaise is disgusting."

"Huh." Niall went back to perusing his choices.

When Gracie came around to their table, Niall ordered the country-fried steak. Mat blushed, then panicked as he attempted to quell the manic butterflies dive-bombing in his stomach, and he ended up ordering his usual.

Niall smirked.

Mat was toast.

Niall made himself comfortable on the vinyl bench seat. He'd been jumpy as hell about dinner until he'd laid eyes on Mat and realized Mat was more nervous than he was. Niall enjoyed having the upper hand. Having Mat nervous suited him—but then again, he was an asshole.

"I see they still have the same art," he commented, glancing around at the decidedly amateur work.

An oil painting hanging on the wall by their table depicted a gritty sailor fighting the elements. One of his eyes was closed against wind and salt spray, the other stared gloomily down at them. It was creepy.

Mat leaned across the table. "It's terrible," he whispered, "but Lulu's grandson painted it."

Ah. He'd probably known that at some point.

The two of them fell into cop talk. It was… Niall wanted to use the word "endearing," but shied away from it… *nice* how deeply Mat cared about not only the Piedras County residents but also the deputies and staff he worked with. He knew all of their stories and their extended families' too—who was having trouble paying bills, who had a new girlfriend or boyfriend, who was worried because their kid wasn't learning to speak as fast as her siblings. He carried all that information around in his head in addition to the department's ongoing cases.

The waitress dropped their plates off, interrupting a story Mat was regaling him with about wrangling raccoons who'd broken into one of the island's coffee shops one night, wreaking complete havoc.

"Because somehow the sheriff's office is also animal control."

"Another beer?" the waitress asked.

Niall didn't recognize her, although her name tag said, "Gracie."

"No, make it a coffee," Mat replied.

Niall raised a questioning eyebrow, also shaking his head. He didn't need another beer. He'd cut back since taking a bottle of Jack Daniel's to bed with him when he first came back to Piedras.

"Technically, I'm backup for Birdy tonight. With my other two regular deputies out and the—" He cut himself off.

"What?" Niall asked.

Mat glanced around. Niall followed his gaze. There were only the three other patrons in the dining room area, and none of them seemed to be paying any attention to their conversation.

In a low voice, Mat continued, "Normally, in a situation like this, I'd ask Duane Cooper to help out… but there's something going on, and until Birdy and I get to the bottom of it, I'd rather not have him in the station by himself."

Niall frowned. "Who's Duane, again?"

"Auxiliary marine search and rescue. I inherited him from my dad, actually." Mat shrugged. "I let things continue as they had been, didn't see the need for change—and until recently, marine wasn't exactly under the sheriff's office umbrella. We were more like sibling agencies, but the county is changing that. Birdy's been going over the budgets he provided from past years so I can give the council an idea of what next year's will look like with marine officially added in."

Niall grimaced. "Things not adding up?"

"Red flags all over the damn place. Not obvious stuff—weird things, like, he actually doesn't spend everything the county allocates. I mean, he gets his salary, and in the summer it's higher because, surprise, there's a lot of overtime, but... there's a new boat out there, and we don't know where it came from. There's no way he could afford it on his salary—plus I know he's still paying alimony—and the county sure didn't pay for it."

"Brand new?"

"New enough. *Fancy*. It's a boat I'd love to have for my team. Sharleen Dixon, she's the dockmaster these days, says Duane started mooring it there not too long ago. When I was out there the other afternoon, he was not very helpful. But maybe I'm projecting."

Mat truly liked most of his citizens, Niall knew that. Even the ones who were perennially in trouble. Not the meth dealers, but apart from those, he found something to like about most. It must have been hard for him to think that someone he'd known and trusted was likely pulling some sort of funny business.

Loud, rough male voices interrupted Niall's thoughts as four burly men spilled into the dining room. The walls quivered as the door banged shut behind them. The waitress stiffened, her welcoming smile turning to a frown when she saw who they were.

Glancing over at the interlopers, Niall recognized one of them as Martin Reynolds. His cop antennae jittered. Martin was never up to any good. The men hadn't spotted Niall and Mat tucked away in the corner yet, but they would soon enough.

The thought had hardly crossed his mind when Martin swung around looking for a spot big enough for his group and his stare caught Niall's. Niall returned Martin's hard look, refusing to drop his gaze. Martin's lips twitched upward in a smirk.

"Look, it's our fearless sheriff and his friend."

The word friend had a certain emphasis, and Niall had a

nearly overwhelming urge to punch Martin—so much so he actually twitched, the fingers of his left hand clenching into a fist. Something brushed against his ankle. Mat's foot. Niall relaxed his fingers and settled for shaping his lips into the facsimile of a smile before finishing his remaining beer. The desire to wipe the smirk off Martin's face remained, but for Mat and Mat alone, Niall would step aside. Still, he didn't know how long he was going to be able to sit in the same room with the man.

"Martin, it looks like you're having a good time tonight." Mat's deep voice carried across the room, calm, yet everyone heard the razor-sharp edge.

One of the other men ignored the exchange altogether, instead walking over to the largest booth and sliding into it. The other two followed his lead, leaving Martin alone at the door. Martin stood there, trying to outstare Mat, before he followed his friends to the booth. The four of them immediately began whispering among themselves.

Mat huffed out a quiet breath. "He is such a pain in my side. The rest of those guys are relatively harmless, but Martin is a loose wheel."

"I should get going." Niall shoved his plate away. He'd finished about half the meal, but his appetite was gone.

To his credit, Mat didn't argue, but the hurt in his eyes spoke volumes.

"Fenrir's in the car."

Which was true, but also an excuse. And what guy liked being put second to a dog?

Niall signaled to Gracie and paid his portion of the check; he wasn't letting Mat pick up the tab when Niall was the one ducking out on him. The murmurs of Martin and his cronies buzzed in his ears. It wasn't that he cared what they said about him, but Niall wasn't sure he was going to be able to control his temper if they started bad-mouthing Mat.

Once he was safely in his car, the tension released from his shoulders. He was slightly embarrassed he'd let Martin get to him. Inside the restaurant his palms had itched with the very primal desire to pummel Martin into a bloody pulp.

Niall was used to anger. Anger was an old friend; it had been his companion for many years. Anger was the driving force behind his solve rate, possibly the reason he was still alive. But Piedras and Mat—they weren't the place for anger. Niall was ready to leave the anger behind. He just wasn't sure it was ready to leave him yet.

Minutes later he found himself bumping down the driveway to his property. Niall had a hard time thinking of the land as his instead of his grandparents', but they were both long dead and Niall was the only Hamarsson left. He supposed it was past time he accepted his heritage.

What if he was related to Shay Delacombe? Even then, Niall was still the last Hamarsson.

He parked next to the pile of ash and debris that had once been Morfar and Mormor's home, the home he'd come to as a feral boy and where he'd reinvented himself into a human. It was less painful to look at these days, but he would be glad when the insurance claim finally went through and he could rebuild. It would be good to start something new.

Fenrir whined, pressing his nose in a most pathetic way against the rear window, adding another smudge to the mural of nose prints already there. Rolling his eyes, Niall opened the back hatch. Grinning, tail high, Fenrir raced down to the beach, sure of where they were headed. Niall took the time to grab his coat and shrug into it. The night was clear but the wind off the water cold, just what he needed to clear his head.

At the beach, Niall claimed his favorite log and let his thoughts wind out into the dark, amusing himself by watching the dog prance and tease the waves. The anger he'd felt at Lulu's slowly seeped out from underneath his skin, absorbed by the wind, the waves, and the stars shining above his head.

Even though the cabin was gone, Niall could still hear his grandparents' voices, especially Od's.

"Life is hard enough, son. Don't go making it harder," he'd say in his gravelly voice with its heavy Norwegian accent, commenting, maybe, on something that had happened at school that day.

Then most likely he'd launch into a drawn-out tale involving Tyr or Odin. Niall didn't know how many of the stories Od had told were made up on the spot and how many were handed down through generations of Hamarssons. He supposed it didn't matter. They were his stories now.

The wind picked up, its wicked fingers slicing through the fabric of Niall's coat—no match for Njord's power—and even Fenrir abandoned chasing the waves to sit at Niall's feet. He wondered if his grandparents had known about Ana and David Delacombe and quickly decided they hadn't. David had been much older than Ana, and he would've been married to Shay's mother at the time. His grandparents definitely wouldn't have approved but that didn't mean they hadn't known about them.

"You cold too?" Niall asked.

Fenrir's tail thumped once against Niall's leg in response.

"Come on."

In the warmth of his motel room, Niall untied his boots, tugging them off while Fenrir flopped elegantly onto the dog bed Niall had sprung for; motel management did not approve of animals on the furniture. Likely another reason they were giving him the boot.

Scooting forward in the remarkably uncomfortable desk chair, he powered up his laptop, idly wondering if the chair had been constructed this way on purpose—just another reason for guests to keep their visits limited to a week or weekend. He opened his email, checking to see if his insurance company had forwarded the paperwork yet. Nope.

But there was correspondence from a former colleague. Niall's first instinct was to hit the delete button, but the subject line grabbed his attention: "Consulting services?"

Leo Zelinsky had been a fellow homicide detective. He'd left SPD a few years ago after a stellar career, and even though Niall had made all the right noises at the time about keeping in touch, he'd never intended to, so Leo's email came as a surprise. Leo wanted to let Niall know the company he was working for, West Coast Forensics, was actively recruiting. Was Niall interested in coming aboard?

Was he interested? And was it merely coincidence Mat had brought up that very thing earlier that day? He didn't think Mat and Leo had any kind of connection, but who knew?

A part of himself stirred, a buzz he recognized as subdued excitement. He didn't want to go back to day-to-day police work. That part of his life was truly over. But after a lifetime of being a homicide cop in a fairly large city, he had a lot of experience under his belt. How else would he put it to use?

Niall closed the laptop's lid. He'd see how he felt about Leo's email in the morning; he wasn't making any snap decisions one way or the other. On top of the photos from Shay and the paperwork from SPD, he didn't have room for anything else.

Instead he'd spend what was left of the evening feeling guilty about coming close to clobbering Martin Reynolds and ditching Mat. Martin deserved clobbering, there was no doubt, but not by him. Justice would find Martin eventually, and Niall would be on the sidelines handing out popcorn.

Regretting how the evening had ended, Niall began to get ready for bed, stripping off his sweater and t-shirt and tossing them into a pile on the chair.

A light tap on the door sent his heartbeat into orbit. Fenrir's ears pricked, and he started to stand. Niall considered ignoring the knock. Maybe it was an accident. Maybe someone walking down the hallway bumped the door. The tap came again, more insistent this time.

Through the door, Niall heard Mat's voice. "Niall, I know you're in there. Your car is parked in the lot."

Mat lifted his hand to knock on Niall's door again. Impatience and the sense that this time he couldn't let Niall run away had propelled him to pass his house and continue to the motel where Niall insisted on staying. When the door opened, Mat swallowed at the sight of him. Niall wore his jeans and nothing else except mismatched socks on his feet, one green, the other black. Mat's gut tightened, and he repressed a chuckle—he had it bad if sock feet were turning him on.

Right, because it wasn't Niall's thickly muscled chest covered with a dusting of dark hair that had Mat needing to adjust himself. If he wasn't careful, he was going to start drooling, and wouldn't Ella have the last laugh then? A door at the far end of the hallway banged, and the ice machine clattered as they stood there staring at each other.

"May I come in?" Mat asked.

Niall opened the door wide enough for Mat to slip past him. Niall's anger from earlier had disappeared. Mat smelled salt air on him and knew he'd been out at the beach.

Mat had stayed at Lulu's for a good half hour after Niall left, slowly drinking his coffee and finishing his meal, making sure

Martin Reynolds understood Sheriff Dempsey would not be cowed. Martin had tried to rile up his buddies after Niall left, but they brushed off his attempts, instead focusing on the motocross race being replayed on the TV.

"What's up?" Niall asked.

Mat shrugged. "Our dinner was interrupted." And he'd obviously lost his mind.

Niall frowned and closed the door. Mat took in the room. It was small, not really big enough for Mat, Niall, and the dog—in fact, it was downright cramped. The only place for Mat to sit was on the bed. The mattress bowed a bit under his weight. Fenrir huffed and shut his eyes, not interested in humans at the moment.

"Did something happen after I left?" Niall asked.

He had no idea what he was doing in Niall's motel room. He had no plan. He just hadn't wanted to go home yet. The evening had ended too quickly and on a negative note. Mat toed off his shoes and unzipped his jacket, tossing it to one side, and it fell down onto the carpet. No, he corrected himself, he knew what he was doing here—he just didn't know if his overture would be accepted.

Niall snatched a t-shirt from a pile on the chair and sniffed it. He grimaced but pulled it on anyway.

"I just thought it was a shame we didn't get to finish our conversation. I know, I know—I said I'd be patient. I didn't come over expecting anything to happen. I mean, no doubt there was a part of me that was hopeful, but." He shrugged. Niall could come to his own conclusions.

"Why did you come over? *Did* something happen?" Niall asked again. His tone wasn't angry or accusatory, merely curious.

Mat lay back on the bed, his arms crossed underneath his head, and stared at the ceiling. "At Lulu's? No, those guys are a bunch of cowards."

The mattress sank further as Niall perched on the edge, pulling one knee up and keeping one foot on the floor for balance.

Neither of them said anything for a moment. Mat shut his eyes and let the silence flow into him. Niall was an easy person to be quiet around; he didn't demand conversation. A memory came to him, an incident when they were children. Another kid had confronted Niall on the playground, asking him if he was deaf and dumb. After a pause during which Niall looked the accuser up and down very slowly, he'd answered, "No," and walked off.

"I guess I came because I wanted to be somewhere no one needed me an hour ago, no one wanted my opinion when they could've just made a decision themselves, no one needed a signature for a form that should've been turned in two weeks ago, and also where no one actively hated me."

"And you couldn't get that by going home?"

"Don't misunderstand when I tell you this. I love my sister and my niece. I'll do just about anything short of murder for them—and even then, *maybe*, if I could hide the body." He chuckled.

"But?"

"But... Ella's getting divorced and moving back home. She'll be living with us for a while. Well"—he sighed—"probably for a more than a while. Her entire life is going to be changing. I adore my niece, and Ella and I have always been close, but I'm starting to feel like there isn't a lot of space for me to be myself.

"Even that's not right, because my mom and Ella would never purposely interfere, at least not maliciously, but when it's just my mom and me, we have a routine. Sometimes I'd come home late, after she went to bed, so I could have the house to myself, and she was fine with that—or she'd stay in her room and watch her favorite shows for the evening. Now I feel like I'll need to be 'on' all the time, cheery Uncle Mat, the caring son, the good brother, the sheriff. I suppose I should be glad Fi isn't moving in—and that's a whole different story. Sometimes I just want to be an asshole, drink a bunch of beer, and walk around in my underwear."

Mat caught Niall's amused gaze, and they both laughed, the sound loud in the small room. He went back to staring at the ceiling.

"I need a secret clubhouse, a tree house or something."

The bed creaked as Niall scooted all the way on, leaning his back and shoulders against the headboard, his denim-clad thigh grazing Mat's hip. "Tell me about it. I need to figure something out too; management is giving me the boot. It's not tomorrow, but they want me gone sooner rather than later."

Mat raised his head. From the look on Niall's face, he wasn't kidding. "My offer is still open. My mom loves you and the dog. We could probably work something out." Even if it would kill him to be that close to Niall every day without being *with* Niall, Mat would offer.

Niall was quiet for a few heartbeats. Mat wondered if he'd overstepped again.

Then Niall muttered, "Yeah. We'll figure something out."

Not the answer Mat was expecting, but coming from Niall, it felt like a promise of some kind. The words made his smidge of hope grow just a little stronger.

"Are you on call, or whatever you call it out here?" Niall asked.

"Yeah. Patrick will be back tomorrow. But I need to be in early, because Birdy's on duty tonight. We've both been working overtime."

"And you lost sleep because some asshole texted you at seven in the morning."

"Yeah." Mat huffed out a laugh. "I forgot about that asshole."

Niall shifted around on the bed. "I imagine you parked in the motel's lot?" he asked.

"Yeah," Mat replied.

"So by now everybody on the island knows we had dinner together, and suddenly your cruiser's parked next to my car?"

Mat looked at his watch. He'd been in the room for maybe a half hour. "Yep, plenty of time for the island gossip to spread the news around. Whatever. I don't care what people think." He did care about some of their opinions, but not when it came to his sexuality.

"Well, then… it's late, and there's no reason you can't stay here. I'm not talking sex, I'm talking sleeping."

Mat glanced at Niall. He could do that. Right? He could *just sleep* in the same bed as Niall Hamarsson.

"I should call home. Mom worries if I don't check in. She has a very active imagination."

"Understandable, with everything going on, and since your dad died on duty."

Mat grunted his agreement, not wanting to think about that day. His mom and then his sisters had called him, overwrought, not knowing what to do and reaching out to Mat for comfort and maybe hoping somehow he could explain what had happened. Even his brother had checked in with him. The accident happened just before the Fourth of July. His dad had been called to investigate a complaint of illegal fishing, a big deal in Pacific Northwest waters. He'd never made it. As far as anyone could tell, the boat he was driving hit something in the water and Sean Sr. was thrown overboard, hitting his head and drowning. The report concluded he'd never had a chance—especially as he hadn't been wearing a life jacket, which Mat would never understand.

He was too tired to think about his dad right now; he let his eyes drift shut.

"So?" Niall asked.

Mat opened his eyes a tiny bit and let them close again. "So what?"

Niall's foot twitched, bumping Mat gently on the leg. He

didn't know if it was accidental or to get him to pay attention. "Are you staying here, no messing around, or are you heading back to the chaos of your house?"

The fatigue he'd been fighting all day had Mat thinking he heard a gentle tone to Niall's voice, one he hadn't heard much before. At least, not when Niall talked to humans. Fenrir, yes; people, no.

Did he want to stay? Yes. Did he want to have to deal with people tomorrow and the next day and forever, fielding questions about his sexuality? The subject of who he slept with would come up, he had no doubt. Mat was continually amazed by what relative strangers thought was their business. He'd have to deal with the talk sometime, though, and after their dinner earlier and the mini run-in with Martin Reynolds, there was bound to be gossip flying around the island already.

"Yeah. I'm gonna stay."

Mat's eyelids felt too heavy to open, and the bed wasn't as comfortable as his own, but he was already sliding into that before-sleep state of being.

Niall poked him. This time it was absolutely on purpose. "You'll regret sleeping in your clothes."

The bed moved, and Mat opened his eyes reluctantly. Niall's back was to him as he rummaged through the dresser drawer. He took the time to discreetly check out Niall's ass, then his gaze meandered upward to where, he realized, Niall was watching him in the mirror, his lips pulled up in a half smile.

Mat shrugged and laughed as he sat up to pull his pants and shirt off, dropping them to the floor. "I didn't agree not to look."

A pair of cotton sweatpants hit him in the side of the head. "You can borrow those. I need to fill Fenrir's water bowl and brush my teeth. I don't have a spare toothbrush, sorry."

Mat pulled on the sleep pants and slipped under the covers. It was a king-size bed, but he knew he'd be hyperaware of Niall all night. No way was he getting a decent night's sleep. He pounded the pillow into submission and lay back, waiting for Niall.

When he opened his eyes, it was daylight. He'd turned onto his side at some point during the night, and Niall was not exactly spooning him but tucked in behind him, keeping him warm.

"The hell." His joints popped as he rolled onto his back and stretched. The clock sitting on the side table said the time was just before seven.

"I was going to wake you up in a few minutes."

"Tell me there's coffee."

"If I did, it would be a lie."

"How do you stand it?" At least the station, with his stash of gourmet beans, was only down the street.

"I spend a lot of time not in this room, which is why I keep seeing that damn RV."

Mat couldn't help but roll his eyes. The camper was really bugging Niall. Personally, Mat didn't think it was anything. RVs made terrible getaway cars.

"Did I tell you an ex-colleague sent me an email about the consulting company he works for that's hiring?"

"Really? Are you interested?"

Niall pushed the covers back, swinging his legs out of the bed. "Maybe."

"Do you ever make snap decisions?"

Niall cocked his head to look at Mat. "Sometimes."

Mat started to ask for an example, but Niall's stare transformed from the raw green of a spring river to something that felt a lot like liquid sunshine on a hot summer day. He snapped his mouth shut.

A whisper of pleasant tension hummed between them as they both got off the bed and stood staring at each other for a minute. It wasn't the right time. *Yet,* murmured a little voice in Mat's head.

While Niall took Fenrir outside, Mat stepped into the tiny

shower-bathtub, which was small enough that the top of his head was actually above the showerhead. How did Niall manage? Sudsing up and then scrubbing down under the spray—barely more than a dribble—Mat allowed himself to contemplate the mystery of Niall. Not his body, though Mat obsessed enough about that, but Niall himself and what it was about the man that spoke to his heart. Mat wasn't going to try and fool himself: if he wasn't already in love with the grumpy bastard, he was teetering on the edge.

He had no idea what he'd been thinking last night, showing up at Niall's room after the man had left Lulu's. Niall could've told him to go away, and Mat would've left… but he hadn't. He'd opened the door and let Mat in and taken care of him.

What had it been like for Niall before he moved to Piedras as a boy—day-to-day life on the streets, his mother a drug addict, Niall never knowing if he would eat or have a place to sleep at night? From what Niall had shared with him, life had been grim. As a police officer, Mat had seen plenty of squats and abandoned buildings shared by drug users, criminals, the homeless. He wouldn't want any living being to experience that.

And yet, Niall had grown into a man who believed in justice, who'd worked tirelessly to bring closure to victims' families—but didn't seem to like many living people. Mat chuckled. Now that he'd thought it, he realized how true it was: Niall judged the living harshly and forgave the dead their sins. He was *complicated*, just like Mat had told his niece yesterday morning. Mat wanted Niall to understand he was safe with Mat—he would guard Niall's heart and soul with his life. And he wanted the chance to prove he was good enough for Niall to take a risk on.

Niall's gravelly voice reached him from the other side of the door. "What're you doing in there? You're going to use up all the damn water in the motel."

Complicated… and romantic. Mat couldn't leave that out.

Because he was like a dog with a bone, once Mat left for the sheriff's office, Niall and Fenrir took the long road out to Killegen's Point. His excuse was coffee and a cinnamon roll, but Niall knew he was actually looking for the camper.

Waking up with Mat in his bed this morning had been... well, dammit, an emotion Niall recognized as satisfaction had welled up in his chest. Something about the other man vulnerable in sleep had Niall's protective instincts on alert and had him hoping for more.

You can tell yourself it's because he was sleeping, but you always feel protective about Mat.

Whatever. Niall didn't want to think about it. He'd never felt that way about his ex. Sometimes Niall had gotten so wrapped up in a case he didn't see Trey for weeks, and it had never bothered him. When he had thought about him, about *not* missing Trey or worrying about him and knowing (because society said so) that he was supposed to worry and miss his romantic partner, he'd just added "fucked up" to the long list of things that were wrong with him. A little voice, growing louder by the day, murmured,

You do worry about Mat, though, so maybe not as fucked up as he thought.

Thankfully, Chester's appeared out of the morning mist, and Niall could quit thinking about Mat and focus instead on coffee and the camper.

He rolled to a stop in the parking lot and glanced across the street to where the general store was getting ready for spring. Fred and someone Niall didn't recognize were helping unload a delivery truck full of garden and nursery supplies. The open area around the business, which had previously been fairly empty except for a few piles of building materials and a wheelbarrow or two, was now filled with ready-to-plant saplings and early-blooming flowers like daffodils and tulips. Off to one side was a selection of premade sheds and other small outbuildings homeowners could put on their property, which gave Niall the barest hint of an idea. Something he needed to think about.

"Are you sure you don't want to purchase one of these refillable to-go cups?" Sage asked him. "You get 10 percent off your coffee, and you're saving the environment."

The cup in question had a lid and was designed by a company out of Seattle that made camping equipment, and it guaranteed liquids would stay warm for hours. Niall had learned to drink his coffee quickly, but maybe Sage had a point; he was at Chester's just about every day. *Every* day, he mentally corrected.

And, since it had a lid, he could take Fenrir for a walk and drink coffee at the same time. A win for both of them.

"Can I leave my car in the lot for a little while? I should take the dog for a walk."

Fenrir thought this an excellent plan. His tail swished back and forth as he strode ahead of Niall, excited to be inspecting new areas. Mist still clung to the trees, but it looked to Niall like the day might end up being pleasant—at least, no rain.

Killegen's Point was really just a bend in the road with a few businesses strung along it. Further along and drivers would reach the island's tiny airstrip and Lulu's; if they took the other road, they'd end up at the bluff where Niall had been the other day. There were homes tucked in behind the businesses; a "Caution: School Bus Stop" sign along the side of the road indicated people did live close by.

Fenrir took Niall on a short tour of the small town. It didn't take long, as there were only three or so blocks. They passed by several abandoned structures that hinted at the history of the island—including what had once been a Mobil Oil gas station, with the faded ghost of a Pegasus flying on the reader board.

"We should get back," Niall said.

To what? He didn't know, but there were things—emails and paperwork he couldn't ignore much longer, and he should probably try a little harder to find a new place to stay.

Fenrir veered off the main roadway toward an alley that ran behind Chester's. It wasn't used much, Niall could tell. Weeds, along with cotton and needlegrass, had begun to take over, and soon enough it would be difficult to drive down. Unexpectedly, the dog jerked against his lead, pulling it out of Niall's grip. He grabbed at the end, but with the damn coffee cup in one hand he couldn't catch a hold of it.

In very un-Fenrir-like behavior, the dog bolted to the side, off the road and into the bushes.

"Fenrir!" Niall called out just as his gray-brown tail disappeared from sight. "Dammit."

There was nothing for Niall to do but follow the dog and hope he hadn't gone too far.

The spot where Fenrir had disappeared had long ago been a well-used path. Carefully, Niall negotiated his way down a slight incline. The recent rains made the path treacherous and slippery.

The path faded into a yard that had lost a hostile takeover by blackberry bushes and volunteer cottonwoods. A house, or what had once been a house, hunkered sullenly about fifty feet from Niall. It was close to collapsing. The windows were broken or gone completely, and the siding had been pulled away or fallen off, allowing the insulation to ooze out.

A shadowy something on the other side of the cottage, something not part of the structure, caught Niall's attention. Fenrir sniffed the ground around it, wagged his tail like he'd found something good, and disappeared around the corner.

"Are you part bloodhound? A truffle dog, maybe?"

Niall pushed his way through the dewy grasses and random trash, his cop instincts practically screaming. Even before he reached the dog, he knew Fenrir had found the camper.

Someone had attempted to camouflage it with branches and leaves, but the larger branches had fallen to the ground, exposing the cracked windshield. And they'd only covered the front of the RV, so when Niall got close enough, he could see the stripe along the side and the side door, which was ajar.

Fenrir pranced back to Niall, a big grin on his doggy face. Niall picked up his leash, gripping it tightly.

"Yes, you are a good dog. You realize, of course, we're trespassing?"

The dog pulled him toward the camper as if he wanted to go inside. Niall didn't think anyone was inside the camper, or the house.

"Hello? Is anyone there?" he called out quietly.

With his luck there *would* be someone there and it would be a freaked-out meth-head, or worse. But no one answered his call, and the birds who'd quieted when Niall invaded the yard began to chirp again, ignoring his presence.

Fenrir placed a paw on the first step, looking back over his shoulder at Niall.

"We really can't."

Jesus, what if this was where Fenrir used to live? What if whoever owned this disintegrating RV was the same POS who'd abandoned him?

"No fucking way." Niall gripped the lead even tighter, as if someone was about to appear and try and take Fenrir away. "No fucking way," he repeated for good measure. He'd done his due diligence plastering the island with "Found Dog" posters when he'd found Fenrir; they'd had their goddamned chance.

Still, the door *was* open, so they climbed inside.

The RV was messy but not a disaster. No one was home, but whoever had been occupying it did their best to keep the camper tidy. A few dishes were in the small sink, but they'd been scraped off and rinsed, and a blue sweatshirt was folded on the tiny countertop. Bench seats in the dining area had been pulled together to make a bed. The abandoned blankets were messy, as if the person had only just woken. Niall felt the cushion; it was cold. He picked up the sweatshirt. It was small, child size.

At the back was another bedroom area. Ugly plaid curtains had been drawn across the window, making the space gloomier than it already was, and more laundry was stacked up along the side of that sleeping area. Niall picked up a t-shirt from a pile, definitely an adult, likely male.

His conscience reminded him that, even if the door had been open, he was still trespassing. There was no legitimate reason for him to be inside the camper. Whoever lived there was not breaking the law by hiding their camper—they were probably trying to keep people just like him from poking their noses where they didn't belong. And there were definitely no signs they'd had a dog.

Still, on his way back outside, Niall opened the single closet door, the cupboard doors, the glove compartment. No guns, no obvious drugs. No wallets or paperwork. Hardly any food. Mat was right: these were people struggling to make ends meet, and not succeeding. Niall felt like an asshole for invading their privacy, but that didn't stop him from taking a final look around.

In the last cupboard, Niall discovered a stormtrooper action figure. He'd had a shitty childhood, not a lot of toys or anything other than the clothes on his back until he came to live with his grandparents. If the toy had been his, there was no way he would've left it behind, not if he could've helped it.

Maybe they'd just left for the day. But where would they go? And why would the door be open? Niall had gone from being suspicious of the RV to worrying about the occupants—with, he felt, justification.

Back outside, he pulled out his phone and snapped a picture of the license plate. He almost texted Mat with the information, but he hesitated. Maybe it would be better to present the data in person.

Just before noon, Mat left the station, leaving Birdy in charge. Patrick would be reporting for his shift that afternoon, so she wouldn't be on her own for long before she could head out for lunch too. Mat berated himself because he'd forgotten to let his mom know he wouldn't be home the night before. He'd fallen asleep before he could make the call.

But from his mom's text earlier in the morning, Mat knew it really hadn't taken long for word to get around the island that Mat's cruiser had been parked overnight at the Orca. Regardless, he owed her and Ella an apology—it had never been his intent to make them worry. And a home-cooked meal couldn't hurt.

When he pulled into his spot in the driveway, the front door flew open and Riley burst out, sprinting down the stairs two at a time. Mat barely had time to get out of the car before her little body slammed into his. He lifted her up and spun her around for good measure. "Hey, kiddo!"

"Uncle Mat! You're finally home!"

"Riley, what did I tell you?" Ella called from the porch.

"You said Uncle Mat is an adult and can make his own

choices. I just wanted to show you my fairy house." Riley pouted, her lips pulled down in a fake frown.

"Your what? Your airy house? Dairy house?"

"Noooo, I said *fairy* house. Gramma and I made it yesterday. It's for all the fairies to come and stay in when they get cold. You wanna see?"

Mat hitched Riley up onto his hip. Her bony kid butt dug into his belt, pinching his side, but soon enough she would be too big to pick up—or she'd stop wanting him to.

"Can I have lunch first? Maybe I need to take a shower. Does Grandma have any chores I need to do?"

"Uncle Maaaaaat!" Riley screeched into his ear.

Mat winced but he deserved that for teasing her. "All right." He set her back on the ground. "Show me this fairy house."

Riley grabbed Mat's hand and led him around to the back of the property. The path, if it could be called that, meandered a bit, finally ending at a thick stand of evergreens. Under the canopy the earth stayed dry, even on the rainiest of days; the branches above were so close together they prevented even the heaviest rain from reaching the ground. The forest floor was carpeted with decades' worth of pine needles, and not much else, because it was so dry. This spot had been Mat's favorite growing up, a secret place away from his older brother and dramatic, pesky sisters. When his mom hadn't been able to find him, she looked here.

Keeping hold of his hand, Riley dragged him forward. He had to duck under branches to avoid being whacked in the face.

"See!" She dropped his hand and pointed at something.

At first Mat had no idea where to look, but then he saw it. Tucked in between two tree trunks was a little house fashioned from bark, sticks, moss, and twine.

"Look inside!"

Mat crouched down to peer inside, where he could see a tiny table and pebbles for chairs.

"I'm going to decorate it with dainty lions!"

"Don't you mean dandelions?"

"No."

Mat smiled. "How about we grab some lunch first? I'm hungry."

"Sorry about that," Ella remarked once she sent Riley off to wash her hands. "She's kind of all over the place emotionally, and she missed you last night."

They were sitting at the kitchen table. Their mom was heating up delicious-smelling chili. Mat crossed his arms and leaned on the table. "I fell asleep."

Ella raised an eyebrow. "Is that what they call it these days?"

"El, jeez, I really did fall asleep!"

"I heard you had dinner at Lulu's," his mom added as she ladled the chili into bowls.

A flare of irritation welled up inside him. He tried to quell it. Ella and Riley were going through hard times, and, for crying out loud, they'd all just said goodbye to a brother and oldest son. But, goddammit, couldn't they just leave him alone about Niall for two seconds so he could figure out what the hell was going on himself? He wasn't sure the elusive man would let him in again if he showed up—he hoped so, but what if Niall changed his mind?

"Can we talk about this later?"

Riley zoomed back into the kitchen, wiping her hands on her jeans. "Talk about what later?"

Mat dropped his head onto his forearms and groaned. He loved his three nosy family members dearly, but he *really* needed a space he could call his own.

"Does your tummy hurt, Uncle Mat? Mommy rubs my tummy when it feels sad. Who rubs your tummy?"

Ella snickered. Mat turned his head so he could melt her with his laser glare.

His mom said, "Uncle Mat's tummy is fine, Riley. Here's your chili."

Ella stopped teasing Mat while they all ate, at least up until there was a knock at the front door.

"Oh, can I get it? Who's that?" Riley peered out the kitchen to the front door. Mat leaned backward so he could see too. Beyond the curtains, a recognizable hulking shadow waited for someone to answer.

"It's Niall. I'll get it," Mat replied.

"Oh," said Riley. "You said he was complicated."

With his sister and mother trying, and failing, to repress their laughter and Riley asking, "What was funny?" Mat went to answer the door.

"Hey," Niall said in greeting. Fenrir wagged his tail and bumped Mat with his nose. Niall looked self-conscious. Mat narrowed his eyes at him, knowing this was about the damn RV again—nothing else would get him to stop in at the house uninvited.

"Come on in." Mat stood back so they could pass by him. "What's up?"

Alyson came out of the kitchen. "We're just eating lunch. Would you like some chili? There's plenty."

Ella scooted over so Niall could squish in at the table, his shoulder brushing against Mat's. It had been a while since the kitchen table had five people sitting around it. Mat met his mom's thoughtful gaze and knew she was thinking the same thing. Mat wanted to hate how right it felt to have Niall at the table. The dog belonged too, curled up against the back door.

"Mr. Niall?" Riley asked at one of those moments when everything was quiet, a sort of lull Mat was beginning to learn was the calm before the storm for her.

"Call me Niall. Can I call you Riley?"

"Okay." Riley fidgeted a bit, and Mat narrowed his eyes,

wondering what she was about to say, when she asked, "Um, why are you complicated?"

Once everyone, including Niall, and Riley, who still had no idea what was so funny but was generally a good sport, managed to control their laughter—Mat thought they were lucky no one had choked or spewed chili across the room—Niall replied.

"That's a good question, Riley. I wish I knew the answer. But we're all kind of complicated. It's not easy being an adult sometimes."

She looked thoughtful for a second before replying, "Yeah, it's hard to be a kid too."

"It is. Being a kid is hard because there's so much to learn, and being an adult is hard because we know so much. It hardly seems fair."

"You want to see my fairy house?"

"Riley," Ella interjected, "Niall is here to see Mat."

Riley flashed Niall a look that clearly said, *See, that's what I'm talking about.*

"Sure. Fenrir would probably like to get outside again."

"Okay!"

Mat fell in beside Niall as they all traipsed out the kitchen door after lunch to go visit the fairy house. It felt comfortable and *right.* "I know you didn't stop by randomly. What's going on?"

Niall glanced at him, and Matt thought he spotted the shadow of a smile. "What do you mean? I've been invited often enough."

Mat huffed. "Yeah, and you've never accepted, so you're here because... you saw the damn RV again, didn't you?" From the slight hitch to Niall's step, Mat knew he'd guessed right, although it actually wasn't much of a guess.

Niall attempted to protest. "I can't believe you'd think I have an ulterior motive."

Mat rolled his eyes.

"Fine, you're right. I stumbled on it today and took a picture of the license plate." He patted his coat pocket, where his phone must've been tucked away.

Together they arrived at the stand of trees. Riley darted back to Niall and Mat, grabbing Niall's hand and dragging him over to her fairy real estate. He followed Riley's lead, crouching down like Mat had to see the house better. Mat caught Ella's amused glance at Niall's compliance.

Niall was bigger than Mat. Normally Mat didn't notice, because Niall was only a couple inches taller and maybe twenty pounds heavier, but his presence was commanding. However, with Riley he was a gentle giant, allowing her to lean against him while she explained all about how she and her gramma had made it: searching for the right bark and sticks, collecting pebbles, finding dry moss.

Niall nodded and offered comments about the construction, wondering whether the fairies would need a garden.

"Maybe. And see?" Riley leaned forward, pointing at something and nearly falling. Niall wrapped a strong arm around her hips, securing her against his side. "There's a spot for them to have flower nectar and drink dainty lion tea."

"Okay, whose idea was the 'dainty lion'?" Mat asked.

His mom answered, "After a discussion about the word 'dandy,' Riley decided she liked 'dainty' better."

"What's wrong with 'dandy'?" Mat asked.

"I have no idea."

FIFTEEN
NIALL

After dutifully admiring Riley's creation, Niall said his goodbyes. He'd never been around children much. As a kid he'd been in survival mode before he went to live with his grandparents, and if his ex-colleagues had kids, Niall had never met them because he'd avoided the summer barbecues and get-togethers. Most of the children he had experience with were the victims of crimes or family members of a victim.

Riley was… a welcome surprise. She didn't make him uncomfortable; she treated him as if he were normal.

"You're always welcome here, Niall," Alyson said as the entire Dempsey family walked him to his car. He'd made some excuse about an appointment, but he could tell by Mat's exasperated expression that he knew better. Niall was running away again. No, not running away—he was done doing that, although maybe he needed to tell Mat—but gatherings like this were overwhelming for him. He could only absorb so much love and happiness before he started to feel twitchy. Probably something he should talk to a therapist about. Maybe when hell froze over.

Standing next to the Subaru, Mat twirled his index finger. Niall rolled down the window. Mat leaned inside, his arm on the roof of the car, his face close enough that Niall could see the striation of dark and darker blues in his irises. They were close enough to kiss. Mat glanced at Niall's lips. Niall knew he wanted to feel Mat's lips again, but not in front of his family.

Mat smiled, hopefully reading Niall's thoughts. "Couple of things. One, I'll be back at the station in about thirty minutes. Two..." He paused, making sure Niall was paying attention.

"What?" Niall asked.

"Two, I'm debating whether you'll run away faster if I kiss you now or if I promise to later."

"I'm not running away."

"Huh. What's this *appointment* about?"

Niall felt his cheeks heat. He never blushed. Luckily, he didn't think Mat could tell. "Okay. I didn't realize, I didn't *think* about everyone being here. I was caught off guard."

"You did great. Riley already loves you, my mom adopted you ages ago, and Ella—well, she's off men right now, but I think she'll make an exception for my—for you."

Niall knew all that, intellectually, but he'd been hiding behind his self-built wall of protection for so many years that he felt naked when he let his guard down. And Riley had definitely slipped past it. He was twitchy.

He stared up into Mat's eyes, trying hard to ignore his own discomfort. "I'll see you at the station."

On his way to Hidden Harbor, every time Niall glanced in the rearview mirror to check the roads, Fenrir's amber eyes were there, silently judging his escape.

"Jesus Christ, I get it, okay?"

And he was back to talking to the dog.

His cell phone buzzed in his coat pocket. As tempting as it was to check and see who'd called, Niall forced himself to keep driving.

Once he was parked behind the station, he dragged his phone out. He expected the call to have been from Mat—no one else bugged him with such regularity—but it was Marshal Soper, a good friend of Mat's and one of the island's ER docs. After a moment's hesitation, curiosity overcame Niall and he pressed Return Call.

"Oh, hey, that was fast." Marshal had a pleasant voice, always calm.

"I was driving, or I would've answered right away."

"Um, no worries."

Marshal and Niall didn't know each other well enough to be calling just to say hi, even if Niall had stayed with him. But then Niall had been in the emergency room only last month. Maybe he'd missed a checkup?

"Are you calling about my hand? It's doing fine, seems all healed to me."

"Your hand? Oh, no. I was wondering—I know this is going to sound weird, but I have a personal favor to ask, and I don't want to ask Mat because—well, I do watch some cop shows, and I know—" His voice dropped lower. "Can you research somebody for me? Like, find out about them on the down-low?" His voice was definitely tense now.

"What for?" Who used phrases like *on the down-low*? Apparently Soper hadn't gotten the memo that it wasn't the 1970s anymore.

"I'll tell you, but not yet. I'm violating someone's trust by calling you, but I need to know if he is who he says he is."

"You're looking for what kind of information?"

"Obviously more than I can find when *I* search the internet. Is this person maybe hiding something? A criminal record, bad debt, I don't know."

"Most of that you can find on your own."

"Not my expertise, and I kind of would rather someone else did it. I'll pay you, if money's an issue."

"No. I can do it."

It would give him something to do besides bother Mat about the RV.

Marshal breathed out a sigh of relief. "Thank you. And please don't tell Mat. He'll get all up in my grill about helping a stranger."

"Okay, give me the name and I'll see what I can come up with."

He felt a bit uncomfortable promising Marshal he wouldn't say anything to Mat, but the man probably had his reasons, and Niall could see where Mat might be a little protective of his friends.

"Trevor Collier."

"Do you know anything about him, like birthday or something, so I don't search some old geezer from Florida instead of the guy you want?"

"Uhhh…" The line went quiet for a second. "I think he's in his thirties, dark hair, white, divorced, has a kid named Caleb. Was a field medic stationed out of Bremerton. I'm pretty sure he's from Washington State."

"Okay, I'll start with that and let you know if I need more."

"Yeah, sure—hey, I've got to go."

Niall did too. He'd spotted Mat's cruiser turning into the parking lot.

The station was empty. Niall raised his eyebrows.

"Deputy Flynn has the afternoon off, and Radden is out on patrol. Thankfully it's been quiet, although Holstrom is still out. His wife keeps calling in telling us how sick he is and how sorry she is she gave it to him. Hopefully the folks on Orcas are feeling better. This is a nasty flu. A week ago, Marshal told me the ER was full—meaning like five patients—of residents waiting to be tested."

"What's the license?" Mat asked once he'd sat down at his desk.

Mat typed while Niall read off the license plate he'd taken a picture of earlier. He turned to Niall once the computer did its magic. The RV was registered to Mark Wallace. His most recent address was listed in Oak Harbor, Washington.

"There, we have a name. I'll check on the RV myself when I'm out that way later. You said it's behind Chester's?"

"Yeah, there's a falling-down cottage back there. The vehicle was very poorly camouflaged with tree branches, or maybe the owner was just hoping if anyone saw it they would ignore it."

"I know the cottage you mean. Cute place once. It doesn't sound like the camper's going anywhere soon."

Mat typed "Mark Wallace" into his system and hit Enter. Niall leaned forward, elbows on his knees, watching Mat's screen over his shoulder and secretly enjoying Mat's warmth. He could admit to himself he liked being around the man. The more time Niall spent with him, the more time he wanted to spend. But he had to constantly fight his knee-jerk reaction to push him away. He didn't think Mat understood how hard it was for him to not disappear.

Mark Wallace's info popped up. He'd had a few parking tickets, but nothing else. It looked like he worked at an auto repair shop in Oak Harbor. His picture showed a white male in his thirties with brown hair that was trying to curl. Nothing about him screamed criminal, but photographs could be deceiving.

"I don't know him," Mat said. "He's not a part-timer on the island that I'm aware of. I'll check with Flynn when she's back tomorrow."

"Okay. I'm sorry I bugged you about this."

Mat swung around to look directly at Niall, bringing their faces close together, taking Niall's breath away. Whatever Mat had been about to say was swept away by longing. How was it possible for him to experience longing when he was literally two inches away from the man?

"I told you I believed you. Something is going on with the camper, and now I have a name to work with."

Niall sat back, giving himself some space to breathe. "Just what you need, more work."

Mat grinned, his smile lines dazzling Niall so he had to blink. Since when did he get googly over smile lines? Apparently, it was the magic that resided in Mat Dempsey, slayer of monsters and tamer of the most fearsome beasts. He blinked again, but Mat's smile was seared onto his retinas.

"Dinner again?" Mat asked.

"When? Two nights in a row and people won't just be talking, they'll be lining up to interrogate us."

"I'm not worried. I talked to Birdy this morning, and I'll catch each of the deputies separately as the week goes on. Maybe one of them will be bothered, but I doubt bothered enough to say anything."

"All right," said Niall.

"All right, what?" Mat grinned at him.

Niall rolled his eyes and smiled back. "All right, I'll meet you for dinner."

"There's a bistro one block over owned by some locals, Joe's Place. They use as many locally sourced supplies as they can. It's supposed to be excellent."

"What time?"

"I should be wrapped up here by seven."

Niall left the station feeling oddly euphoric, like maybe he'd forgotten to breathe for a few minutes. Maybe he could do this and it wouldn't break him.

SIXTEEN

MAT

Mat kept the thrill of Niall agreeing to join him for dinner—again—secreted away like a talisman for the rest of the afternoon. The day dragged along forever, much like when he was a kid and the holiday season was in full swing. He forced himself to concentrate on his work—and there was plenty he needed to take care of.

Alongside attempting to reduce the mound of paperwork threatening a takeover of his desk, Mat fielded phone calls from two separate irate drivers who'd been ticketed for speeding. He put in a request with the WSDOT to see if he could get more information about the boat out at East Bay Marina, and he started the files for annual reviews. When his phone rang again, Mat expected it to be another rant about how the sheriff's department was targeting specific drivers. And um, yes, they were targeting a certain population: speeders.

The wail of a siren outside as he reached for the phone had Mat standing up, sending his chair into the table behind him. He snatched up the handset and attempted to put on his jacket at the same time. Sirens were never good news, and the sheriff's office hadn't been called in first, which usually meant a fire. He had hoped the arsonist was finished with Piedras.

"Where is it?"

"East Bay Marina."

"Shit. On my way."

Mat was at the marina in under eight minutes; he chased the two fire engines and the battalion vehicle all the way to the turnoff. The drive gave him time to speculate, and he didn't like the suspicious turn his thoughts took. He had the sinking feeling the fire was the work of the arsonist—who'd finally escalated—or possibly Duane Cooper trying to hide whatever shady activities he was up to.

Even before he had a visual on the marina, the acrid smoke from diesel engines made his eyes water. He parked next to Devon's SUV, and Devon immediately handed him a face mask.

"Wear it, Sheriff. No need to be taking you to the ER tonight."

"Are we taking anyone to the ER?"

"Don't know yet. Sharleen called it in, so she's alive, but I haven't talked to her in person yet."

Devon strode away from Mat, yelling out orders to his team, who were already pulling the hoses off the trucks.

The north side of the marina appeared to be fully engulfed in flames. As Mat watched, they licked their way along the wooden pier toward the sailboat that was being restored. Firefighters tried to stop them, but the fire was too fast and too hungry. Within minutes the boat went up in flames and sank into the water, along with the mysterious Boston Whaler and the rescue boat. He regretted not acting on his misgivings about Duane and putting the marina under surveillance. Who was he kidding? With most of his deputies out sick, he didn't have the staff anyway.

As Mat was wondering when the county fireboat would arrive, he spotted it in the distance, powering through the water from where it was docked on Orcas. It was old, inherited from a small city in California, but they were lucky to have it. The fireboat began pumping hundreds of gallons of seawater from the bay onto the flames. That, in tandem with the water from the fire engines, soon brought the fire close to under control—at least, it wasn't spreading to the south side. The teams were working hard to protect the remaining vessels and the boatyard. He quickly radioed Deputy Radden with instructions to barricade the upper road.

Mat spotted Sharleen at the edge of the parking lot, as close as she could get to the marina. She didn't look good. Birdy stood with her, wearing street clothes. Mat wondered how she'd gotten here so quickly, but Devon was her older brother, and like as not they'd been at home together when the call came in. Birdy turned, catching Mat's glance and shaking her head as she put an arm around Sharleen's shoulders. Mat wound his way through the emergency vehicles, hoses, and equipment to where the two women stood.

"What happened?" he asked.

Sharleen didn't appear to hear his question.

Birdy shook her head, lips pressed together. "She was in the office and smelled smoke. That's all I know," she answered for Sharleen.

Mat's main duty in this incident was to keep rubberneckers from trying to get close to the scene. The last thing they needed was civilians interfering with the firefighting efforts or, worse, getting themselves injured. And no doubt there were boat owners on their way. Patrick arrived a few minutes later, and Mat watched him block the road with his cruiser.

Birdy whispered in Sharleen's ear. The older woman turned to look at him, her face a mask of grief, cheeks streaked with tears and smudged with soot, hair a wild mess.

"Sharleen, I'm so sorry." Mat felt as if he were consoling her on the loss of a loved one. Maybe he was. She'd devoted her life to this small marina and the residents who docked their boats there.

"I don't understand." She looked bewildered, her voice begging Mat to have an answer for her. "We just had the electric upgraded. How could this happen?"

The three of them turned and looked back out at what remained. Devon and his team of volunteers were doing their best to protect the remaining boats, but the entire north side of the marina was already gone. Smoldering remains floated half in, half out of the cold waters. Masts jutted from the surface—a last, desperate call for help. The end of the pier was gone, whether sunk under the water or burned away, Mat didn't know.

The sun had begun to set, adding an eerie glow to the scene, shades of orange and red mixed like finger paints reflecting the flames licking the waterline.

Devon appeared beside Mat. "We need everybody to move back," he said.

"Can you save it, Devon? What's left?" Sharleen's voice was small. She seemed to have shrunk in the few minutes Mat had been at the scene.

Devon grasped the top of her arm with his gloved hand, leading her away from the shrinking flames toward the ambulance that had arrived and was parked by the entrance. "Sharleen, we'll do our best, you know we will. While we're working, I want you to let Foster check you over, okay?"

She nodded. Mat wasn't sure how much she was comprehending; she was definitely in shock. "Birdy, will you stay with her?" he asked.

"Of course. Come on, Sharleen, let's let that hunk Foster take a look at you."

The ghost of a smile flashed across Sharleen's face. "Okay."

It was kind of a running joke on the island that Foster Jennings, one of the EMTs, was Hollywood handsome. He caught the eye of many of the island's women residents—the men too, more than were willing to admit it. Aside from his outward appearance, people were naturally drawn to him. He had a kind word for almost everyone. However, as far as Mat knew, Foster never took anyone up on their offers of companionship, instead spending most of his days training border collies and caring for his younger sister, who used a wheelchair.

"Thanks, Birdy. Be sure to put in for OT. I'll have it authorized."

Birdy shook her head. "I'd be here no matter what. This is me helping a friend." She led Sharleen over to where Foster waited, and Mat turned his attention back to the fire.

It looked as if most of the damage had occurred before the fire engines and fireboat arrived. The flames were mostly out now, but the trucks and fireboat would remain on the scene for hours making sure every last flicker of fire was extinguished.

There were quite a few residents at the scene besides the volunteer firefighters and the EMTs, more than Mat liked, and now Patrick had a group of people at the top of the road wanting information—boat owners, likely. They were not going to be allowed to come closer until the morning at the earliest.

As he scanned the crowd, Mat realized that, of all the people he saw impatiently waiting for news, good or bad, he didn't see Duane Cooper.

Sharleen had been coaxed inside the ambulance and was lying back on a stretcher. Foster had his hand on the door as if he was about to shut it.

"Hang on a second," Mat called out as he trotted over to the ambulance and poked his head inside. "Sharleen, was Duane here? Have you seen him today?"

"Duane?" she repeated huskily, her voice rough from the smoke. "I don't think so."

"Can I ask just a few questions, Foster?" Mat asked.

Foster nodded his agreement. "Keep it quick." In a lower

voice, he said, "She's had some chest pain, so I want the doc to check her out."

"Sharleen, can you tell me what you were doing when you noticed the smoke?"

"I was working on the certification renewal for the state and some paperwork for our fueling pump—it was due for inspection. I hate doing that stuff and always put it off to the last moment." She stopped to take a shaky breath and coughed. Mat waited, not wanting to upset her any further. "I didn't see Duane today, but if he didn't stop in the office I might not have seen him walk by. Sometimes he just comes out to work on the boat. If he was doing something in the boathouse, I wouldn't have seen him either."

"Thanks, Sharleen. I'll need to question you later, okay?"

Tears welled in her eyes. She sniffled but nodded. Birdy, who was also inside the ambulance, handed her a tissue.

Sharleen asked, "You'll find out what happened, Mat?"

He wanted to promise her he would. Instead, he said, "We'll do our best."

Mat turned away. That was enough for now; Sharleen needed medical attention. Foster shut the door behind him. "Thanks for taking care of her, Foster," Mat said.

Foster nodded. "This is a terrible blow to everyone in the community. I hope you find who did this."

"You think it was on purpose?" Mat asked.

Foster shrugged, a careless movement that was at odds with his words. "Maybe. Maybe it was negligence, but I've known Sharleen all my life, the marina is her whole life."

SEVENTEEN

NIALL

Before he could talk himself out of it, Niall did two things.

One, he responded to Leo's email, asking for more information. He was interested but didn't want to commit. And wasn't that a slogan he needed printed on a t-shirt.

Then he spent an hour going over the retirement paperwork, checking boxes, signing on the indicated lines, and declining an offer for in-person advising. After scrawling his name one final time, Niall quickly folded the papers into the included envelope and left his room to drop it into the mailbox in the lobby.

There, he'd done it.

The blare of sirens interrupted his internal victory dance. He recognized the first tone as that of the fire brigade. Almost immediately a police siren joined in, its shorter staccato burst of sound at odds with the long cry of the engine.

Ricky had been sitting in his spot behind the reception desk, but he rose to his feet and peered out the window.

"What's going on?" Niall asked.

"I don't know yet." He picked his cell phone up from where it lay on the desk and began texting.

Niall waited while Ricky texted back and forth for a minute or so.

He looked up at Niall. "East Bay Marina is on fire. Sounds like a big one, not just a single boat or something."

Mat wouldn't be making it to their dinner. Niall refused to call it a date. It was just a dinner they could eat together another day. He might as well spend a few hours investigating Trevor Collier for Marshal Soper. And the other idea that had come to him that morning. Maybe it would pan out and maybe it wouldn't, but he'd have to look into it to know for sure.

Back in the room, Fenrir waited impatiently, giving Niall a sniff and a lick on the hand when he came through the door.

"It's okay, buddy, I'm back."

Checking his email one last time, Niall found a message from the insurance agency. He clicked it open to read it and then reread it very carefully and slowly. Yes, they were proceeding with the claim, but they had more questions. He sighed and tugged at the hair falling across his forehead. He'd let it grow longer than he usually did. He continued reading. Because the fire had been started by arson, they wanted to be absolutely certain Sean Dempsey—now conveniently dead—had no connection to Niall. Niall needed to come in for one last interview.

"Jesus fucking Christ."

This was par for the course, but he'd never been on this end of an arson claim before—and hopefully never would be again. And, while they were giving him a stipend for his lodging, he didn't know how long it would last. Another thing he had to deal with.

Putting the email aside—it would do little good to brood over it—Niall typed "Trevor Collier" into his search bar.

It always surprised him when a search turned out to be easy. He wondered if Marshal had even tried looking on his own.

Trevor Edward Collier, age thirty-six, former field medic in the navy, had graduated from medical school in 2007. He was divorced and the father of a son, Caleb Augustus Collier, aged seven. When not deployed, he'd lived in Bremerton and Oak Harbor and, most recently, Everett. Niall noted the address, then called the phone number shown for Collier and was informed the number was out of service.

Nothing on the surface indicated Collier was anything more than divorced and ex-navy, but no recent job records showed up. Niall searched Snohomish and Kitsap County records for Collier's divorce filings. He had to pay a fee to access them, but, in all likelihood, any scandalous information would be found in those pages. As a cop, he considered public records a dream come true. As a private citizen, he was horrified by the ease with which he was able to access information most people wouldn't want their best friend to know.

Collier had filed for the divorce. His spouse, Emma Collier, née Whaley, left him while he was serving overseas, the location of his deployment redacted from the papers. She'd left their then-five-year-old son alone for several days more than once—neighbors testified they heard the boy calling out and ended up taking him into their home. Those same neighbors managed to contact Trevor's commander, and he was able to return home to care for his son.

Emma Collier never appeared before the judge, although the state requested her presence, and she was found to be irresponsible and unable to care for Caleb. An interesting note in the various declarations, especially surrounding Caleb's custody, was the maternal grandfather's, who clearly thought Trevor was the one responsible for his daughter's behavior.

Niall dug further, discovering Emma had signed paperwork relinquishing parental rights, although her father had vehemently opposed her decision. Franklin Whaley, Niall learned, was a one-star admiral based out of Naval Base Kitsap. Not actually far from Piedras, just southwest of Anacortes. Nothing Niall found indicated Trevor was anything other than a respectable veteran.

The few pictures Niall discovered of Trevor Collier showed a man with jet black hair—longer than Niall would expect for the military, but everything was changing these days—striking pale blue eyes, and a mouth that didn't look like it was used to smiling. Late in his search he stumbled upon a snapshot of Trevor laughing as he held a baby, presumably Caleb, on one hip—perhaps on vacation, as he was wearing a colorful pair of swim shorts and the baby wore a hat protecting it from the sunshine. He was one of those people whose entire appearance changed when they smiled. The man was quite attractive, rugged, obviously fit. Niall knew he'd have looked twice at him if he'd seen him on the street.

Not now. Before Mat.

Niall sighed and picked up his phone to let Marshal know Trevor Collier seemed to be exactly who Marshal thought he was. Mat hadn't texted to cancel dinner, but Niall didn't expect him to; he'd be busy with the fire. He was tempted to see if Ricky had any more information about what was happening at the marina but decided against heading out to the lobby. He was mostly trying to stay out of Ricky's, and hence Orca's management's, sight.

He turned the TV on and, after flipping channels, found a show about a guy his age in England who'd sold all his belongings and bought a narrow boat to live on. The man had a very soothing voice, and Niall's eyes drifted shut while he listened to his stories.

The knock on his door startled him out of a doze, and Fenrir let out a quiet woof.

The thought that maybe he shouldn't be knocking on Niall's door after a long, shitty day crossed Mat's mind just as his knuckles met the hardwood. He was tired and strung out from trying to get everyone affected by the fire settled. The fire was a catastrophe; the marina had moored mostly working boats, and people were going to be hurting financially from it. Maybe he should have gone home and tried his best to hide how tired and worn down he felt from his mom, sister, and niece. But he didn't want to. He wanted Niall.

It didn't *feel* wrong to be standing at his door. Of all the people in his world, the only person he felt like seeing right now was Niall. Niall was a grouchy, uncommunicative ass, but he was Mat's grouch, and Mat could be himself with Niall. Niall understood the effect of police work—hell, he'd retired because of it. Mat shook his head. He wasn't ready to retire, far from it, but he was bone-tired tonight.

He'd parked his cruiser next to Niall's Subaru again, figuring that ship had sailed. No one had said anything to him today—the scene at the marina had been too chaotic, not the place for confronting someone about their sexuality—but Mat had no doubt that some kind of reckoning was coming.

The door was opened by a rumpled and sleepy-looking Niall.

"Did I wake you up?"

Niall shook his head. "I was watching TV."

The TV was on; Mat could hear a man speaking with an English accent.

"Do you always watch TV with your eyes shut?"

"Fuck off." Niall scowled. "Did you come here just to give me a hard time?"

"Can I come in?" Mat belatedly asked as he brushed past Niall.

Niall shut the door. "You look like shit."

"Gee, thanks."

"And you smell like smoke. Did you just get finished at the fire?"

Mat peeled off his jacket, wrinkling his nose. Now that he was away from the scene, he could smell the heavy odor clinging to him. "Yeah, sorry I didn't text. Can I take a shower?"

"Go ahead. I'm gonna finish up watching this guy navigate his boat along the English canals."

Over Niall's shoulder, Mat glimpsed a picturesque scene with a guy standing at the back of a very narrow boat as he floated past lush trees and a path with people jogging.

In the tiny bathroom, Mat stripped off the rest of his clothing, balling up his uniform and tossing it on the floor. It was going to take an act of god to get the smell out. At one point the wind had changed, bringing great billows of smoke inland. He'd been glad for the face mask.

The Orca wasn't a luxury hotel, but standing under the meager spray was close to heaven. Mat began to feel human again as the dust and grime sluiced off his body and disappeared down the drain. He squirted a bit of Niall's shampoo into the palm of his hand and scrubbed his scalp, letting out a little groan of pleasure.

Fires were always frightening, something about watching what may have taken months or years to build be destroyed in minutes, turning order into chaos. Mat shivered and shut his eyes. That was the wrong thing to do, because he instantly saw the flames again, burning high into the evening sky.

"Fuck." Opening his eyes, he reached out a hand to steady himself against the tiles.

"The fire?"

Mat started, but strong, warm hands kept him from falling. "Jesus Christ, I didn't hear you come in. How are you so damn quiet?"

Niall was in the shower with him, entirely naked. He didn't have to turn around and confirm it, he just knew. He could feel the heat of Niall's body surrounding him, enfolding him like an embrace.

"Being quiet has its benefits," Niall rumbled.

The shower stall was barely big enough for the two of them. Niall moved a few inches forward, and now he was close against Mat's back. Mat could feel Niall's cock pressed against the top of his ass. He'd have thought he was too tired, but his own cock throbbed in response to Niall's touch. "If we do this, are you going to quit speaking to me for a month?" he asked.

Because even though he wanted to—so much; his dick was continuing to harden—Mat wasn't going to jeopardize the progress they'd made over the past few days.

"I'm sorry," Niall replied.

"Sorry? Sorry for ghosting me? Sorry for getting in the shower now?" His dick started to deflate.

Niall moved even closer, his rough chin coming to rest on Mat's shoulder. "I'm sorry I hurt you."

His hands settled on Mat's hips, and Mat's cock changed its mind, wanting nothing more than to feel Niall's strong fingers around it. Niall shrugged, his bristly chest rubbing against Mat's back. Even if Niall told him this would be the only time, Mat wanted Niall to fuck him. His ass clenched at the thought, and he had to force himself to focus on Niall's words.

"I needed to think."

"Personally, I think you need to quit thinking." Mat allowed himself to push back against Niall.

"Yeah, probably."

Niall's low chuckle rumbled in Mat's ear, and he went from half hard to fully erect. One hand left his hip, coming around his pelvis to stroke him. Not hard, not aggressive—although Mat wouldn't have minded, he liked rough sex sometimes—no, this was fucking tender and kind, as if Niall was treasuring Mat. "Jesus, Niall," he gasped.

"This okay?"

He gripped Mat a little harder, twisting upward and running his thumb up and under the tip of Mat's cock. Mat groaned and had to reach out one hand to support himself against the wall, the chill of the tile in juxtaposition to the heat coursing through his body.

"That's a yes?"

Mat wasn't sure which was turning him on more, Niall's hand on his dick or Niall's cock rubbing between his ass-cheeks. Both, it was both. Mat's body felt like he was on fire—the good kind. Flames of need and want licked between his thighs and his groin as Niall pumped him. Shamelessly, Mat pushed harder against Niall's body, needing more, anticipating more, not wanting Niall to stop until he came. When Niall's other hand left his hip and drifted upward to twist his nipple, Mat barely kept himself from shouting. He managed to clap a hand over his mouth.

When he more or less had control of himself, he released his death grip so he could speak. "I want you to fuck me."

"That's excellent," Niall growled, "because I want to fuck you."

"But not in the shower." Mat's legs were shaking, and if he was quite honest with himself, he wasn't sure they'd hold him up with Niall pounding into him.

Niall released him to step past the shower curtain, laughing when he saw the amount of water on the floor. "Probably a good thing. Management's already itching to get me out of here."

Right. Mat had forgotten about that. At the moment he also didn't give a crap what management thought.

It was lucky the bed was just a few feet away from the bathroom door; Mat didn't think he would've made it much farther. He fell facedown onto the mattress with abandon. "What made you change your mind?" he asked into the covers.

The bed moved as Niall climbed on board, his heat once again stoking Mat's fire. "I didn't."

Mat twisted his head around to stare at Niall. His agate-green eyes seemed to glow in the dim room, the only illumination came from the muted TV.

"I've always wanted you, Mat. Look at you."

A thick finger stroked down Mat's spine. If it could've, his cock would have hardened further, but he was trapped against the covers.

"You're one of those people who's beautiful on the inside and out."

"Beautiful. That's something no one's ever called me before." Mat knew he wasn't a troll, but his body definitely showed signs of age. He liked to think his body had a history, but not when he was lying on a bed, exposed to the man he'd wanted for ages.

"I don't want to think about anyone else calling you beautiful," Niall growled, moving so he straddled Mat's legs.

"Well, don't worry. No one has."

"Their mistake."

Niall's finger made its way to Mat's ass, sending another shock of need through his body. He spread his legs, inviting more of his touch.

"Not just like this, lying in front of me, open and wanting, but when you're fully dressed, when you're bossing around your deputies, when you're with your family. You're beautiful because you're a good person, Mat."

"I'm not Mother fucking Teresa. Quit with the fucking poetry and fucking fuck me already."

The bed shook with Niall's laughter, a sound so foreign Mat wondered if he'd ever heard it before. "With that mouth, why wouldn't I want to fuck you?" Niall rasped out when he was able to speak.

"You're not going to run away?" Mat's question from earlier had gone unanswered.

"I'm not going to run away."

Then Niall proceeded to fuck Mat out of his ever-loving mind.

Mat didn't know what he'd expected when he and Niall finally came together. Whatever it had been was nothing like the reality of Niall touching him, caressing him, taking care of him.

By the time Niall was finished prepping him, Mat was shaking. His fingers dug into the sheets so deeply he hoped he didn't shred them. At first he'd begged Niall to hurry, but that had only made the infuriating man move even slower. Mat learned to keep his mouth shut.

Niall tapped his hip, and Mat shifted so his knees were underneath his body and his butt was completely exposed. It had been a long time since he'd had sex of any kind. He'd thought he'd feel more nervous or uncomfortable about it, but Niall was taking care of him, and now all Mat wanted him to do was fill him up. The sound of Niall ripping open a condom packet reached Mat's ears, soon followed by the glide of Niall's finger between his ass-cheeks.

"Ready?"

"Yesterday already."

Niall chuckled again, the sound rumbling from somewhere

deep in his chest. "I don't know where you get the idea this is going to happen quickly."

"Fuck me," Mat groaned into the pillow jammed under his head. The words were muffled, though, and again, all Niall did was chuckle. Then the thick head of Niall's cock bumped against his hole, demanding entrance. Instinctively, Mat pushed back as Niall pressed forward, the heavy stretch of his ass around Niall's cock keeping Mat grounded.

"Yes," Niall muttered. "You feel incredible around me. I'm going to make you forget anyone else you ever fucked."

"It's never going to happen if you don't hurry the fuck up," Mat panted as he pushed more forcefully, jamming Niall's cock inside. He stopped for a second to get used to the feeling of being stretched, being full, then did it again.

"It's probably not a coincidence the marina burned down," Niall said as his cock dragged across Mat's prostate. A lightning bolt of pleasure crashed through Mat, momentarily removing his ability to speak.

"If... you can talk about work now... you're not doing it right," Mat grunted when he could put words together again.

"It's the only way I can keep from coming."

NINETEEN
NIALL

"Don't let me sleep late."

Mat had barely managed to whisper the words to Niall before he fell dead asleep. Niall was decidedly not sleepy. His brain was bouncing furiously between two different reactions to "What have I done?" He never should've gone into the bathroom, but something—*Mat, it was always Mat*—had drawn him like he was a puppet. Seeing Mat's figure on the other side of the flimsy shower curtain had ripped away the last shred of his self-restraint.

His attraction to Mat was intense and out of his control and therefore something he couldn't trust. But tonight, over the last few weeks actually, Niall had gotten to know Mat, and his sharp intellect was as attractive as the body he resided in. And now that man had trusted Niall to take care of him during sex and as he slept afterward. A gift Niall cherished.

Sex with Mat had felt like coming home.

As he lay on his back in the dark motel room with Mat sleeping peacefully beside him, Niall rubbed his chest. An emotion that fucking scared him was making itself known. It wasn't something he'd ever felt before, and he wasn't going to try to give it a name at this point for fear of killing it.

Instead he turned onto his stomach, battered his pillow into submission, set his internal alarm for around six, and shut his eyes.

Morning came far too quickly, and Niall was the first awake. Rolling over, he glanced at his phone: 5:46. His bed partner had hardly moved in the night except to close the small space between their bodies, so their feet had been tangled together when Niall first surfaced from sleep.

"Mat," Niall whispered.

He was answered by a groan.

"You said not to let you sleep late. It's almost six."

The man in question rolled to his back, causing the duvet to slide off his body. Niall drank in his physique. No, Mat didn't hit the gym every day and had the tiniest beginnings of love handles; his body was not perfect. And yet it was. In the dim light coming through the curtains that were not quite pulled closed, Niall could see Mat's heavily furred chest and the trail that began at his belly button and led to his crotch, where Mat's semihard penis was waking up along with the person it belonged to.

Without volition, Niall reached out and traced a finger from Mat's chest to the tip of his erection, loving how he twitched under his touch.

"Jesus, Niall," Mat complained, "I have to go back out to the marina. I'm meeting Devon at the scene."

Niall had no idea who Devon was, but he had no intention of Mat meeting someone without a very recent memory of what Niall could do to him. Instead of answering, he wrapped his fingers around Mat's cock, leaned down, and swallowed him.

"Oh, shit!"

Niall allowed himself a grin before going back to the work at hand. It had been a long time since he'd wanted to give a blow job. It wasn't something he always enjoyed, but with Mat this morning it felt right and perfect. Niall licked around Mat's tip and tasted a little burst of precome.

"Niall," Mat panted, his fingers clenched into fists, "I don't—oh, god."

Niall let Mat slip out of his mouth for a moment, saying, "You can touch my head," before getting back to work. One of Mat's hands came to rest gently on the side of Niall's head, caressing his ear and face, while the other clutched the sheet in desperation.

He was hard too, so much so precome was dripping onto the sheets, but it wasn't himself he was concerned about. This was about Mat. He sucked again, running his tongue along the underside of Mat's erection. He felt him harden further in his mouth. Mat was about to come.

"I can't—oh god, Niall."

And Mat was shooting into his mouth while Niall drank him down.

"Come here," Mat demanded. "Let me."

"I'm too close," Niall managed to grind out. "Touch me and I'm gone."

"Come on me, then."

Jesus fucking Christ, the words alone had Niall seconds from erupting. Getting up onto his knees, Niall straddled Mat's thighs. He had to keep a tight grip on himself, the urge to come was so strong. All it took was two pumps as he stared into Mat's heated gaze, those blue eyes promising everything. Streams of come shot out of Niall, pooling on Mat's stomach and abdomen.

He collapsed onto the bed next to Mat, his chest heaving from the intensity of his orgasm—and his reaction to marking Mat as his own. Mat was still catching his breath as well; he turned his head, looking at Niall with a massive grin.

"That was hot. You're welcome to wake the sheriff up every day with a blow job—or whatever."

"Did you just refer to yourself in the third person?"

Mat laughed. "I have expectations now."

The smell of sex was heavy in the room. Just another reason for management to hate him.

"We both need to shower again."

"Probably best if we do it one at a time this time around. But seriously…" Mat propped himself up on one elbow. "I may have fallen asleep—"

"Passed out, more likely."

Mat's dark eyebrows drew together, creating a V. "Don't interrupt. I may have fallen asleep, but are you okay with this, with what we did? You're really not going to disappear for weeks?"

Niall wanted to avoid the conversation, not because he was planning on disappearing, but because exposing himself to Mat—leaving himself vulnerable to this man who was coming to mean a lot to him (internally he scoffed at "a lot," but that's as far as he was willing to go)—was a step farther than he'd ever gone before. Mat's clear gaze became shadowed. He shifted on the bed, and Niall realized he'd taken too long to answer.

Sitting up, he gripped Mat's shoulder, not letting him escape. "I'm not good with this… stuff, with relationships in general, but I promise I will try." Keeping his grip on Mat, Niall leaned in and took Mat's mouth with his own, trying to tell him with his body what he had a hard time saying with words.

Kissing Mat was addictive, Niall mused as he sucked on Mat's lower lip and licked his way into his mouth. Their tongues tangled, rough and slick, and Niall felt his dick perk up. Reluctantly, he pulled away. They would have to follow up later.

"I won't run away again." He could say the words now. "Go take a shower before we lose all control."

Mat rolled his eyes. "Fine." But he rolled off the bed and stepped into the bathroom, shutting the door behind him. A moment later, the shower came on.

Niall lay back and stared at the ceiling, listening to the spray of water against the bathroom tile. A rustling sound caught his attention, and he turned his head to see Fenrir standing next to the bed, an expectant look on his furry face.

"You're going to have to wait until I get out of the shower. If anyone saw me like this, we would be evicted immediately."

Fenrir continued to stare at him until the shower turned off and Mat appeared, drying himself off with one of the postage-stamp-size towels.

"It's all yours. Hey, Fenrir! Who's a good boy?" He reached for his clothes and wrinkled his nose. "Holy crap, my uniform smells like I've been camping for weeks with no shower and only a campfire for warmth."

"Borrow something of mine. We're close enough to the same size. I'm only taking a quick shower, because someone here"—he pointed at Fenrir—"wants a walk and his breakfast."

Mat looked startled by Niall's offer and then pleased. Niall brushed his lips quickly across Mat's before heading in for his own shower.

Once in the bathroom, Niall realized he loved how open Mat was with his feelings and wished feelings were as easy for him—while also being thankful that Mat was apparently attracted to emotionally stunted men.

The door opened a minute or so later. "I'll take Fenrir out."

"Don't you have to go? Isn't this why we're up so fucking early?"

Mat laughed. "Yes, but ten minutes longer is acceptable. Besides, I want to stay on his good side." The door shut, leaving Niall alone.

Niall was pulling a t-shirt over his head when Mat tapped on the door again. He and the dog both looked pleased with them-selves as they brushed past Niall.

"Why are you smiling?" Niall asked.

"Fenrir doesn't like Martin Reynolds. He must've been on his way to the Hook. I know," Mat said as he bent to unclip Fenrir's leash, "I should be scolding him. It was probably bad form, as sheriff, to not even try to stop him from growling." He straightened and shrugged. "Ah, well, I guess I'm not perfect."

Niall glanced from Mat to Fenrir, who was also still smiling. "What am I going to do with the two of you?"

"You're going to accept us for the wonderful gift we are to your life."

"Have you been reading motivational shit? I hate that stuff."

Mat chuckled. "I really do have to go. I have a spare uniform at the station to change into. Devon's going to be out at the marina in about—well, in all likelihood he's there already." Mat glanced down at his watch.

"Who the fuck is Devon?"

Mat looked at him, his eyes widening before his grin broadened. Dammit, that grin was impossible. Niall hated that he was jealous.

"Devon Flynn is the fire chief. He may swing our way—I've never asked—but this morning we're looking for evidence at the scene." He looked out the window. "I think the weather is going to cooperate too, no rain. Anyway"—Mat's smile turned wicked—"you're the only one I want, Niall."

The door had almost closed behind him when Mat poked his head back in. "I haven't had time to run a search on Mark Wallace yet, by the way." Then he was gone again.

Fenrir stared at the closed door for a second, letting out a little whine. Niall looked down at him. "You too, huh?"

Mark Wallace. Niall had actually forgotten about the name and the RV he'd been so worried about. Niall rummaged in the drawer and tugged on an old sweater, handmade, alternating cream and navy stripes. It was his favorite, and today he wanted its familiarity.

From the small box on the desk, he pulled out the film canisters. They felt heavy in his palm, more than the cheap metal and the undeveloped negatives hidden inside. He'd found a place in Seattle that still developed 35 mm film, and all they needed him to do was send it in; he'd even prepaid for the service. Since the lab had no connection to Piedras Island, the chance of them knowing anyone pictured was slim, which was for the best. Before he could second-guess himself, he tucked the canisters into an envelope, addressed it, and carried the small package to the lobby.

"Can you have this mailed for me?" he asked.

Ricky looked up from the reception desk, where it looked to Niall as if he was studying. He pushed his glasses to the top of his nose before nodding and taking the envelope. "Sure, I'll drop it in the post tomorrow."

"Thanks."

It was done, out of his hands for now. In a few days Niall would have more information and could decide how—or if—he should respond to Shay Delacombe's message.

"This is depressing," Mat said to the man standing next to him.

He and Devon had managed to arrive at the marina almost at the same time. In the early-morning light, the devastation was savage. A few of the boats had escaped the blaze, by what miracle Mat had no idea, but the majority were damaged or completely destroyed. The building where Sharleen had worked and shared space with Duane was gutted.

"How's Sharleen?" Mat asked. Surely Devon had talked to Birdy since last night.

The ambulance crew had transported Sharleen to the ER. The island didn't need to lose another resident so soon after Chas Reynolds and Sean—his brother may not have lived there, but he was one of theirs.

"They kept her overnight for observation. Birdy stayed with her for a while, and it sounds like she'll be fine."

"Good, good."

The marina was not good. By mutual agreement, he and Devon moved closer to what was left. Mat had his phone out, recording his observations and snapping pictures. The biggest mystery was, where was Duane Cooper? He was nowhere to be found, and attempts to reach him last night had gone unanswered.

"Cooper show up, by any chance?"

"I haven't heard from him," Devon said, looking up from where he was picking through a pile of ash.

"Fuck."

Mat called Deputy Radden and asked him to drive by Cooper's again and do a wellness check. When he clicked off, Devon had moved on, nudging odds and ends with his booted foot, making notes, taking lots of pictures. Mat rubbed his chest. He had a bad feeling that Duane was a key player in the fire. Even though Mat didn't have all the pieces, it was highly suspicious that the marina burned almost as soon as he and Birdy began to look into Duane's business activities.

"We're going to need a diver, likely," Devon muttered.

"Oh, sure. Let me just reach into my magic bag."

Devon straightened to his full height. He wasn't much shorter than Mat, his dark gaze sharp. "Yeah, this sucks. Thing is, Sharleen had the electrical upgraded last summer, and I did the inspection myself. It was a solid job. This fire was either complete negligence on the part of one of the boat owners or it was set on purpose. Which in itself is interesting, with all the other smaller fires."

"The Hamarsson place, which Jackson said my brother set. This one, the Wainwrights'. I was thinking—hoping, I suppose—that the garage fires were copycats. Teenagers, maybe."

"First, we don't know that Sean actually set the fire. Jackson only said he didn't and *claimed* Sean did," Devon replied.

This bit of information, looked at from an entirely different angle, settled uneasily in Mat's head. He'd been there when Trey Jackson had said the fire was Sean's doing and had no reason not to believe him—Sean had disliked Niall intensely—but what if Jackson was wrong? Sean was dead, shot to death by Trey, so Mat hadn't been able to question his brother about it. Had he been looking the wrong way, assigning to Sean a crime he hadn't committed? It made him wonder how else he might have been looking at things wrong.

He'd broken one of the most important rules of an investigation: never assume anything. Find the evidence to back up your belief.

"Refresh my memory on the other fires." He hadn't personally responded to all the small fires over the past few months.

"A garage out past Killegen's Point was the first, in January."

"I remember that one. It's a seasonal rental property. Didn't it just sell last summer?" One of those that sold every couple of years to someone wanting to make an investment.

"Think so. Then there were two other small garage fires in empty houses and that fire in the public restroom at the state park."

Mat had forgotten about that one. "Crap."

"Yep. And I wouldn't worry about trying to find a diver. I think Jennings is certified with the state."

"Foster dives? Why didn't I know that?"

Devon shot him a half smile. "Foster is a man of many talents, and he doesn't like to brag about any of them."

Mat continued to stare out over the devastated marina. Clouds scuttled across the sky, making the water appear both blue and gray, the ever-present wind sketching out whitecaps on the waves. His phone buzzed, snapping him out of his thoughts.

"Dempsey here."

"Sheriff, Deputy Radden. Cooper didn't answer the door and his place seems empty. I've walked around the property. Do you want me to go in?"

"Wait for me, Patrick. Don't do anything. I'll be there in ten minutes."

His bad feeling was getting worse. Deputy Radden was still learning the job, and Mat wanted to be there as backup. On his way out to Cooper's, Mat called Birdy to hear what she had to say about last night, but there was no answer. His worry ratcheted up. Deputy Flynn always answered.

Where was Duane?

Duane Cooper's home was located on the outskirts of Killegen's Point, not far from the marina. The cottage hunkered, like so many of the older island houses did, in a carved-out hollow of Doug firs and cedars. There was no lawn because the trees didn't let enough sunshine through to encourage the grass to grow. Instead, a cement walkway cut across bare ground through a few hardy tufts of native grass that dotted the landscape. Patrick's cruiser was parked out front, and he was sitting in the driver's seat. Mat pulled in behind him and turned the engine off. They got out of their cars at the same time, Deputy Radden hitching his uniform slacks up over his narrow hips.

"What's going on, boss?"

Funny how when Patrick used the term it didn't bother him the way it did coming out of Cooper's mouth.

"Cooper seems to be AWOL. With the marina burning down last night, I'd think he'd be on the scene, and he's not answering his phone. We're just going to check and see if he's here." Which didn't seem likely, since he hadn't answered Patrick's earlier knock and his truck wasn't in sight.

Patrick nodded, and together they crossed to the front door. There was no porch, only a small overhang that did nothing to protect visitors from the wind or rain.

Mat banged on the front door, loud enough it echoed across the yard. They waited, listening for a voice calling out or someone moving toward the door, but there was nothing. The only sounds were the evergreen branches brushing against each other in the wind and a raucous Steller's jay who was displeased they'd invaded his territory, his dark head ticking back and forth as he cawed at them.

"You wait here while I go around back. Step back from the door so he can't see your shadow if he's here. If he tries to bolt, take him down."

Mat didn't think Cooper or anyone else was inside the small house. It felt empty to him. But better safe than sorry.

The house was a one-story, no-basement, shotgun-style design, the back door almost directly in line with the front, and again, no porch or deck. Mat banged on the door as he called out Duane's name; there was no answer. He waited a minute before knocking one last time, also having a quick debate with himself about how much heat he'd catch for breaking in. He decided he could weather the storm. This was, after all, a wellness check on an island resident Mat was legitimately concerned about. Although... he bent down and after a moment claimed his prize.

The house was empty, as he had suspected. Nothing seemed unusual—not that Mat had been there before, but he didn't see evidence of a hurried departure, scattered clothes or a convenient gasoline can lying around. He and Patrick quickly walked through the house without touching anything. Front room, kitchen, bathroom, and the single bedroom were all empty. Mat didn't see anything indicating where Duane might have gone and, sadly, no notes admitting he was a criminal mastermind.

"He's not here." Patrick sounded as disappointed as Mat felt.

"Nope."

They locked up the house, using the key Mat had discovered hidden under the doormat. Why people thought that was a sneaky place to keep a key, Mat didn't know, but he didn't have enough fingers to count the times looking under the doormat, flowerpot, or closest rock had revealed a key.

"Radden, stay here until I can get Deputy Holstrom on the line. He may be under the weather, but he can sit in a cruiser and watch the house. After he takes over here, I want you to patrol the island—every single road. If you see anything weird, out of the ordinary, downright suspicious, *don't do anything*. Make a note and call me. Got it?"

"Got it."

Mat needed to get back to Hidden Harbor. He'd remembered —with a sinking feeling in his stomach, causing coffee he hadn't even had yet to sour—that Duane also had a boat at the dock where the Marine Safari was. Whale watching and tours around the San Juans during the summer months were Duane's official second source of income. It was the only other place Mat could think to look for him.

TWENTY-ONE
NIALL

By midmorning Monday, Niall had set up an interview later in the week with Leo Zelinsky and his boss from West Coast Forensics. All without coffee—but as soon as he was finished making phone calls, he was heading to find some.

"We'd love to talk to you sooner, Niall, but Kimball's out of the office on a case—we're swamped right now." Leo sounded tired but also excited to get Niall's call.

Ten minutes after that, Niall had agreed to meet with the insurance representative one more time. He was on a roll, taking care of business, even as he'd put off thinking about Shay's note and the box of photos. Shay was someone he'd been unsure of as a teen. When Niall had moved to Seattle and Shay had shown up a few years later, hanging out his shingle as a defense attorney, Niall had decided he really didn't like him. He forced his attention back to his current phone call.

"It's merely a formality, Mr. Hamarsson, just dotting i's and crossing t's." Roger Johnson had an irritatingly smooth voice, like he was so used to calming people down he forgot to change modes and now only spoke in a grating monotone.

Niall thought the company was dragging its feet as long as

possible, grabbing at straws to keep from settling with him, but maybe that was his pessimistic outlook. Maybe he needed to take a leaf out of Mat's book and think positive.

He snorted. Positive was never having to talk to these guys again. There: he'd done it.

Regardless, Niall was meeting Johnson at the man's Anacortes office Friday morning, and hopefully he'd be walking out of the interview with a check or the promise of one. Ha, another positive thought.

The rest of the day loomed ahead of him. Mat was busy dealing with the marina fire. Niall hadn't seen him since he'd left the motel the previous morning. Without dwelling too much on what he thought he was doing, Niall loaded Fenrir into his car and headed toward Killegen's Point and the promise of caffeine.

The RV was still parked behind the house. Most of the branches covering the windshield had fallen to the ground, indicating to Niall that the owner had not returned. Gripping Fenrir's leash, Niall walked around the vehicle but was certain it hadn't moved since the last time he'd been there—two days ago. It seemed like longer. A lot had happened in two days.

For one thing, he'd fucked Mat Dempsey.

No, he corrected himself. He'd had sex with Dempsey, and it had been unlike any sex Niall had had in his life. It had been give and take, strengthening the connection between them—every movement, every sensation between their bodies resonating like ripples in a pond. Even Niall was unable to deny it. He hadn't been joking when he'd said he had to think of cases in order to keep from coming... or possibly breaking down from the sheer intensity. Even now, envisioning Mat lying underneath him, giving himself to Niall with abandon, demanding Niall hurry up —Niall suppressed an erection.

The two of them were lucky the Orca was largely vacant. Niall was pretty sure they hadn't been very quiet by the end. Which was going to be a problem if they continued this... whatever it was. Relationship.

Did he want to continue? Did he want something with Mat, with the sexy sheriff who witnessed Niall's dark core and wasn't afraid of it? Hell, Niall was afraid of it himself. Mat and Fenrir seemed to be the only beings who ignored the warning signs.

And Alyson Dempsey.

And Riley.

And Ella.

Niall felt maybe the entire Dempsey clan had a problem with boundaries, as they flagrantly ignored his. Fenrir whined and tugged on his leash. Niall started walking again, leaving the abandoned house and empty RV behind them.

After grabbing a coffee from Chester's, Niall headed across the street to the general store. The truck he'd seen unloading a few days earlier must have been packed to the gills. Spring flowers, some in decorative pots and others ready to plant in people's yards, were everywhere. The other day when he'd been here he'd spotted little sheds, and they'd sparked an idea he wanted to research.

Inside the store were Fred and two teenagers Niall didn't recognize. Fred smiled at him and motioned for him to come closer.

"Morning, son. What brings you here today?"

Niall outlined his idea. "Do you think it would work?"

Fred nodded, but in a way that meant he was thinking, not agreeing. "Maybe. You're a big man, and they're awfully small. And, of course, they're not rated for habitation. No ventilation and the like. Maybe you should talk to Stu."

"Why Stu?"

As he organized a pallet of something that looked like petunias, all purple and dark blue, something Niall's grandmother would have liked, Fred answered, "His grandson Ian owns a business selling yurts. Seems to me—and don't get me wrong, the store could use the sale—a yurt might work better for what you need. I can't see you living in a 150-square-foot shed. If you want to talk to Stu, odds are he'll show up at Lulu's or the Hook for lunch. But I think he favors Lulu's grilled cheese sandwiches right now."

The idea of a yurt rolling around in his brain, Niall wandered back to the little free library Fred had stocked with romances, Westerns, and thrillers. He rummaged around for a bit before picking out a dog-eared Louis L'Amour and heading out to his car.

Fenrir greeted him with joy, something Niall was getting used to. "Let's go see if we can get some lunch and find Stu," he said to the dog.

Niall debated leaving Fenrir in the car, but most places on the island were pretty lax when it came to health codes, and the look Fenrir shot him was pathetic. He figured he'd give it a try.

"Want a table, honey?"

Gracie had been at Lulu's for years, Niall realized. Niall remembered her being much younger, but he supposed he'd been younger too. "I've got my dog with me." As if Gracie might have missed a dog that was nearly as tall as she was.

Gracie glanced at Fenrir. "Hey, sweetie, do you promise to behave?"

Fenrir did his best to look meek, thumping his tail against the floor. Niall could swear the dog winked at her.

"I'll seat you two in the back. No one's there right now."

Niall and Fenrir followed Gracie to the back of the restaurant.

"Take your pick. I'll be back in a sec."

• • •

Niall chose a booth by the window facing toward the entrance, not the one he'd sat at with Mat the other night. That seemed ridiculous, and he hated having his back to doors. Fenrir sniffed once or twice and then thumped down next to the table with a decidedly expectant air. Gracie returned almost immediately with a large mug of coffee and a plate of waffles.

"What's this?" Niall asked.

"Oh, CeeCee let them overcook." She smiled. "I thought the pup might take care of them."

"He's going to get spoiled. And his name is Fenrir," Niall grumbled.

"He's skin and bones! A couple plain waffles aren't going to hurt him."

Niall shook his head but picked up a waffle, tore it in two, and handed a piece to Fenrir. The dog delicately took the offering between his lips and actually chewed it before swallowing.

"He's so funny, seems almost human to me," Gracie remarked. "Do you know what you want to eat?"

Niall ordered a burger, and Gracie bustled off. "You're one lucky dog, that's all I have to say," Niall said to Fenrir, who finished the rest of his waffle without answering.

Niall's burger arrived promptly, and he made short work of it, doing his best to ignore Fenrir's hopeful eyes. "You already had a whole plate of waffles," he told the dog, but he might possibly have shared a french fry with him too.

As Niall was taking the last sip of his coffee, Stu Dennis strolled in. Niall nodded at him, and the older man walked over to Niall's table.

"Mind if I sit with you?" Stu asked.

"Sure, have a seat. I was hoping to find you here, actually." Stu was another one of those people Niall remembered being much younger. It had taken him a little while to put a face to the name. Years ago, Stu had been the history teacher at the local high school. He must've retired around the time Niall graduated.

Now, as he watched the older man, Niall wondered if Stu might have known about David Delacombe and Ana. Stu didn't seem to miss much.

Stu made himself comfortable, scratching Fenrir on the head as he did so. "How's the wolf doing?"

"Ha. He's more of a sheep in wolf's clothing. I don't think he'd hurt anyone."

"He is fierce-looking, though. I had a dog as a boy, meanest beast you ever came across. That dog terrorized my sister and me for its entire life. The only person it liked was my mother."

"What kind of dog?" Niall was expecting Stu to say Rottweiler or Doberman.

"Golden retriever. Mean as a snake."

Niall chuckled along with Stu.

"Now that the dust has died down from the murders, how are you doing?" Stu asked with an air of innocence Niall did not fall for.

"Are you trying to get information out of me?"

"Just making conversation, just making conversation." Stu smiled and Niall knew he'd been right, but Stu took the hint.

They sat for a while talking about nothing and everything. Stu knew a lot about what was happening on Piedras—Niall would learn more from him than he ever would from a community bulletin board.

"Everyone wants to know what you're going to do with Od and Jo's property."

"The insurance inspector was out a couple weeks ago. Surely 'everyone' knows that."

Stu nodded. "But what have you decided? There's a pool going, you know."

"A pool? People are betting whether I'm going to stay or go back to Seattle?"

"Yup."

"What are the odds?"

"Right now, about three to one in favor of you leaving."

"You mean they want me to leave?"

"No, no, three out of four think you're too chickenshit to stay."

Niall laughed. "Chickenshit, huh?"

"Pretty much."

"And where do you stand?" Niall asked.

Stu inspected Niall carefully, his eyes narrowing a bit. "I think you're probably going to stay. Piedras gets in your blood. You were gone for a long time. Things change, even in a place like this. But I think you're going to stay."

"What do you mean, things change?" He'd been meaning to bring up Stu's grandson and the yurts, but now he was curious. What was the other man hinting at?

Stu leaned back in his chair. Gracie chose that moment to come over with the carafe and refilled Niall's mug. They watched the stream of dark liquid splashing into his cup. Gracie smiled at them and headed off to caffeinate other patrons.

Once she was gone, Niall repeated his question.

"I mean"—Stu paused, clearly searching for the right words— "society has changed. Piedras is more accepting these days, we're more liberal. Even old coots like me."

Niall leaned forward, his elbows on the table. "Stu, what exactly are we talking about?" He had an idea what the old geezer was hinting at, at least he thought he did. Goose bumps broke out along his arms underneath the warm sweater he was wearing.

Stu rolled his eyes. "Homosexuality, Hamarsson. That's what I'm talking about. For a cop, you're mighty obtuse. Mat's car has been parked outside the Orca overnight for two days running. That has people talking, but not in the way you probably think. Well, not many, anyway," he amended.

Niall narrowed his eyes. He felt certain Martin Reynolds was the source of much of any negative gossip about him and Mat, especially after Mat's run-in when he was walking Fenrir the other morning. Martin irritated Niall's last nerve.

The old man confirmed Niall's thoughts. "Don't worry about people like Martin Reynolds. He's a shit heel, no doubt, but he's also too caught up in his own wacky theories to be any harm. I think Claribel would take him out of her will if he did anything more than blow off steam, and he knows it. No, I knew about you before you came back to the island. I get to Seattle. You were out there, no reason you can't be here. Nor that foolish sheriff of ours either. I think I'm actually offended if you two men think you can't be yourselves here."

"It's not that easy," Niall grumbled.

"The hell it isn't. I'm an old man, and I'm here to tell you nobody's gonna live your life except you. Is somebody going to act like a jackass? Hell yes, and it'll probably be Martin Reynolds or one of his so-called friends. But the rest of us, we don't care. If your grandparents were still alive, they'd say the same thing. You think they didn't know? Maybe not Od, but Jo sure did. Kids these days." Stu shook his head.

"How long have you had that little speech ready?" Niall inquired.

What Stu said was true. He hadn't tried to hide his sexuality once he moved to Seattle. He hadn't actually tried to hide when he was a teen either, but there hadn't been anyone else for him to be with—he'd thought, anyway. He hadn't known about Mat. Hell, he'd hardly paid attention to him. Niall was older than Mat and too focused on his own survival and escape plan to notice Mat.

Stu sat back again, grinning, "A while now. Felt good to get it off my chest."

"Well, thanks for that. Getting back to me staying." And off the topic of his sexuality, he sincerely hoped. "Fenrir and I have been politely asked to leave the Orca," Niall said.

"Hmmm." Stu crossed his arms across his chest.

"Fred from the general store said that your grandson sells yurts."

Stu nodded, clearly following Niall's train of thought. "He does. Runs a good business off Lopez."

"A yurt, though?" He pictured windswept plains, huge hawk-like birds, and cattle with extremely long horns.

Stu waggled his eyebrows. "Ian designs them himself. He has a degree in something fancy to do with sustainability. The fire didn't do anything to the sewer and water on the property, right? You could plop a yurt down, bring in a temporary shower and toilet, and call it good until the insurance company gets done diddling you around. They can be converted to permanent structures as well."

The tingle of excitement Niall had felt when he spotted the garden sheds at the general store returned. "What about this time of year? Do you think he'd have anything?"

"If you think you're serious, I'll give you his personal number and you can find out for yourself."

After departing Lulu's, Niall retraced the route to Hidden Harbor. As the road brought the Subaru close to the Dempsey homestead, Fenrir stood up in the back seat, blocking Niall's view, his tail moving back and forth with a hopeful swing.

"We are not stopping," Niall told him. "We haven't been invited."

Fenrir caught Niall's glance in the rearview mirror.

Dammit.

"He's not even home. He's out investigating crime."

Like Niall would've been had he not bailed on his career. The guilt over Tanya Nichols, her family still grieving and not able to bury her remains, ate at him every day.

Fenrir didn't drop his gaze.

"This is a bad idea," Niall said to the dog. And himself. It was a really bad idea, but he wanted it as much as Fenrir did. "I'm only stopping for you."

Mat's cruiser was nowhere in sight. Disappointment warred with relief in Niall's gut, making his lunch churn in his clenching stomach. Maybe one of these days he'd figure out his feelings. He snorted. Maybe pigs would fly. He pulled in and parked beside Alyson's car.

Niall lifted the hatch and Fenrir bounded out of the Subaru, heading to the back of the house where his favorite spot to pee, apparently on the entire island, was. Niall grabbed a plastic bag, just in case, and followed him. It was hard not to be at least somewhat cheerful when a big gray doofus of a dog was bounding in front of you.

While he waited for Fenrir to reappear out of the bushes, the back door opened.

"Niall!" Alyson called. "And Fenrir too. Two of my favorite people."

"You shouldn't call him a person, Alyson, it only encourages him." Niall was puzzled at the pleasure in Alyson's voice. He knew she adored Fenrir and liked him—he just couldn't figure out why.

"Come in. I have fresh coffee."

Alyson's kitchen was bright and cheery and smelled like freshly baked cookies. Mat's sister Ella sat at the kitchen table, turning as they entered. Fenrir went to her side, and she began to coo and pet him, but not before Niall noticed she'd been crying.

"Is this a bad time?"

"No, not at all, Niall. I think maybe you and Fenrir are exactly what we need this afternoon."

As Alyson poured coffee for Niall and got out plates for the still-warm cookies, Riley came into the kitchen. The little girl was cute. Niall thought she was around six or seven years old. She was the spitting image of her mother except for the shape of her eyebrows and the color of her eyes, which were a clear mahogany instead of the Dempsey midnight blue.

Niall sat across the table from Ella and Alyson. After Riley had a glass of milk and a cookie, Alyson had sent her and Fenrir out into the yard where, Niall could see through the window, the dog was grudgingly retrieving a stick over and over again. Albeit as slowly as possible, humoring the small human.

"They're going to get wet and muddy."

"That's not a problem," Alyson responded airily.

Niall felt uncomfortable and out of place, but Alyson had insisted he stay.

"I'm sorry," he said to Ella. "About…" He wasn't sure how to put it, so he settled for a vague hand gesture.

Ella smiled grimly. "I am too, and it's all my fault. I never wanted this for Riley." She swiped at her face as another tear slipped out.

"Baby girl, we will get through this, and it is not your fault," Alyson told her.

"I feel like I've let everyone down. Riley, most of all."

Alyson put her arm across Ella's shoulders, pulling her in for a hug. "Kids are pretty resilient, and you have family to back you up. We'll get Riley all settled in. She can probably start school right away—or in the fall, whichever is better."

Ella lifted her head to look first at Alyson, then at Niall. "Before we left Houston, she asked if Richard and I were getting a divorce. I didn't know how to answer, because… why would she ask that? I almost said yes right then, because having her ask me that, it was like something inside me unlocked and now I could admit how unhappy I was... and I realized too that staying together when everything is so toxic was the worst example I could give her. But I don't know if I'm strong enough."

"I should probably go," Niall said.

This kind of conversation made him nervous. Niall knew next to nothing about families and how they worked. He itched to escape.

He glanced out the kitchen window again. Riley and Fenrir were now playing some kind of game where she spun in a circle and tossed the stick. Fenrir trotted over and picked it up, but instead of returning it, he stood there with it in his mouth. Riley was laughing at... Niall had no idea at what, but she was enjoying herself.

Alyson had followed his gaze. "Don't go yet. Riley and Fenrir are busy. Have another cookie. We're having a hard day. Ella got some paperwork from Richard."

Ella smiled at him. It was a little watery, but she managed. "Riley loves dogs, and Richard never let her have one."

The sound of the front door opening distracted Niall from whatever he'd been about to say. Seconds later Mat strode into the kitchen, his dark hair sticking up in all directions as if he'd been tugging it. He didn't bother to stop and take off his jacket or shoes but headed straight for his sister, engulfing her in a hug. Ella burst into tears again, and Mat rocked her back and forth. Alyson winked and pointed toward the back door.

Quietly Niall stood, moving to the door with Alyson behind him. In a quiet voice she asked, "Do you mind taking Riley for a few minutes, maybe to the park? One of us will come get her, but I think Ella needs space to talk, and Riley makes it impossible."

"I don't have a car seat."

"My car's unlocked. There's a booster seat you can borrow. Her rubber boots are in the trunk. Hang on, I'll walk out with you."

Mat and Ella didn't seem to notice Niall's departure, and Riley was thrilled when her grandma told her Niall would be taking her on an adventure. Niall didn't know what to think about being assigned kid duty. Who in their right mind thought he was fit to entertain a child? Alyson Dempsey, apparently, because she put Riley in the car seat and waved goodbye to them without another word.

He ended up taking Riley to his beach. The public beaches on the island would be deserted this time of year, but someone would still complain about Fenrir, and Fenrir did not appreciate being on a leash when there were waves to herd.

"Where are we?" Riley asked as they bumped down the driveway.

My home. My heart's center. The only place I feel peace.

"This is where I live," Niall answered.

"But there's no house."

Niall unbuckled his seat belt and sent Alyson a quick text so she'd know where they were. Wind buffeted the car, and the few leaves that had hidden from the wind all winter gusted up and flew past them. Unlocking the door, he got out and went around to help Riley out too. Her bright purple rain boots were too big. One slipped off as she slid to the ground, and Niall helped her put it back on. "There was a fire, and the cabin burned," he told her.

Riley looked over to where the ashes were. The remaining yellow tape fluttered wildly. She cocked her head, looking very much like her uncle, and stated, "You're going to put it back."

Fenrir woofed impatiently at them, wanting to head down to the rocky beach.

"I am. Let's go see what he's all excited about."

The temperature had dropped so it was freezing on the beach. Niall didn't care, and neither did the other two. For a little while,

Riley helped Fenrir chase the waves back to where they belonged, then she began to hunt for "the perfect rock." What that was, Niall didn't know. All his suggestions were considered and then promptly dismissed.

They'd been out there about half an hour, by Niall's calculations. Riley had to be cold. Her clothes were wet from the drizzle, and there was no way seawater hadn't splashed inside her boots. Niall was chilly too, but to his surprise he enjoyed Riley's company. He had no experience with children other than as witnesses to crimes. Almost as if she was reading his thoughts, Riley chose that moment to speak.

"My daddy and my mommy yell a lot."

She'd come to stand next to him. Niall tried to shield her from as much of the wind as he could while she examined a greenish rock about the size of a quarter in the palm of her hand.

"Sometimes adults yell." Niall picked up another rock, wondering, as he did so, how many of the rocks on this particular beach he'd touched over his lifetime. Half? More?

"My daddy doesn't like to go to the park. I like the park."

"This is my favorite place," Niall replied by way of an answer.

Riley beamed up at him, her brown eyes warm even if the rest of her must've been freezing. "Can it be my favorite place too?"

"Sure, kid."

"Was this your house always?"

"It was. Not at first, not when I was your age."

"I'm almost seven."

"Well, I guess around your age. I moved here when I was eight."

"Did your mom and dad yell too? Is that why you came here?"

Niall scrabbled around inside his messed-up head for any answer that would satisfy Riley. Yes, his mother had yelled, but her vitriol had been aimed at Niall. He was the root of her problems. He'd wrecked her life, she wished he'd never been born, he was a demon. That final memory startled Niall. It wasn't until the end, he thought, that she started accusing him of being Satan's spawn. It was hard to reconcile his memories with the photos sitting on his desk.

"I came to live with my grandparents," he said, hoping that would do. "My grandpa would tell me all sorts of stories about Vikings, and we'd build rock castles together."

"Can we build one?"

"Sure," Niall replied, glad for the change of topic.

They'd decided on the location and were well into framing out the foundation when Fenrir let out one of his rare woofs. Niall looked up from plunking down a rock the size of two of his fists to see not one but two cars heading down from the road.

"It's Gramma!" Riley shouted. "Hi, Gramma!"

Following Alyson's car was Mat's cruiser.

Niall was forced to swear on Fenrir's fuzzy head that Riley would be allowed to return and finish building the castle before she allowed herself to be led away by her grandmother.

"You created a monster," Mat commented as he watched his mother's car drive away.

Niall shrugged and tried to pretend the sight of Mat wasn't having an effect on him. "Ella going to be okay?" he asked.

Mat shrugged. "I guess. Eventually."

Niall wanted to tell him she would, that everything would be okay, but in his experience that was unlikely. Things rarely turned out the way you wanted them to. He looked over at the castle he and Riley had started. He wanted to keep working on it. Anything to distract himself from Mat.

"I was jealous Riley had you to herself." Mat uttered the words while leaning closer, invading Niall's space and sucking away all oxygen in Niall's vicinity.

He opened his mouth to protest, but instead his gaze latched on to Mat's mouth and there was nothing to say. Mat erased the space between them, bumping his nose against Niall's. The day was chilly and quickly heading toward late afternoon, but the drizzle had stopped while Niall and Riley were planning the castle, and the wind had died down to a mild breeze. Mat's mouth settled against his own, warm, and inviting. Reflexively Niall's tongue flicked out, licking his own lips and then Mat's.

Mat groaned, low and soft. Niall could barely hear it over the waves, but he did hear it and knew what it meant. Mat wanted him as much as he wanted Mat.

They met with unintended force, teeth clashing as they remembered how to fit against each other's bodies. Mat's hands, much warmer than Niall's, rose to cup his face, to hold him still and allow Mat to control the kiss. Niall didn't mind. When it was his turn, he'd reciprocate.

Kissing Mat was liquid fire. As the waves crashed around them and Fenrir let out the occasional whoop, reminding the water where it was supposed to be, Niall lost another slice of himself to Mat—maybe this was the time he gave in and lost it all. Mat groaned again, pushing harder against him. Even through their layers of clothing, Niall could feel Mat's erection, and the memory of the last time they'd been together on this beach surfaced. Niall forced himself to pull away from Mat's embrace.

They were both panting. A half smile flitted across Mat's handsome face. "I need to get more exercise if I breathe this hard after we kiss."

Niall started to say something, to tell Mat Niall wasn't good enough—not for someone as upright and honest as Mat. Mat must've suspected, because he pressed his index finger against Niall's lips. "Don't. Okay? Just don't. Let me drive for a while. I don't know what's going on in that head of yours, but I'm sure it's *complicated* and you have all sorts of reasons why we can't or shouldn't be together. The thing is, Niall Hamarsson, you're still here on the island and I've stayed at your room twice—the ship of secrecy has sailed.

"You haven't left the island, even though you are twitchy as hell, and you showed up at my house today with that damn dog and then brought my niece here while we had the family talk. You think you're not a good man, but you are. So here's what's going to happen: we're going to date."

Niall squinted at him. "Date?"

"Yes, date. You are familiar with the word?"

Niall rolled his eyes, moving a little away from Mat—but not too far, not so far that he couldn't feel his warmth or smell his particular scent. Fenrir was off snooping in the shrubbery. Niall could barely see his gray tail. The thing was, Mat was right. Niall was invested. He wanted Mat in every way. He just didn't know how to get his heart to open and worried he would never be able to be who Mat deserved. "Do you really want the whole island up in your business?"

"I don't really care. And everyone already knows anyway."

"Stu Dennis talked to me about it."

"Of course he did. I'm sure he won't be the last. Big deal."

Niall turned to stare out over the dark, turbulent waters of the strait. Something in his gut warned him that being together wasn't going to go the way Mat hoped it would. Something was bound to go sideways. Maybe that was just Niall's hard-won sense of self-preservation. Maybe he gave too much credit to his instincts, especially where Mat Dempsey was concerned. "Mat," he began, but he didn't know what he was going to say or how to articulate his feelings.

"Do you still blame me for what happened in high school?" Mat asked, a pained edge to his voice.

The question took Niall by surprise. "What are you talking about?"

"I should have done something, something more. I knew my brother, Martin, and some of the other boys were bullying you."

"They would have pummeled you into the ground," Niall

replied with a snort of laughter. "If I recall, you weren't exactly a giant."

"Still."

"Still, *nothing*. What they did was nothing, Mat. They thought they were tough, but I'd already been through hell. They couldn't touch me."

When Niall said things like that, that what he'd been through was so awful that the bullying later had been nothing, anger welled up inside Mat like lava. He had to take a breath to get himself under control. "Thanks for watching Riley," he said. Riley was at least a safe subject.

"No problem," Niall said, a gruff edge to his voice.

Mat cocked his head and gazed intently at Niall. "You sure?"

Niall kicked a pebble into the waves. He had his hands jammed into the pockets of his jeans. He and Riley'd been at the beach for an hour. He must be freezing.

"I don't know, Mat," he said. "I mean, yes, I'm sure it wasn't a problem. I just—I don't know anything about kids. I think she had fun."

Jesus Christ, enough with this space between them. If Mat had learned nothing else about Niall, he'd learned that talking about his feelings—Niall's—and it appeared others', was almost impossible. For Niall a whisper was a shout, and they were too far apart, the waves were too loud for Mat to hear. "You know about people, and from the look on her face and the amount of sand she was covered with, yes, Riley had fun," Mat replied.

Stepping in close again, Mat pressed himself against Niall's strong back. The small incline gave him enough height to lean his chin against Niall's shoulder while he wrapped his arms around Niall's waist.

"Is this okay?" he whispered, Niall's ear chilly against his cheek.

Niall nodded, tugging his hands out of his pockets and resting them against Mat's.

"Thank you for taking care of Riley. Now that she knows about this place, she's going to be relentless wanting to come back. You did great with her. She loves you."

"Mghrg."

"That's not a word."

Niall shrugged.

"I wish I could stay here until dark and just be *Mat* with you—mind, I'd probably freeze to death—but I need to get back to the station. If Mom hadn't called me earlier, I wouldn't have come home, but I'm glad I did."

Before rushing home, Mat had issued a BOLO for Duane Cooper and made a phone call to the district attorney's office about subpoenaing his bank records. Birdy was following up with Cooper's ex-wife in the hopes that maybe he'd been in touch with her in recent weeks.

Niall gave another unintelligible response, but Mat thought it was agreement. Niall whistled, and the bushes at the far end of the rocky beach moved wildly before Fenrir burst from the scrub and raced toward them. Who knew what he'd been doing back there. The closer he got to them, the more obvious it was he was filthy: covered with dirt, moss and twigs clinging to his coat. He looked pleased with himself.

"You were right, you know, the other night," Mat said.

He was remembering Niall pounding into him, his heavy body keeping Mat from floating off the bed, Niall's skin against his own and Niall thinking about the case to keep from coming. He chuckled.

"What?" Niall tried to turn and look at him, but Mat held him in place.

"I'm sure the fire was arson. So is Devon. Something about the way it burned so fast and the patterns of the flames. Devon thinks the accelerant was gasoline, like the Wainwrights' barn and the other fires, which would explain the speed. One of the deputies and I were out at Cooper's place earlier today checking if I could cross him off my list, but no luck."

"He wasn't there?"

"Nope."

"What did you find at the marina?"

"No smoking gun, if that's what you mean. There's a state fire inspector coming out again tomorrow. I think they're getting tired of the ferry ride. Maybe they'll take a room at the Orca." That actually wasn't unusual. When an investigator thought they had a serial arsonist, they often stayed close to the scene to see if the perpetrator returned to see their handiwork.

"What's next for you?"

"I need to officially interview Sharleen, the dockmaster. She was pretty shaken up, ended up in the ER. They kept her for observation, but she should be home by now, and I need to talk to her." Dropping his hands from Niall's waist, Mat stepped away, immediately missing Niall's warmth and strength. Niall swiveled around, and Mat was taken by surprise when Niall's large hands cupped his face and his lips claimed Mat's. It was quick and dirty, Niall sweeping his tongue into Mat's mouth, tasting him, a bit ravaging. Mat didn't have time to react before Niall had pulled away again.

"What was that for?"

Niall's mouth pulled up into a half grin. "You hear the things I don't say. It's a little unnerving, but I think I like it. Go do your job. Find me later if you have the time."

"I'll always have the time for you, Niall." Mat batted his eyes.

Niall's laugh echoed out over the water. "Get to work. I'll see you tonight."

As he drove toward Sharleen's, Mat was starting to think this thing with Niall might actually work out.

Sharleen lived in an enormous log house on a big piece of property. The two-story home faced west, and large picture windows reflected the quickly setting sun; it was a beautiful location, and the logs had obviously been well maintained over the years.

There were two other small buildings on her property: a detached carport that protected her truck and a shed with gardening tools leaning up against the outside like she'd been working in her yard recently. Mat climbed the porch steps to the front door and knocked.

After this interview he was heading back to the station, writing up his notes for the day, then tracking down Niall again, though only for a while. Tonight he would need to go home; he'd used his last spare uniform at the office, and he should check in with his family again, see how Ella was feeling. He wasn't eighteen; he didn't need to spend every night with Niall.

Didn't mean he didn't want to.

As he waited for Sharleen to answer the door, he stared out over her property. A few of the flower beds were freshly cleared, the winter mulch pulled away so the spring blossoms would feel the sunshine. Here and there purple flowers were blooming, along with some tiny white ones.

After a minute or so, the door opened a crack. Beyond it, Mat could see a hint of Sharleen's peach-colored hair and her dim shadow.

"Sharleen, Sheriff Dempsey. Can I speak to you for just a moment? About the fire at the marina."

"Right now?" Her voice was husky. She opened the door a bit farther, but it wasn't an invitation to enter.

"Well," he said, smiling, "the sooner after an incident the better. What you saw or heard will still be fresh in your mind. I'm sure you understand we all want to figure out what happened and find who did this."

"I know, I suppose you're right. I'm awfully tired though. Will it take long?"

Now she opened the door enough so Mat could slip past her into the mudroom. Sharleen shut the door and led Mat through the small room to another door and into a short hallway that led into what he supposed was a great room.

The semi-open kitchen was located behind the wall of the hallway. On one side of the great room was a massive, ancient dining room table. To his right was a living room area with two comfortable-looking couches, and a wood-burning stove separated the two spaces. The picture windows had a magnificent view of the strait.

"Beautiful place. I don't think I've ever been here."

The house seemed even bigger from inside. The dining room ceiling was open to the roof, making it two stories tall. There were windows set high in the interior second-story walls, creating a courtyard effect and allowing afternoon light into the upstairs rooms. It was beautiful.

Sharleen sat at the table and with a sweep of her hand indicated Mat should sit opposite her.

"I've never been questioned by the police before." She pulled her garish housecoat tighter around herself.

"I'm just going to ask you questions about the day of the fire, get your impressions."

Mat took her through the day, starting from when she woke up to when she arrived at the marina. Sharleen's day had consisted of grocery shopping, visiting a friend, and working in her yard.

"I'm not normally there on Saturdays, but I was working on the state certifications. I wanted to get ahead of the game for once. I was so focused I don't think I heard anything."

"I know people come and go," Mat said encouragingly. Saturday would doubtless be a busy time at the marina. People who worked during the week would have time to work on their boats, even if it was only just spring.

"All the time, you have no idea. It's amazing how many people think I'm there just to chat with." She shook her head at the people who had the gall to bother her.

"And you didn't recognize anyone?"

"Oh, well, not really. I mean, like I said, I was working." Sharleen had been leaning toward him. Now she sat back in her chair, her hands in her lap.

"Mm-hmm. Does the marina have a security camera?"

"Oh, yes, but I imagine it was destroyed. It hung on the corner of the office."

Mat made a note for Devon to double-check. It was unlikely the camera had survived, but weirder things had happened.

"Just to be clear, you didn't see or hear anyone before you smelled the smoke? There was no one, as far as you know, working on their boat? No one who'd just stopped by? We haven't been able to get in touch with Duane—he wasn't there? Just relax and let yourself think back."

Sharleen pinched her lips together, pulling her robe around herself again as if she was cold. "I decided to come down after lunch with my friend. There was no one outside when I arrived, but there were a few cars parked." She bit her lip, trying to remember. "Everything is just so jumbled, I can't remember. I was working, you know, and all the noises kind of turn into a rhythm and it helps me to concentrate on the numbers." She met Mat's look. "I'm so sorry. I wish I could remember more."

"But you're certain Duane's truck wasn't there?"

"No. I don't think so. But if he'd been there in the morning, I wouldn't have seen him."

"Any thoughts on where Duane might have gone, or where he might be now?"

She shook her head. "Maybe to his other boat? The one he uses for his Marine Safari business. He moors it at a private dock in Hidden Harbor. Maybe he had business off the island; sometimes he does odd jobs for that ex-wife of his."

"You don't think it's odd we can't locate Duane and that he's not answering his phone?"

Sharleen shook her head, her distress obvious. "Duane is a good friend. I hope nothing has happened to him. I would've thought he'd try to contact me." Her eyes filled with tears.

Mat couldn't put his finger on what, but something was bothering him. He needed to get back to the station and write all his notes and impressions down. It was an old habit from working in San Francisco, and it often helped him see unexpected patterns.

He made another note to check and see if Duane's other boat was still there. His bad feeling about Duane was getting worse. The marina fire would be very convenient for him if he was somehow diverting money from Piedras County. Mat didn't want to think that someone he'd known most of his life was responsible for this fire, but so far the evidence was, if not pointing in Duane's direction, at least hinting strongly at it.

What they needed was to actually interview the man himself instead of speculating about a bunch of maybes.

That morning, he'd talked to the district attorney again about Duane's bank records, and he'd added East Bay Marina to the list as an afterthought. Cathy DeWitt, a young and very promising attorney in the prosecutor's office, had agreed to put a rush on the request.

"I'll see what I can do, Sheriff Dempsey. Sometimes the wheels of justice need a little encouragement."

Didn't he know it.

Arson was often about money, but not always. Best to rule out the money angle so he could focus on finding whoever had done this. If money wasn't the motive, next in line was drugs.

"I just don't know what I'm going to do." Sharleen swiped at a tear that dared to escape down her cheek.

"I'm sure the doctor told you to rest. If I have any further questions, I'll let you know."

He left Sharleen sitting in her chair, staring out the window. As he maneuvered his cruiser up the driveway to the main road, it occurred to him he should've asked if she had copies of the information and documents stored at the marina office. He almost turned around but instead decided to have Birdy check in on Sharleen tomorrow morning and ask her then.

Back at the station, Mat pulled a battered spiral notebook out of his desk. He opened it and flipped through to a blank page, then began jotting down his thoughts. First he created a timeline of the suspicious fires since the beginning of the year, referencing the police reports for the details. The first three were the empty garages and a public restroom. The first two had occurred on Friday nights in January—a traditional night of no good for the teen crowd.

The third was on a Wednesday the first week of February. The Wainwrights' barn had been a week ago—a big step up from a small garage fire—and now the marina on a Saturday. He tapped the notebook with his pen, scanning his list. After staring at it, he went back and added "Hamarsson cabin" between the last garage and the Wainwrights'. What was he missing?

The obvious conclusion was that someone was trying to claim insurance money, but that was a lot harder than it sounded these days. Insurance companies didn't just hand out checks, as Niall knew. The marina was a disaster. There were so many claims from that fire alone it would take months to investigate. If this was about insurance, which fire was the one? Mat could rule out Niall's cabin; Mat had witnessed Niall's pure grief.

And where the hell was Duane? That was another burning question—Mat chuckled at the tasteless humor. Deputy Holstrom had had Cooper's home under surveillance since the morning, and Deputy Radden had been patrolling the island. There was no sign of Duane or his pickup. Duane's second boat was snug in its mooring in Hidden Harbor—and yet no one had seen him. Mat would think *someone* would've spotted his vehicle.

Yes, Cooper could've taken the ferry and left Piedras, but Mat and Birdy had already looked at the terminal's video feed, and, between the time the marina fire was reported and now, no one driving a truck like Cooper's or a pedestrian looking like Cooper had boarded.

"Where is he?" Mat asked out loud, though he wasn't expecting Birdy to have an answer.

"He knows his way around boats. It's possible he could've taken a different one," Birdy commented.

Mat rubbed his eyes, unsuccessfully stifling a yawn. He looked at his watch. It was just after seven. "True enough. And with all the vessels destroyed last night, it will be hard to figure what's missing and what simply burned."

Mat didn't want Duane to be the one behind the fire. He'd known the man most of his life. Duane had been one of the first people to encourage Mat to go into law enforcement when he found out Mat was interested; he'd been to Dempsey family barbecues and birthday celebrations.

He needed to steer himself away from the past and focus on the present.

"If he's responsible for the fire and on the run, I'm surprised he didn't take the boat moored here—what did he name it?" Mat thought for a moment. *"Pirate's Dream?"*

When Birdy didn't immediately respond to his speculation, Mat glanced over at her. Her cheeks were red, and she was biting her lip. He raised his eyebrows, a trick he'd learned from his mother.

"I think his fuel tanks might have been empty."

"You think his fuel tanks might have been empty," Mat parroted.

"Yes, sir. Very possibly. And maybe a spark plug or two went missing."

"How odd."

"Yes, Duane always brags about how he's ready for everything, that he's never caught off guard. He quotes the Boy Scouts a lot: 'Always Be Prepared.'"

He did actually say that a lot, so much that Mat had started to tune it out.

"I wonder what could've happened." He stopped any confession from his deputy with a raised palm. Whatever Birdy had been up to between leaving Sharleen at the emergency room and right this minute, he didn't want to know.

Taking his hint, Birdy said, "And of course, when you issued the BOLO, I took steps to impound the boat pending the investigation."

"Of course." Mat wasn't sure why he hadn't done that himself. To be fair, he'd been a bit busy and maybe distracted. Birdy was on the ball, as usual, even if she had apparently started tampering with suspects' property.

"Should we keep Deputy Holstrom at Cooper's?" she continued, giving him a look of wide-eyed innocence.

Mat thought for a moment. They needed to be careful. The last thing he wanted was for Cooper to get a whole bunch of evidence excluded because of police overreach.

No. The *last* thing he needed was for Duane to hurt anyone. The marina fire could easily have killed someone. It was pure luck no one had been working on their boat. It made sense to have Birdy keep her eye out for the missing man. "Holstrom is still recovering from the flu and could probably use a break. Why don't you head over there for a few hours and relieve him? But keep your distance, and call for backup if you have reason to believe something's going on there. You're a valuable member of my team, so don't put yourself in any more danger than you have to."

Birdy grinned. "Thank you, sir. And, I'm just saying, please keep that value in mind when annual reviews come around."

Mat chuckled and nodded. "I'll do that. I'm heading home, but consider me on call."

"Yes, sir. Go home and get some sleep."

Mat yawned again on his way out to his car. The only time he'd slept well this past week was in Niall's bed—and it still hadn't been long enough. He was exhausted and wanted nothing more than to spend the rest of the night in that bed at the Orca, but his family was waiting for him at home—and so were clean uniforms. Still, he could spend a little while with Niall before he headed out. Checking his phone, Mat saw he had a text from Niall saying he was going to the Hook for dinner. Maybe Mat could catch him there before he finished.

"No sleep for the wicked," he muttered as he unlocked the car door.

TWENTY-THREE
NIALL

After returning from his romp on the beach and impromptu child-watching session, Niall did his best to clean Fenrir up before using the side entrance of the Orca to get to his room. The towel he'd left in his car, for just this purpose, looked like he'd given the dog a mud bath, and Niall didn't look much better. No reason to give the evening desk clerk more to complain about.

His was the second-to-last room from the entry, and the motel didn't have many other guests, so Niall was surprised when the door across from his opened and two women emerged. Fenrir stayed close to Niall but didn't bark; that he saved for the beach.

The taller woman's face paled. "Is that a wolf?" She moved backward, putting her partner or friend between herself and Fenrir.

Niall gathered all his patience and replied, slowly and clearly, "Fenrir is an Irish wolfhound, most likely." Before the woman or her friend could utter another word, Niall let himself and Fenrir into his room, shutting the door behind them. Fuck.

He was going to have to work a little harder to find a new place. He pushed contacting Stu's grandson, Ian, to the top of his to-do list. There was no doubt in his mind he'd be hearing a complaint about Fenrir the next time they passed through the lobby—which he was going to try to avoid from now on.

After a quick shower, Niall discovered he didn't need to pass through the lobby to get into trouble; trouble had been slipped under the door. "Dear Mr. Hamarsson... we appreciate... blah blah blah..." Niall wadded the paper and the envelope into a ball and tossed them into the trash can by the desk.

"Two points," he muttered to the dog.

It was now early evening. He wanted something to eat, and there was no telling when Mat would be done at the station. Niall texted him to meet him if he could, then donned fresh jeans, a t-shirt, and a sweatshirt and escorted Fenrir to the car. Niall sniffed. The interior of the Subaru smelled musty, the wet, muddy towel making itself known. He'd need to do laundry at some point, some point soon.

If it hadn't been a chilly evening, he would have walked the few short blocks to the Hook, but he didn't want to leave Fenrir sitting outside. What a sucker he was. Niall glanced in the rearview mirror. Fenrir was curled up in the back seat, his eyes already closed in contented sleep—lucky dog.

Who was he fooling? Niall was the lucky one.

And Mat Dempsey—turning Niall's private beach into fodder for a personal sexual fantasy—added another whole layer to the idea of luck. Mat's scent was so strong in Niall's memory he could've sworn the man was sitting in the seat next to his. For a moment it even drowned out the heady aroma of damp dog and dirty towel. Niall adjusted himself.

That afternoon Niall had almost passed the Dempsey property without stopping. But he'd allowed Fenrir to be an excuse to turn in, even knowing by doing so he was close to accepting what was being offered him: family, warmth, a place to rest his head and his heart. It was frightening to contemplate, but it didn't seem his heart was giving him a choice.

As terrible a mother as Ana had been, she'd been his mother, and her disappearance had shaped the rest of his life. The nightmarish thought of exposing his wants and needs to someone else —to considering someone else family—was not as bad as the knowledge that, if he did, that person could be taken away again. Niall didn't know if he would survive such a loss. The only way he'd made it this long was by building walls inside himself, walls so high Niall didn't know if he could scale them… until Mat had come along and blown them away.

Niall parked on the street a few doors up from the Hook and turned off the engine. Looking over his shoulder, he spoke to Fenrir, who'd stood up when Niall pulled over. "You're guarding the car, big guy. I don't want to get in trouble here."

Fenrir mumphed but sat back down; he was very well-behaved, much better than Niall.

"I know, but you're not an assist dog, you're just… a dog."

Niall rolled the back windows down enough to give Fenrir all the fresh air he could want before climbing out and heading into the café.

He was one of the only customers that evening. The well-used space smelled like coffee, bacon, and freshly baked bread. A few people he recognized came in as he ate, nodding toward him as if he was a local. Maybe he was.

Had he accidentally become an islander, reclaimed his birthright? The thought would've had him running for the hills a few weeks ago, but now? Now it felt very close to comfortable.

He finished his meal without seeing hide nor hair of Mat. Leaving enough cash to cover his bill and a tip, Niall went back to let Fenrir out of the car and snapped his leash on.

"We'll just walk down to the station and see if he's there, all right?"

. . .

They had another block to go when Niall heard something he'd only heard once before in his life. The staggering reverberation of an explosion came from the direction of the station. He didn't remember breaking into a run; he only remembered arriving at the scene and seeing a Piedras County Sheriff's Office cruiser with its front end smashed to bits, the engine smoking, flames billowing from it. He tasted metal and burning plastic, and the odor of gasoline filled the air. Was he crying, or were his eyes watering?

Fenrir pulled at his leash. The nightmare was real, and Niall needed to act. The doors of the station opened as he ran toward them, and he dragged Fenrir inside. Where was a fire extinguisher? This was a fucking police station. There had to be one somewhere.

Birdy was at his side, her face a mask of fear and something else Niall wasn't going to identify. Her lips moved, but Niall didn't hear her words.

Dropping Fenrir's leash, Niall ripped the fire extinguisher from the wall in the lobby and bolted back to the parking lot and the burning cruiser. It had taken him maybe thirty seconds to return. Mat was alive—he had to be. Niall couldn't allow his thoughts to go sideways, not now. He had to act.

Now he could hear sirens, fire trucks responding to the explosion, but there was no time to stand around and wait. Every second mattered. He clawed the pin out of the handle, shredding his knuckles in the process, and recited RACE and PASS. Every year the SPD had a required safety training—he knew how to use a fucking fire extinguisher.

His eyes streamed from the smoke and heat, and his hands were too hot, but still he couldn't see Mat. He kept moving the extinguisher back and forth, watching the white foam spray uselessly onto the flames. Someone wrestled the extinguisher from his grasp. He turned to tell whoever it was to fuck off and saw a firefighter in full turnout gear. The man's mouth moved behind his mask, and he gestured Niall aside as another pair of hands pulled Niall away from the wreckage.

"We need you to step back now, sir. Let Devon do his job. He's good at this."

Niall allowed himself to be led to the back of a waiting ambulance. The EMT, a woman his age, motioned for him to sit on the bumper.

"Are you injured?" she asked. The badge clipped to her uniform identified her as Meredith Asher.

Niall shook his head. "No, I don't think so." He looked down at his hands. His knuckles were bleeding and blackened, covered with smoke, dust, and god knew what. Meredith started to say something when a shout from the other side of the wreckage interrupted her.

Dropping Niall's wrist, she commanded, "Stay here."

She raced into the dark to where the shout had come from. Niall wanted to follow her, but all his adrenaline was gone; he felt himself shaking. Reluctantly, he stayed where he was. His ears were ringing, and he couldn't distinguish sounds very well, just yelling and the wail of sirens. Seconds, maybe minutes, later Meredith was back, reaching into the back of the ambulance and grabbing a stretcher.

"Is he...?" Niall couldn't bring himself to say the word.

Meredith didn't answer, just shot him a grim look and disappeared into the fray again. The cacophony of sirens and lights swirled around Niall as he sat. There was nothing he could do. He'd been too late; he'd waited too long to realize what Mat meant to him, and now he'd never get the chance to tell him. What a fool he was.

Whoever had done this had just signed their death sentence. The fury Niall was so comfortable with rose up inside him.

"Um. Sir?" Another person in uniform stood just off to one side, as if she was afraid to approach him.

Niall looked up. Oddly, his vision was fucked up too. "Deputy

Flynn, right?" he rasped out, realizing she was struggling with an animal on a leash. "Fenrir," Niall whispered.

His dog shot out of Flynn's grip and to Niall's side, whimpering, trying to crawl into Niall's lap, but even Niall wasn't big enough for that. Fenrir settled for rearing up and resting his paws on the bumper of the ambulance, licking Niall's face with his rough tongue. Niall embraced him, not caring that the dog still stank from the beach. Fenrir was real and alive, and Niall needed him.

"He was digging at the door of the station," Deputy Flynn said. "I thought he would hurt himself, so I brought him to you…"

She may have stopped speaking, or Niall may just have lost the ability to hear. He sobbed into Fenrir's coat, anguish and grief possessing him as he grieved for Mat, for never admitting how much he cared, that he probably loved him. That he'd been too scared to face his emotions, and now the man had been taken from him. Another person ripped from his life, just like his mother, his grandparents. He thought about the last time he'd cried like this, in Alyson Dempsey's kitchen.

"Fucking fuck," Niall rasped out. He wasn't the only one who'd lost someone important tonight. He lifted his face from Fenrir's neck, managing to bring himself back under control; tears were useless. They never brought anyone back.

Alyson Dempsey had lost a husband and possibly two sons now; Niall would pull his head out of his ass and be there for her and Ella. And Riley. He could do that much. It might kill him, but he could do that much.

He took a deep breath, wiping his face on the sleeve of his jacket.

"Sir, stand away from the ambulance. We need you to move out of the way."

Niall jerked his head up to see the EMTs wheeling the

stretcher back toward him. He stood quickly, too quickly. He was dizzy and almost fell on his ass, but Flynn propped him up.

He almost couldn't bear to look. Fucking hell, he was a homicide investigator. He'd seen bodies in all conditions. Steeling himself and gripping Fenrir's fur, Niall forced himself to focus, to witness as Mat's body was placed into the waiting ambulance.

The still form on the stretcher *wasn't* covered head to toe with a sheet. One of the EMTs was holding oxygen over Mat's face while the other collapsed the legs of the stretcher and slid it inside. Niall felt a surge of hope that almost knocked him flat.

"He's alive?" That was Deputy Flynn; Niall couldn't speak.

"For now," the EMT said grimly. "Dempsey's tough, he's holding on, but we need to get him to surgery."

Flynn asked, "Is it Marshal? I mean, is Dr. Soper responding?"

Meredith nodded, coming around to shut the doors. "If we get him there alive, Dr. Soper will do his best to keep him that way. Stand aside."

And then they were gone.

"I need to stay here and take care of things, sir," Flynn said. "I'll call Sheriff Dempsey's mother. You go on to the hospital. Please call or text me with updates."

Niall looked down at Flynn. She stared back at him with a confidence Niall was envious of. "Okay, give me your number." Niall unlocked his phone and handed it to her.

As she gave it back to him, her mask slipped a little. "Please let me know as soon as there's any news. Sheriff Dempsey has always believed in me. I wouldn't be a deputy today if it weren't for him."

Yeah, Mat had a way of believing in people so hard they started believing in themselves. If Mat lived, Niall was never letting him go.

. . .

Niall arrived at the hospital only a few minutes before Mat's family. Ella was holding Riley, who looked lost and scared.

Alyson took one look at him, and Niall could practically see her refusing to break down.

"Niall, honey." She crossed the waiting room to stand next to him. "You look terrible. Maybe you should go wash up?"

Niall made the mistake of looking at himself in the restroom mirror and was surprised the staff had let him come inside. Using hand soap and paper towels, he did the best he could to wipe the soot, dirt, blood, and mucus off his face. Maybe Riley had been scared of him rather than for her uncle.

Back out in the waiting room, the family sat huddled together. Niall wasn't sure if he should join them, but Alyson must've been watching for him and waved him over. "They've taken him into surgery. There's a more private room we can wait in."

Niall wasn't sure he could handle a more private area, but Alyson led the way and he followed along behind Ella and Riley.

"I'm sorry," he said.

Alyson frowned as she passed through the doors to the private waiting room. "Sorry for what?"

Niall shrugged; he didn't know for what. Sorry for being in the way? Sorry for not protecting Mat?

He was saved from answering by a loud voice in the hallway that only got louder as it approached the waiting room.

"I don't care—get him rights. The man was a field surgeon. He served in Iraq and Afghanistan. It's not as if he's forgotten how to diagnose and operate."

The quiet response must not have been satisfactory.

"I. Don't. Care. I am not familiar with these kinds of injuries. This is not my specialty. Give me gunshot wounds all day long; explosive injuries are completely different."

"The best the hospital can do is allow your"—the words were muffled—"scrub up and be in the operating room giving instruction, but he cannot be awarded privileges on this short notice."

"Fuck my life. You know what I hate?" Marshal Soper burst into the room, and Niall figured they were all going to learn what he hated. "I hate fucking red tape. I hate bureaucrats who are more worried about saving their asses than saving lives."

Marshal was dressed in scrubs. The man with him was wearing what Niall called administrative attire: a button-down, slacks and suit jacket, leather loafers. He looked like he'd been called in from somewhere else.

"Alyson, Mrs. Dempsey." Marshal approached Alyson looking like he wanted to hug her but remembered he was in his scrubs. "I need to ask your permission, as you are listed as Mat's next of kin."

Alyson nodded, leaning hard into Niall. He wrapped his arm around her, wanting to protect her from the world. "Okay, what do you need?"

"We could go somewhere more private..." Marshal offered, his blue eyes full of compassion and concern.

"No, here is fine, with my family around me." Ella came forward to stand on the other side of her mother.

"I'll be honest..." Marshal looked around the room, his attention landing on Riley.

Ella followed his gaze. She reached out to her daughter. "Riley, honey, let's go get something to drink for everyone. Niall, will you stay with Mom?"

The door swished shut behind Ella and Riley. Niall tugged Alyson to the set of chairs so they could sit down. He kept his arm around her shoulders, not sure who needed the contact more, Alyson or himself.

Marshal spoke. "I'm not going to sugarcoat it—Mat's injuries are serious. He's in critical condition. At the least he has a collapsed lung, broken ribs, and a broken clavicle from where he hit the curb. He banged his head, hard—I ordered a skull X-ray to rule out hemorrhaging—and there are likely internal injuries from the blast. Blast injuries aren't my specialty, but I have a"—

his eyes wavered—"friend who is experienced with them. He was a field medic in the navy, a licensed doctor, and his experience could be what saves Mat's life. Blast injuries are incredibly serious, Alyson. I can't get privileges for him, but with your permission, Trevor can come into the operating room and observe."

The name Trevor rang a bell, but Niall couldn't remember from where at the moment.

"You trust this person?"

"With my life."

Without hesitation, Alyson answered, "Where do I sign?"

The next hours were grueling, some of the longest Niall had experienced in his life. If it was hard for him, he couldn't imagine what it was like for Alyson and Ella. At first they were quiet, as if any second the doors would open and Soper would be there to tell them Mat's status. As the minutes passed, Riley became restless and Ella let her play on her cell phone, which eventually devolved into watching a movie.

Niall couldn't do anything. He couldn't speak. Words had never been his strong suit, and now it seemed he might have to find the right words to console the Dempsey family. He texted Deputy Flynn, basically telling her he had nothing to tell her. An hour or so in, he remembered Fenrir was in the car and excused himself to go check on him.

Fenrir seemed to sense Niall's tumultuous feelings. He greeted him with a lick on the hand before hopping out. Niall walked him around one of the flower beds and then let him back inside the car. "I'll be back," he promised.

Fenrir gave him a look Niall wanted to interpret as hope, but he was just a dog. Niall turned away, making his way back to the waiting room.

Alyson glanced up when he returned, answering his unasked question. "Nothing yet."

He sat down next to her and stared at the wall. Riley had finally fallen asleep on a makeshift bed Ella had created for her using two of the chairs and all their jackets.

There was nothing for Niall to do but think. Brood, whatever. His fingers hurt from clenching them into fists; whoever had done this was going to be sorry they were ever born. This fucker had crossed the line, making it personal for Niall. Mat was out of commission and Deputy Flynn was going to need help, and Niall was damn well going to do what he could.

Around midnight, the doors opened again, revealing a tired Marshal Soper.

They all stood and Alyson went to meet him. Marshal grasped her shoulders with both hands, speaking to her directly. "He's going to be okay. His chest injuries were bad, but not as bad as I'd imagined. He came through with flying colors, and if he follows instructions while he heals, he should make a full recovery."

"When can I, we, see him?" she asked.

"He's in recovery for the next few hours. You should go home and get some sleep, come back around noon. He looks pretty bad, Alyson. He'll be okay, but there's a lot of scrapes and significant bruising."

"Thank you for saving my son, Marshal." Alyson leaned in and wrapped her arms around him.

"It wasn't me, it was Dr. Collier."

She leaned back, looking Marshal in the eyes. "Marshal, if it wasn't for you, Mat wouldn't be alive. So yes, thank *you*. When can we meet Dr. Collier and thank him as well?"

Marshal shrugged, glancing at Niall. "I'll ask him. Maybe tomorrow when you come visit Mat? Call me and I'll try to be here. We'll go over expected recovery and physical therapy then as well."

. . .

Niall followed Alyson and Ella out to their car, carrying Riley. A deadweight six-year-old was heavier than he expected.

"Thank you, Niall," Ella said as he tucked her into the car seat.

"Niall," Alyson said, "please come and stay with us. You can sleep in Mat's room, and Fenrir will be much happier. I don't know why you insist on staying at that motel." She made the word "motel" sound like something she'd scraped off the bottom of her shoe.

He opened his mouth to argue that Alyson didn't want him staying at her house, but she shot him a look that had him snapping his mouth shut so quickly his teeth clicked.

"That's settled, then. We'll see you there."

After stopping at the Orca for a change of clothes and dog food, Niall made his way along the dark roadway to the Dempsey household. Fenrir sat up when Niall made the turn into their driveway.

"Don't get used to it."

Who was he kidding? Piedras was home, but Mat was his shelter.

TWENTY-FOUR
MAT

Mat slowly drifted to awareness. Sleep wanted to hold him down, but he had a mother of a headache and there were all sorts of beeping sounds disturbing him. He didn't remember having too much to drink. Was that his alarm? Crud. One of the beeps gained speed and volume. Someone needed to turn it off.

He tried to roll over. Pain shot through his upper body, and he groaned.

"What happened?" he asked no one in particular.

"Are you ready to open your eyes, Sleeping Beauty? Your family's worried about you, even though I told them you're fine, just sleeping and healing."

Mat dragged his eyelids upward; it took a lot more effort than if he just had a hangover. The light was too bright, so he settled for leaving his lids at half-mast. Marshal was standing over him, wearing the doctor's jacket Mat teased him about.

"What are you doing here?" he rasped out. His throat felt like he'd swallowed glass.

"Checking on my favorite patient. Tell me, how are you feeling?"

He was actually in the hospital. What the hell had happened? His head was fuzzy, probably from pain medication.

"Like I was hit by a truck."

"Not surprising. What do you remember? Can you tell me your name and birthday?"

"What is this, twenty questions? What happened? Mat Owen Dempsey, December 10, 1982."

Marshal smiled at Mat's answer, but it didn't reach his eyes. Looking closer, Mat realized his friend was exhausted. His eyes had dark circles underneath them, and the lines on his face were accentuated.

"Good. Now I need you to tell me what the last thing you remember is. This is part of me being a doctor."

"I suppose being in the hospital is a clue something bad happened," Mat groused.

The beeping and antiseptic odor were big clues. Mat's brain felt foggy, and he shut his eyes so he could think better. There'd been a fire. He'd been investigating it. The fire had been at the East Bay Marina. Then he... something else, shadowy, irretrievable. His memory seemed jumbled together, a tangle of images that didn't make sense to him, but he remembered he'd been at the station late talking to Birdy about something.

"I think I was at the station, talking to Birdy. I was going home but told her I'd be on call."

"Very good. I'm impressed. I'm going to quickly take your vitals, because you've got family waiting to see proof of life. I kicked them out for a few minutes. Niall's been prowling around like a caged panther, scaring the nurses and techs."

"A panther, huh? That's pretty specific."

"Absolutely a panther. Okay." Marshal stepped back from the bed, tucking his stethoscope into the pocket of his jacket. "Your heart rate and pulse are good. I'll be back to jab you with sharp instruments later."

"Your bedside manner needs work."

"This is the friends and family deal. Most of my patients don't get such specialized service."

Mat fell asleep while his mother was visiting. He'd only meant to shut his eyes for a minute and listen to her voice, but sleep had taken him to a place where his head, chest, and shoulder didn't ache. Before he opened his eyes again, he knew a different person was in the room with him. At some point since he'd fallen back asleep, the beeping had been reduced to just one monitor. For that he would forever be thankful.

"I can tell you're awake."

Niall's deep rumble had Mat prying his eyes open. Niall was crammed into one of the visitor chairs against the wall. He couldn't possibly be comfortable.

Mat wanted to say something clever, but "Hey" was all he could come up with.

"How are you feeling?" Niall asked.

"Aside from like I was run over? I guess better than the last time I was awake. What happened?" Niall looked horrible.

"Someone rigged your cruiser with a bomb. But something happened to the explosive device or it was poorly put together to begin with, and it went off before you got inside. If you'd gotten in that fucking car, I wouldn't be talking to you right now." Niall looked away; Mat barely caught the stricken expression on his face.

"But I didn't. I'm still here." He attempted to spread his arms, proving he was in one piece, but his body said otherwise, his shoulder shrieking in pain. Mat wasn't quite able to muffle his yelp.

Niall glared at him. "*Barely* fucking here."

His voice was rough, sounding as terrible as Mat's did. He knew Niall's anger wasn't directed at him but toward whoever had landed Mat in the hospital. "Tell me."

"You nearly fucking died. If I never have to go through something like that again, it will be too soon. You were critical, with something Marshal called blast lung. Don't ask me, I've never heard of it. A couple cracked ribs, shattered your collarbone—oh, and a collapsed lung. Doc says you'll heal, but the PT's going to hurt, and it looks like you used your face to scrub the parking lot."

"I'm touched by your kindness." His face did hurt a bit. Nothing like his other aches, though.

Niall stood up, stared at Mat, walked to the door, turned, and strode back again. He repeated this several times before halting at Mat's bedside, his body quivering with barely leashed emotion. Mat remembered Marshal saying something about Niall being a panther, and he was leaning toward agreeing with him.

"I don't know what to say," Niall rasped.

Reaching out with one very shaky hand, Mat grasped Niall's forearm, stopping him from continuing his pacing. Mat could almost feel the confusion and despair coursing through Niall. He wanted to make a joke to lighten the mood, to distract Niall, but he couldn't think of anything. He supposed nearly dying wasn't a joking matter.

"I'm here. I didn't die. I'm going to recover."

Niall collapsed into a chair that had been pulled close to the bed. Mat thought he remembered his mom sitting there and holding his hand.

"I just... I just don't know what to do. I can't help—I mean, any more than I already am, which mostly involves texting back and forth with Deputy Flynn. Don't get pissed at her—she asked for my help, and I've been advising her, but Flynn's been making the decisions. She's good."

"We're lucky to have her. Tell me what you know."

Niall nodded. "She's been by a few times to talk to you, but you seemed determined to sleep. I'll let her know you're awake if you think you can manage another visitor. Then there's your family."

Mat didn't want to think about how much worry he'd put his mom and sister through. Instead he asked, "Have we found Cooper yet? *That's* what Birdy and I were working on." He remembered he'd been at the station after unsuccessfully searching for Duane Cooper.

"No sign of Cooper, and no sign of his truck. The state investigators have been snooping around, but if they've found anything, they're keeping it close to their chests."

"How long have I been in the hospital?"

It wasn't until this moment that it occurred to him; he'd probably been there longer than it seemed.

"Four fucking days. Soper seems to think you can go home Sunday or Monday if there aren't any setbacks, but you aren't going to be allowed back to work for something like six weeks." Niall smiled, but it held no mercy.

"Six weeks?" Mat collapsed into his pillows—a long half-inch distance. Six weeks was going to be forever. Surely that just meant no physical duty. He would be allowed to investigate from his desk. "First, tell me everything you know. Don't think about leaving anything out. Then ask Birdy to get over here."

Since the bombing, Birdy had stepped up, leading Mat's ragtag team of three remaining deputies as well as teaming up with her brother Devon in his capacity as fire chief. Mat would've preferred not to have almost died to have it confirmed Birdy was an excellent leader, but he'd always known she had it in her.

The IED had been crudely attached to the undercarriage of Mat's cruiser and was most definitely homemade. As Niall had said, state investigators had already been out. They took assassination attempts very seriously and would be back to interview Mat any day. They were working on tracing the bomb materials. One thing about the state, it had a lot more resources than Piedras. If there was a fingerprint anywhere, they would find it.

No progress had been made on the marina fire, except the investigators had confirmed it was arson; gasoline residue was found on and around the dock area. Yes, there were plenty of fuels in a marina, many of which could cause a fire, but this was set purposely, demonstrated by the pattern the fire burned in. According to Niall, who'd gotten the information from Birdy, arson investigators from the Washington State Patrol had questioned Sharleen again but learned nothing new. She still claimed she hadn't seen anyone, and, unfortunately, it seemed the surveillance cameras had not been online and now were gone, destroyed by the fire.

There was a tap on the door. Mat called out, "Come in," and the door opened and Birdy entered. Her face lit up at the sight of him.

"It's great to see you awake, sir!"

"It's good to be awake, Birdy." He was feeling a bit tired, but hopefully he'd get through this interview. Then he'd take a nap. "Have a seat." He gestured toward the visitor chairs.

Birdy dragged a second chair up next to Niall's.

"Tell me everything, including what you didn't share with Niall. You can trust him. He won't do anything with the information—will he?" Mat narrowed his eyes at Niall.

Niall raised his hands in surrender. "I promise not to morph into the Punisher." He muttered something else Mat didn't quite catch.

Birdy didn't have much to add to the facts Niall had already shared with Mat. Her biggest addition was that she was as close to 100 percent positive as she could be that Duane hadn't left the island—not by boat, anyway. They'd had eyes on the ferry terminal since the morning after the fire. It was possible he'd used a kayak or canoe, and if that was the case, he'd managed to escape—or he'd drowned in the attempt and they'd find his remains one day.

Niall frowned. "How do you know he hasn't left by boat?"

"If he'd stolen a working boat, one of the residents would've reported it by now, especially with this attack on Sheriff Dempsey. People are pretty upset someone tried to murder you, sir; I don't think anyone would help Duane."

"What about his own boat?" Mat asked.

A sheepish expression flitted across Birdy's face. "I told you, sir, his fuel tanks were empty—and since the night of the explosion, his boat's been impounded."

Mat chuckled. He'd forgotten about that little nugget of information. He wondered what else he'd forgotten. Then, as hard as he tried to suppress it, a yawn escaped him. Niall frowned harder, his thick eyebrows drawing together in a V.

Mat wanted to reach out and smooth the line between his eyebrows with his finger, but the distance was too far. And Birdy was in the room. She didn't care about the two of them, but it felt like a personal gesture—maybe one Niall wasn't ready for yet.

"If I get my hands on whoever did this to you, you're never going to solve the case because the perpetrator is going to be wearing cement shoes in a watery grave." Niall smiled when he spoke, but it wasn't nice at all.

"We're close, sirs, I know it." Birdy's eyes had widened at Niall's statement. "I've been going over the timeline Sheriff Dempsey wrote down and trying to fill it out. There are definitely things that don't add up. Not all of these fires are the same, and that's a clue in itself. We'll figure out who did this."

Mat added, "I thought you just promised not to go vigilante, Niall. *Right?*"

Niall nodded, but Mat wasn't convinced. He narrowed his eyes, hoping he was getting the message across.

They talked for a bit longer, but Mat could feel himself tiring. As much as he wanted to find the bomber, he was going to need a nap first. And no matter what direction they approached the case from, it seemed the key was Duane Cooper... but no one had seen the man in over a week. The last known sighting had been by Mat himself, when he'd gone down to talk to him at the marina on the Thursday before the fire.

"Come back later?" Mat asked when it became obvious he couldn't keep his eyes open any longer.

They nodded. Birdy left the room first, leaving Mat and Niall alone. The only sounds were the rustle of nurses moving around in the hallway and the soft beeping of that one damn monitor.

Mat started to speak. Niall shook his head, stopping Mat's words. His eyes were dark with an emotion Mat couldn't decipher, what with all the pain medication coursing through his system. He shut his mouth, not knowing what he'd been about to say anyway. Maybe there was no need to say anything.

Niall reached out one hand, his fingertips gently skimming Mat's face, moving up to his forehead and brushing the too-long hair back. Then, without words, he too was gone, leaving Mat alone in the room.

Had he ever experienced anything as tender as that gesture from a lover before? Mat didn't think so. Niall was not good with words—he had varying grades of the word "fuck," ranging from a slight inconvenience to the world coming to an end, but emotions were hard for him to articulate. That didn't mean he didn't feel them, though, and nothing in the world would sway Mat's belief that Niall had just declared his love for Mat.

Before he was pulled under, the thought struck him that maybe this had been a bad time for Niall to realize how he felt—with Mat trapped in a hospital bed, unable to reassure him that everything would be okay, that they could love each other and nothing else mattered.

TWENTY-FIVE
NIALL

Niall had been serious, although it was best that Mat and Deputy Flynn believed he was kidding. If he managed to get his hands on the perpetrator who'd put Mat in the ICU, Niall would give him a lesson he wouldn't forget—up close and personal. Niall had never met Duane Cooper, or at least he didn't remember him from when he lived on the island before. That Cooper was somehow involved in this string of arsons, Niall had little doubt.

He'd looked the man up online, combing through his Marine Safari website, the only online presence he had. Cooper was in his sixties, a grizzled man who looked the part of a ship captain. Mat had said Cooper had been with the sheriff's department for years, originally hired on by Mat's father, and Mat had kept him when he took over. He'd been in the first Gulf War; he could fashion a bomb. In between working marine rescue, Cooper ran a whale watching business. Niall wondered how he managed working the two jobs—in the summer, either of them would've been full time.

The Dempsey house was empty at the moment, the only sound caused by a March wind making the house creak and groan as it tried to sneak inside. Ever since the night Mat had nearly died, Alyson had insisted Niall stay with her, Ella, and Riley. The first night he'd agreed because, by the time they knew Mat would survive, it had been late. The second, third, and fourth were less easy to explain.

Niall was sleeping in Mat's bedroom, in his bed. Nothing on earth would get him to admit he'd been staying because he needed to be as close to Mat as possible and this was the only way he could do it. He slept with his nose pressed into the sheets, inhaling Mat's unique scent. After days of sleeping there, the sheets now just smelled like Niall, but he hadn't packed up his belongings yet.

Yesterday or the day before—Niall had lost track of time— he'd stopped by the Orca to pick up more clothes. He'd considered checking out but put it off. He'd actually been paralyzed by the thought of having nowhere else to go and had to force himself to pick up his backpack of dirty clothes and take it out to his car. The motel room was a security blanket, an escape, a "just in case." Relying solely on Dempsey hospitality was tempting too many fates.

The silence of the house wrapped around him like a blanket, and Niall could almost hear his grandmother's voice admonishing him for making life more difficult than it needed to be.

Niall, life is already hard—and you've had a harder one than most, sure —but let's not go borrowing trouble.

The thing was, trouble usually found Niall whether he was looking for it or not. Surely Mat would realize that soon enough.

Out of habit, Niall looked around for Fenrir, forgetting for a moment that the traitorous animal was out with Alyson, Riley, and Ella. He hadn't even given Niall a backward glance when Riley asked him—the dog, not Niall—if he wanted to go to the beach. It worked out, though, because Niall was taking the late-morning ferry to Anacortes to meet with the insurance adjuster, which would've meant a long time in the car for Fenrir. He'd rescheduled his appointments, since there'd been no way he was going to leave the island—or be in any condition for a job interview—before Mat regained consciousness. Thankfully, both the guys at the consulting firm and, more surprisingly, the insurance adjuster had been willing to meet on the weekend. Niall didn't want to drag this out any longer than necessary now that he knew Mat really was going to be okay.

Snapping his laptop shut, Niall headed upstairs to Mat's room. He would really have to start thinking about finding somewhere else to stay soon, because Mat would need the space as he recovered from his injuries. Opening the bedroom door, Niall saw that someone—Alyson—had left a stack of clean and folded laundry on the bed. *His* clean laundry. He froze for a minute, bemused by the gesture; Alyson didn't need to do his laundry. But it was nice not having to pick out his least-smelly shirt for a trip to the mainland.

As he drove, Niall kept finding himself glancing in the rearview mirror to see if Fenrir was staring back at him with some sort of judgmental expression on his furry face. He felt *alone*, and it was weird to recognize the feeling as something he'd forgotten about, something that used to be how he always felt… and now was slightly uncomfortable.

Before returning to Piedras, he'd always been alone—even when he was with Trey. Possibly even more when he was dating Trey, because neither of them gave each other anything. The relationship had been selfish on both of their parts. Niall supposed being a manipulative asshole was part of Trey's problem. What was his?

The turbulent waters of Rosario Strait weren't as soothing as they usually were. Niall's metaphorical feathers were ruffled, and he was having a hard time calming himself. The night of the explosion he'd believed Mat was dead, *known* that he was dead and Niall's effort to put out the fire was useless. Because he was emotionally stunted, it was only when he knew he'd lost Mat that he realized what they had—what he'd been too afraid to accept. Was still afraid to accept. Fuck, he was messed up. The little voice that sounded like his grandfather said, *You can be afraid. That's okay. You can be afraid and still take the hand, accept what Mat is offering. You want it, accept it, and* then *get used to it.*

The fact that Mat was alive meant Niall would have another chance with him. Once they found the fucking bomber, because no one on the island was safe until Duane Cooper was dead or under lock and key. Blinking at his reflection in the ferry's plate glass window, Niall dug his phone out of his pocket. His fingers hovered over the screen for a moment, then he sent a text to Mat.

Heading to Anacortes, see you when I get back

He didn't know if Mat would reply or if he even had access to a phone—his old one had been destroyed by the blast—but it felt good, like Niall was a plant sending out a little tendril, a root, hoping to take hold.

Anacortes was a sleepy town. It splayed lazily across a jut of land and ended at the ferry terminal. Rush hour occurred when the ferry came and went, and in the high season, cars lined up for miles waiting their turn to board.

Niall followed the line of cars exiting the ferry, most making their way up the hill into the city, some turning to the right and into neighborhoods. He found the insurance office with ease. Roger Johnson met him at the door. He was a tall, slender man with thinning brown hair and a firm handshake.

"Sorry to make you come all the way out here."

Johnson led him back to a small office furnished with only a desk and a set of shelves with thick, heavy-looking books stacked on them. A window looked out onto the street. Niall could see his car and an older woman walking by with her dog leading the way.

"Have a seat. Do you want something to drink? Coffee, water?"

Niall refused the offer and took the seat. Over the next hour, Johnson took Niall through his account of the fire at the cabin and his relationship with Trey Jackson dragging up painful details like the fact that his real identity had turned out to be Jeffrey Reynolds and his motive for being with Niall, had been money. The latter was something Niall would have rather not talked about with a stranger. However, by the end, the trip proved to be worth it.

"Again, I'm sorry we had to put you through this. It really is just a matter of dotting i's and crossing t's. I'm sure you understand we need to make absolutely certain claims are handled properly." Johnson sat back in his chair. "This is the part where I get to tell you the company will approve your claim. The settlement may be less than you hoped for; the cabin's footprint was small, but—"

Johnson quoted a figure that gave Niall hope he would be able to rebuild or replace the cabin sooner rather than later, and he made a mental note to contact Stu's grandson.

Leaving the office feeling lighter than when he'd arrived, Niall headed to Slo-Jo's, a coffee shop on the main drag. His interview with Leo and his boss was supposed to be informal, so they'd set up an online meeting.

Niall hated being able to see himself in the little square at the top right of his screen, but he couldn't figure out how to turn it off. He was jabbing at his keyboard when Leo and his boss appeared on screen, greeting him from somewhere in San Francisco.

Leo introduced him to Kimball, then launched right in with, "I should let you know right off, the interview is just a formality. If you're interested, we want you on board with us, yesterday." The connection made his voice a bit crackly.

"That's quite a compliment."

Leo shrugged. "There are only four of us right now, and let me tell you, we could use twice as many experienced investigators. When I retired, I kept my feelers out for detectives like you."

"Jaded and overworked?"

Kimball chuckled. "Done with the establishment. Ready to work outside the lines a bit. Not breaking the law, of course—"

"Of course," Niall agreed blandly.

"—but, you know, taking advantage of being in the private sector to help out small police forces and others solve cases that might otherwise go unsolved. We do some cold case work too, but with our current workload we have to have compelling evidence for a cold case."

"How do people find you?" Niall asked.

"I have no idea." Leo winked. A mug appeared in his hand, and he took a sip. "We network, of course, but many of our cases come via word of mouth—and we are swamped. I lied earlier; we could use eight more investigators at the least. I hate having to choose who we can help and who has to wait."

Niall's last case, the one that had been the final straw, was exactly the kind of case Leo was talking about. Tanya Nichols's family would have to wait for justice, and who knew when or if it would ever arrive. But now West Coast was giving Niall a chance to help other families get closure. And in situations where the responding department—like Piedras—didn't have the resources to examine the evidence and go after the perps, Niall could help pursue those cases as well.

"The sooner you start, the better," Kimball said. "You know the backlog isn't getting any smaller. But we're flexible and won't ask you to relocate. Most of the investigators work remotely because we take jobs all over the country. Once a month we fly everybody into Orange County and have a face-to-face meeting."

"Okay. Let's make a deal." Saying the words felt easy and right. Something settled deep inside him.

Leo beamed and pumped a fist. "Welcome aboard. You won't regret your decision. We have a great team."

"Can I ask a favor?"

Leo nodded.

Niall outlined what had been happening on Piedras, the fires and then the explosion that had nearly taken Mat's life.

"One of the deputies told me they recovered a gas can from one of the earlier fires but weren't able to get any prints off of it. I'm wondering, if we send it down, can one of your guys take a look?"

"*Our* guys," Leo said. "And yes, one-day it down here and we'll get a tech on it ASAP. If there's something to be found, I'll let you know."

"Thank you. It means a lot."

"Don't thank me yet."

By the time Niall departed Anacortes, he had a new job and had negotiated what felt like a ridiculous salary and benefits package, and he had the promise of money to replace the cabin. Things felt right. He could breathe a little easier. He wasn't a cop any longer, but he was putting his years of experience to use. Now, if he could use his detective skills to find Duane Cooper, Niall's day would be complete. For now, his number one priority was getting that gas can to Leo.

Back on Piedras, after first stopping at the station and convincing Deputy Flynn that sending the gas can to the West Coast Forensic Investigation and Consulting team for fingerprint analysis needed to happen and then helping her wrap it properly for shipping, Niall retrieved his dog, mostly to prove to himself he was still Fenrir's favorite. Then he returned to Hidden Harbor to visit Mat at the hospital. From the hallway he could hear another visitor speaking, a woman whose voice he didn't recognize. It wasn't his intention to eavesdrop—not much, anyway—but he couldn't help but stop and listen to what she was saying.

"You almost died!"

"But I didn't. I'm still here, alive and—well, I will be kicking soon enough. I can't wait to get out of this place," Mat grumbled.

"When Mom called, I almost didn't answer the phone, that's how stupid and mad I was. I'm so sorry."

Niall peeked around the slightly open door to see Mat awkwardly trying to stroke the head of the woman sitting in the visitor chair. She was slumped over the bed, her shoulders shaking as she sobbed. Mat looked up and caught Niall's questioning gaze.

"Fi?" Mat said. This was his other sister, the youngest one. The one he'd told Niall wasn't speaking to the family. "Fi, there's someone here I'd like you to meet."

The woman sat up and grabbed a tissue to wipe her nose with. "I told you I hate that nickname, but if not hearing it means you're dead or something…" She squeezed her eyes shut to keep more tears from flowing. "Who am I meeting?"

Mat pointed his chin at the door. Fiona followed his movement, her eyes landing on Niall.

"Niall, come in. Fiona, this is Niall Hamarsson. Niall, Fiona Owens, my youngest sister."

"Oh, are you Mat's boyfriend? And if you must, you can call me Fi."

Niall walked all the way into the room, his focus on Mat. He hadn't seen him since yesterday. He looked better this afternoon, less like a Mack truck had hit him. Mentally, Niall was downgrading him to a run-in with a small SUV. The scrapes on his face were healing quickly, and his two black eyes had faded to a light yellow.

Mat wore an expression Niall couldn't figure out until he replayed Fiona's greeting in his head.

"A pleasure to meet you, Fiona. I guess I am Mat's boyfriend."

He spoke to Fiona, but he was looking at Mat as he did so, and Niall didn't miss Mat's flush of pleasure at the words.

"Fiona just got here. Oh, and Marshal was here earlier. He says I can go home tomorrow."

"That's good news."

Mat waved a hand toward one of the other chairs. "Have a seat."

Niall dragged the chair closer and sat down. "I have some news too," he said.

Mat's eyes widened, and Fiona turned her head to look at him.

"Should I go?" she asked.

Niall shook his head. "No. I accepted a job with West Coast Forensic Investigation and Consulting and met with the insurance guy, who authorized the funds for the cabin."

Mat beamed. "That's great!"

"I'm pleased."

Shaking his head, Mat chuckled. "Don't go overboard with your excitement there. I might have to call one of the nurses."

"Fuck off." Niall raised one finger in case Mat didn't understand the phrase.

"I think it's genetic," Mat said to his sister. "It's a Scandinavian thing or maybe just a Hamarsson thing, but believe it or not, this is Niall really, really excited."

"Congratulations, Niall, and it's a pleasure to meet you too."

Fiona was plump, her skin tanned from the Texas sun. She had the same dark brown hair all the Dempsey family did, but like her niece Riley, instead of the deep blue eyes, her eyes were mahogany brown. Niall wondered what side of the family the brown came from.

"It was good of you to make the trip." There'd been some tension when Fiona was out for Sean's funeral, but he'd never learned what happened and had not met Fiona at the service.

"I feel terrible it took Mat nearly dying before I realized I couldn't cut myself off from my family. I'm so sorry, Mat."

Mat smiled up at her. "No family is perfect, Fi. We all miss Dad and Sean."

"I know, *I know*, I've just been so selfish."

Niall's phone buzzed in his back pocket. He couldn't have wished for a better excuse to stop interrupting the lovely family reunion. He had a missed call from Marshal Soper, probably calling to let him know about Mat's impending release.

He returned the call from the parking lot, where spring had officially arrived. The sun shone brightly, and Niall wondered where the hell his sunglasses had ended up since last summer. The flower beds around the hospital were bright with red and yellow tulips.

He leaned against his car, enjoying the warmth of the sun on his vitamin D–starved skin, and returned Marshal's call. Fenrir's thumps from inside made the car shake. "We'll get out in a bit, buddy," Niall said to the dog. "Soper," he said when the doctor answered.

"Ah, Niall. Thank you for calling me back. Where are you?"

"At the hospital. I just left Mat. He's pretty excited about getting out."

"I bet he is. I just hope he listens to his doctor's orders. Do you have time to stop by my place?"

"Sure?" He didn't have anything to do except brood about who had put Mat in the hospital.

"Okay, thanks. We—I'll see you in a few."

The drive to Marshal's took about ten minutes. When he pulled into the driveway, a young boy was kicking around a soccer ball, but he darted inside when he saw Niall's car. Niall climbed out and shut the door, hearing the boy shouting something that sounded a lot like "Dad."

He didn't think Marshal had a son. There hadn't been any sign of a child when Niall had stayed with him, no snapshots on his refrigerator or framed photographs. He rolled down the car windows for Fenrir, not sure if Marshal would want him inside. Then he walked around to the front to knock on the door.

Marshal opened it almost immediately. "Heya, come on in."

Last time Niall had been in Marshal's house he'd been recovering from slicing his palm open. Marshal had kindly offered him a place to stay for a few days. Marshal's home had been clean, clear of knickknacks, almost sterile. The home of a single person who didn't have to worry about a kid running around.

While his place wasn't a wreck now, there were clear signs Marshal wasn't the only one living there. A half-finished jigsaw puzzle waited on the breakfast bar, a couple of kids' books with colorful covers were stacked on the windowsill, a single sock too small to be Marshal's lay crumpled under the coffee table, and an unidentifiable stuffed animal was crammed into the corner of the couch. Niall wondered if Marshal was seeing someone. He and Mat were close friends, and Mat hadn't said anything to Niall, but maybe it was a new relationship.

He followed Marshal into his open kitchen with its gleaming stainless steel appliances. The kitchen, at least, looked the same as it had when Niall had been there before.

"Grab a stool. Would you like a cup of coffee or something else to drink?"

Niall didn't know Marshal all that well, but he seemed a little nervous or uncomfortable.

"Sure, I can always use coffee."

He sat on one of Marshal's tall kitchen stools next to the breakfast bar. While Marshal fiddled with his espresso machine, Niall looked out the ceiling-to-floor plate glass windows. Marshal had an incredible view with no obstructions, and his house faced to the east, the opposite view from the one Niall's property had.

"Here you go."

Marshal set a cup in front of Niall. The steamy contents smelled delicious. Niall inhaled deeply.

Niall was lifting the coffee to his lips when the little boy he'd seen ran into the room.

"Marshal, Marshal, there's a dog in the car outside!"

The boy had straight black hair, blue eyes, and was missing one front tooth. He looked to be about Riley's age, maybe a little older. When he saw Niall, he came to a halt, his eyes wide and apprehensive.

"It's okay, Caleb. This is my friend Niall."

"That's my dog. His name is Fenrir," Niall said.

"That's a funny name."

"He's named after a Norse god."

"Oh, like Thor?" Caleb cocked his head.

"Fenrir didn't like Thor. In the stories he was supposed to"—Niall glanced at Marshal, who nodded—"eat Odin, Thor's father. The gods kept him in Asgard, where they could keep their eye on him, but he grew quickly and was very large. So they tried to trick him into accepting a rope or chain, but Fenrir was always too strong and broke out of them. Finally, they cheated and made a chain that would be impossible for him to break."

"Can Fenrir come inside?" Caleb asked.

Niall glanced at Marshal, who, he could tell, was trying to decide. "He's fine in the car. I'll take him for a walk after we're done."

"Please, Marshal?"

Oh, the kid was good. His big blue eyes and pleading expression sealed the deal.

Niall left his coffee on the counter, and together the three of them went out to Niall's car.

"He's magnificent," Marshal said when he saw Fenrir. They trooped back inside, Caleb in the lead, Fenrir next, Niall and Marshal behind.

"He's mellow, except at the beach. And he loves kids. He's got Mat's niece wrapped around his paw." Niall dropped his voice. "Enough about the dog. Why I am here, and what's going on? I remember who Trevor is now, and Caleb is his son. Why did you have me research him? And why didn't you want Mat to know?"

Marshal released a deep breath. "Let's drink our coffee. Caleb, maybe Fenrir would like you to read him a story?"

Caleb asked Fenrir what story he'd like to listen to and plopped down on a cushion next to the window, picking up one of the books from the stack. Fenrir lay down on the area rug, his chin on his paws, appearing to listen as Caleb began to read aloud.

Niall turned his attention to Marshal and raised one eyebrow, waiting for him to talk.

Marshal sighed. "Mat doesn't approve of me taking in strangers. I mean, honestly, most people who stay here are people I have some connection to, and if I can give someone a safe place to recuperate, or heal in your case, I'm going to do it. It's a way for me to help those less fortunate. But I knew Mat would throw a fit about me bringing a complete stranger home."

Marshal checked over his shoulder, making sure Caleb was still occupied, and lowered his voice further.

"Caleb approached me about two weeks ago, asking if I'd come help his dad. Trevor had a severe case of the flu—high fever, everything. I wanted to take him to the hospital, but considering they were living in a terrible situation, a broken-down camper, I figured he didn't have insurance. He was pretty sick and had a secondary infection... I broke a lot of rules treating him, and Mat would be pissed."

"But you had him in Mat's operating room."

"Niall, the man is a decorated navy field surgeon. He's treated soldiers with far worse injuries than Mat's—he knows about blast injuries. I don't."

"What's he doing living in a RV with his kid?" Niall had to ask. Everything was falling into place about the camper he'd been seeing, a big fucking light bulb flashing on and off in his head. It had been Trevor and Caleb, and Trevor *had* been hiding from someone. Whether he'd borrowed the vehicle or whatever —it hadn't been reported as stolen, so he presumably was entitled to use it, one way or another. It wouldn't be the first time that someone had sold a vehicle and not filed the paperwork to make it official. And the fact that Trevor hadn't registered the vehicle under his own name yet—well, the tabs hadn't expired, so police wouldn't have a reason to pull him over. Yeah, it was risky if he got caught, but maybe that was a risk he was willing to take.

A third voice cut across their conversation. "My ex-father-in-law is trying to ruin me so he can get custody of Caleb. If he doesn't know where I am, he has no power over us."

Caleb took after his father; he even had the same dimple on his right cheek. Caleb, however, didn't have dark circles under his eyes and a haunted look about him.

"Not to be harsh, but shouldn't he be in school? Hiding out in an RV is exactly the kind of thing that can lead to—"

Trevor Collier had a limp, but that didn't stop him from getting right up in Niall's face in less than a second.

"—having your kid taken away," Niall finished under his breath.

"Are you threatening me?" Collier whispered hoarsely.

"I'm a cop. I'm telling you what I know."

"Trevor," Marshal interjected quietly, which of course got Caleb's attention.

"Daddy! You're awake! Come meet Fenrir. He's—uh, what's your name again, mister?"

"It's Niall," he answered, but he directed it to Trevor, holding his hand out, palm up. "I don't mean any harm."

"One second, Caleb," Trevor said.

"Trevor," Marshal said, "I asked Niall to come over because I think he might be able to help us—you."

Niall did not miss that Marshal had said "us" first.

"How can he possibly help?" Trevor's protective posture

disappeared, his shoulders slumping in defeat as he heaved himself onto one of Marshal's tall chairs.

"I'm not sure, but he's an ex-cop and a pretty smart guy. Maybe if you tell him what's going on, he'll have some ideas."

An hour later, Niall was unlocking his car and sliding behind the wheel, his head full of the story Trevor Collier had shared with him.

Some of it Niall already knew from snooping through Trevor's divorce records, but Niall didn't think Trevor needed to know that. What Trevor added was the dark underbelly, the stuff that even the lawyers and courts didn't know about. Niall also knew Marshal had feelings for the other man. It was obvious every time Marshal looked at Trevor, but Niall wasn't sure Trevor was aware of it. Or if the man was gay.

Trevor's ex-father-in-law was doing everything he could to ruin Trevor so he could take Caleb. Whaley's actions ranged from trashing Trevor's reputation as a field medic to spreading rumors about his wild life. The former had cost Trevor job opportunities when he left the navy, and the latter had resulted in people he'd trusted no longer speaking to him.

"If he gets custody of Caleb, I'll never see him again." Trevor had leaned in closer to Niall and Marshal, saying quietly, "That can't happen. Frank Whaley is a POS, and I won't have my son around him. Unfortunately, he's also an admiral and has the power to do exactly what he wants. I have no chance against him. I'm lucky I had a damn good divorce attorney at the time Emma and I split; he's spread so many lies about me, I'm almost starting to believe they're true."

"I'm wondering if you could dig into Frank Whaley's life," Marshal asked. "I can't help but think that someone who spreads lies like those has something to hide himself. There must be some way to stop him."

Niall had agreed to see what he could do. He had the resources of West Coast Forensics behind him now; he'd see if they were able to deliver.

"What about Mat?" he'd asked. Keeping a secret from his… boyfriend… felt wrong.

Marshal grimaced. "I'll talk to Mat. In fact, I'll take Trevor to meet him."

"You will?" Trevor looked startled.

Marshal grinned. "You'll like him. After he gets over his protective grizzly bear act."

A stray thought had Niall asking Marshal, "Have you treated anyone else lately? Someone like Trevor, someone who couldn't or didn't want to go to the hospital?"

He was thinking about Duane Cooper and wondering, if he'd been injured, would he try to get the kind doctor to help him?

Marshal frowned. "No. Usually it's people like you, Niall, with nowhere else to go, or the seniors who just need a little TLC." He stopped, obviously remembering something.

"What?"

"Every once in a while, someone on this side of the island will stop by with a minor injury—just to make sure they don't need the hospital. Joella Wainwright was here the other day, worried about her ankle, and Tress Black is always stopping by with one of her kids. What she really needs is an ER punch card. Her kids throw themselves out of trees, off garage roofs with no regard for their safety."

"You haven't seen Duane Cooper, have you?"

"No. Cooper would never ask me for help. The gay might rub off."

After five days in the hospital—even if he'd been asleep for the better part of them—Mat was about ready to murder someone. He liked to think he was an easygoing kind of guy, but apparently that was a myth. Not being able to do things for himself rubbed him the wrong way, and it didn't help that he felt weak as a kitten and could only expand his ribs and lung the tiniest bit before he wanted to throw up from the pain.

"You're in good shape. The next few days will be hard, but by Wednesday or Thursday you'll feel a lot better," Marshal said cheerfully.

Mat glared at him. "Is that the truth, or are you just trying to get me to stop bitching?"

Marshal shrugged. "I do know if you keep that language up you're going to end up teaching Riley some new words."

"Fuck."

"Yes, that would be one of them." Marshal sat on the edge of the bed. "So, before you leave…"

Something about his tone had Mat paying close attention. Marshal seemed off-kilter somehow, but Mat couldn't put his finger on what it was. "What's wrong?"

"Nothing's wrong," Marshal said. "I just want you to meet the doctor who's really responsible for saving your life."

Mat frowned. "What are you talking about? You're the only qualified surgeon on the island." To be honest, after he'd learned the extent of his injuries, he was surprised he wasn't in Everett or Seattle.

Marshal called out, "Trevor, come on in. I want to introduce you to Mat when he hasn't just been blown up."

A man about Mat's age appeared in the doorway; he must've been waiting just outside the room. He was tall and lean, almost too lean, with dark hair and shockingly blue eyes. He was in street clothes: worn denim jeans, a t-shirt, and an unzipped hoodie over it. He came over to the bed.

"Hi, Mat, it's nice to see you awake." Trevor had a soft voice.

"Marshal says I owe you my life."

"Well, I don't know about that. He's pretty handy with a scalpel."

"I'm grateful. Grateful to both of you."

"Now comes the hard part," Trevor said. "You have to rest and let your body heal."

Marshal snorted. Trevor glanced at him and rolled his eyes. "It's much easier to play doctor than patient."

"How do you guys know each other?" Mat asked.

He would've known, he thought, if there was another doctor on the island. He glanced between them when neither of them answered right away.

"Marshal?" Mat asked.

Marshal released a big, gusty sigh, but before he could say anything, Trevor spoke up.

"Marshal took me in when I was in a bad way. Technically, I'm still in a bad way, but at least now I don't have the flu."

"What happened?"

"My son, Caleb, violated every rule I ever taught him about

safety and strangers. He stopped Marshal in a parking lot and asked him for help."

"It's a good thing too, Trevor. You had an extremely high fever, chills, and a secondary chest infection. If you'd been sick much longer, you could've contracted pneumonia and died. And then where would Caleb be?"

This went on for a while and Mat listened with fascination. Was this some sort of odd doctor mating ritual? There was no doubt in his mind that Marshal and Trevor were attracted to each other.

Finally Mat squeezed a few words in. It was like they'd forgotten he was there.

"Um, don't mind me, but I think my mother is supposed to be here in a bit to pick me up, and I'd like to be wearing actual clothing, not this ridiculous gown that doesn't shut in the back, leaving my ass hanging out. Thank you again, Trevor, for what you did while I was on the table."

Trevor nodded and shook his hand. "You're welcome, but it was nothing. I need to go anyway. Caleb is waiting just down the hall."

By the time Mat was dressed and ready to go, he was ready to get back into bed again. Everything hurt, especially breathing. He'd never admit it, but the fact that he was required by the hospital to be transported to his mother's waiting car in a wheelchair was a damn blessing.

"Hi, sweetie." His mom leaned down and kissed him on the forehead. Mat was feeling grouchy enough that he wanted to wipe it away. Instead he snapped his jaws shut and tried for a smile.

It was a victory that he managed to get from the chair into the car without screaming.

"Take your damn pain medications, Mat," Marshal said

before he shut the car door. "You'll feel better, your family won't want to kill you, and your body will heal that much faster."

Mat was relieved when his mom finally turned onto their driveway. He'd felt every single bump and pothole between the house and the hospital. He had a few choice words for the island's road maintenance crew. Relief turned to disbelief when his attention fell on Niall, who was loading a suitcase, or something resembling a suitcase, into his car.

"What is he doing?" Mat ground out the words as he tried to unhook his seat belt without screaming and launch himself out of the car.

"Honey," his mom said in a warning tone.

"I *don't care*. I want him to stay here."

Alyson narrowed her eyes *and* raised her eyebrows at him. "What I was going to say is, maybe you should talk to him before you assume anything."

Mat huffed. "Talk. Fine, I'll fucking talk."

"And maybe clean up your language a bit. Hold on, I'll help you get out. Oh, never mind, here comes Niall."

Mat looked up from where he was struggling with the seat belt to see Niall striding toward their car. He came around to the passenger side and opened the door. Without saying anything, he reached across Mat and unlatched the seat belt. Gently he drew it back, away from Mat, careful not to jostle his shoulder or bump his chest.

"Thank you, Niall," Alyson said. "I'll meet you two in the house. If he's anything like he was getting into the car, you have your work cut out for you. Mat, I'll take your prescriptions with me."

Niall had the audacity to chuckle. "I'm sure I do. Thank you for bringing him home, Alyson."

Mat batted away Niall's hands as he tried to help Mat lift his legs out of the car. "I can do this."

"You can. But Marshal said you should have help for the first couple of days. Still, if you'd rather get out of the car by yourself, rip some stitches, maybe end up back in the hospital, go right ahead—but you're the one who's going to have to tell Marshal what happened."

"What were you putting in your car?" Mat demanded.

Niall leaned down again, and this time Mat allowed him to lift his legs out of the car. Once Mat was positioned correctly, Niall helped him to stand, wrapping a strong arm around him from Mat's less injured side. Slowly and carefully, they made their way together to the front porch.

Mat stared at the steps. "Fuck, those are a lot of stairs."

"We've got all day. I'm not going anywhere."

"Then why were you putting a bag in your car?" Mat demanded again.

Niall glanced over at him, amusement evident in his expression. "Is that why you're being all pissy?"

"I am not being pissy."

"Let me be the first to assure you, you are being pissy."

Mat glared at him.

"I'll tell you when we get to the top stair."

The five stairs seemed to take an hour to mount, but finally Mat made it to the top, dripping with sweat. Niall had stayed next to him all the way, not once letting go, only shushing him when he was about to swear.

"What?"

"What, what?" Niall repeated with exaggerated innocence.

"Why were you putting a bag in your car?" he ground out.

"Making space."

Mat blinked. "What?"

"Was your head injury worse than Marshal thought? *Space*." He sounded out the word slowly, enunciating each letter clearly.

"But…"

"The house is full. I was just putting my suitcase in the car so I could get it out of the way."

"Oh. I thought you were leaving," Mat confessed.

They'd stopped moving, Niall letting Mat get his breath. He could hear Riley on the other side of the front door, Ella answering her, and their voices fading as they moved to the back of the house.

"I thought about it," Niall admitted.

"Can we sit down for a minute?" Mat asked. He wasn't ready to go inside after being cooped up in the hospital. Niall had *thought*, past tense, about leaving.

Niall guided him to the bench in front of the big window and eased him down. It hurt, everything ached, but it felt good to feel the breeze against his skin and see the sun as it peeked out from behind fluffy white clouds. The bench creaked when Niall sat down next to him, but Mat knew it would hold. He'd watched his dad build it when he was ten or so.

They were both quiet for a few minutes. Eventually Niall spoke.

"I did think about leaving." Niall sighed. "I'm used to being alone, and I gotta tell you, your family doesn't give a crap about personal space. But I figure if I need to be alone, I can go down to the beach, work in the yard, or take the dog for a walk. I may leave, but I'll always come back."

The words Mat heard the clearest were, "I'll always come back." They made his heart pound, and he forgot about his aches and pains.

Niall wasn't looking at Mat while he spoke. Instead he was staring out into the yard, but Mat didn't think he was seeing anything.

"For about ten minutes, I thought you were dead." His voice

was bleak, as if the bombing was happening again right in front of him. "I'd been so caught up in worrying what would happen if we, uh, tried to make things work and how it would feel if I... shit..." He took a deep breath, still not looking at Mat. "If I let you in... because I was sure you'd leave like everyone else has." Another breath. "In those ten minutes, I realized I was too late. My heart already needed you, and you were gone—taken from me."

Niall turned, looking into Mat's eyes. Mat was stunned by the intensity of emotion there. Niall turned away again as if looking at Mat and speaking was too difficult.

"So, yeah, I'm going to stick around. I'm going to let your mom give me lectures about family and teach your niece how to make the best fortresses like my morfar did for me. If you'll have me, of course."

Niall glanced at him again, the emotion in his eyes changing from undefinable to embarrassed. Mat wasn't sure he had the right words to accept the most precious gift he'd ever been given: Niall Hamarsson's heart.

"I'm pretty much guaranteed to piss you off on a regular basis. I don't exactly know what I'm doing with my life, although at least now I have a job. I've got more baggage than one of those carts that loads airplanes, and who knows if I'll ever get my sh-stuff figured out. I honestly don't know what you see in me, but that's your problem, I guess."

"Niall," Mat interjected. He had a feeling Niall was going to spend the afternoon listing all the reasons Mat should keep away from him if he didn't stop him. "I'm not perfect either, you know. You won't have to go far to find that out. Ask my mom or my sisters, or any of my exes—if we were still friends. I've been informed that I'm demanding and controlling, and that my job is more important than my relationships." He almost shrugged but stopped himself at the last second. "We'll muddle along and figure it out, okay? I want you for who you are now, Niall, not who you could possibly be or who you think you could have been. And I hope you want me how I am, because I've been told I'm stubborn too."

"Mmph."

Mat figured that was as close to an answer as he was going to get at this point. He was going to assume it meant yes. And he was good with that. He'd had time to think in the hospital, time at night when he didn't have visitors or medical staff checking on him. Nearly dying was one of those things that made a person think about their life and how they were living it. He and Niall would work their way to each other. They had a pretty good start; Mat just needed to keep Niall from second-guessing himself.

It felt like hours, but Niall finally got Mat to his room—his new room, which had been his mother's but was on the main floor of the house.

"Look." Niall frowned at him. "Don't argue. Another set of stairs and I'll be taking you back to the f-ing hospital. This way you'll be able to join everyone in the kitchen when you feel up to it."

Right now, Mat felt like roadkill, and he really hadn't been looking forward to another set of stairs. "Fine. But I think it's underhanded of you to spring this on me."

"Oh." Niall raised his eyebrows. "You would've been more agreeable at the hospital?"

Mat didn't answer.

"You will be sleeping in this room, and I will be sleeping on the couch because"—he raised a thick finger, waving it in Mat's face—"*don't argue,* that way, if you need something, I will be right here." He motioned toward the sectional couch that had graced the living room since Mat was in high school.

Mat was exhausted and sweaty. He let Niall lead him over to the bed. His sisters, niece, and mom were hiding out in the kitchen or upstairs while Niall dealt with Mat, and he was thankful for that.

"Why don't you lie down. Do you want anything to drink? Are you hungry?" Niall lowered his voice. "Please be hungry. There is so much food in the house. Your mom's been cooking every day, all day. I think the freezer is overloaded and she's going to need to buy another one."

Mat leaned back against the mountain of pillows and let out a sigh. It felt good to lie down. "I could eat. Bring yours in here too, and we can talk about the case."

Niall was back in five minutes, carrying a breakfast tray. He carefully set it across Mat's lap, and suddenly Mat was hungry; the food in the hospital tasted like dirt compared to his mom's cooking. There were two large sandwiches, a stack of chocolate chip cookies (his favorite), and two bottles of water. Mat peeked under one slice of bread: bacon, lettuce, tomato, and avocado. Also his favorite. His heart swelled a little, knowing his mom had gone to the effort.

But it was evening before he and Niall were able to talk about what had happened. After their lunch he'd fallen asleep, only to be woken about an hour later by Riley, who insisted on reading him a story. Then Niall had made him get up and walk around the house, and his mom and sisters came to ask how he was doing when the only person he felt like seeing or talking to was Niall. Mat was beginning to understand the man's need to escape.

"What has Birdy told you?" he asked when they finally had a moment's peace.

Birdy was being tight with information, insisting it was more important that he recover than work. Her heart was in the right place, but Mat wasn't going to be able to rest until they caught whoever had done this. The perp had already had a week to disappear; there was no more time to waste.

Niall had pulled one of the dining room chairs in, positioning it next to the bed. "Well, I convinced her to send off the gas can from that barn fire. They were able to lift a print, but it wasn't in the national database."

"Crap."

"She let it slip that the state investigators found a print on what was left of the bomb. Also not in the system—so, not Duane. Which doesn't mean he's not involved. He could have an accomplice, or it could be a print from an innocent guy who works at some random home improvement store where he bought supplies. Now, if I, *we*, could have the two prints compared—at least maybe we could figure out if we're dealing with one perp or two."

"What about the financial records?"

Niall shook his head. "Haven't heard anything about records."

Mat bit his lip. Had he told Birdy about talking to the district attorney? With everything that had happened, the request could've been lost—or the answer could be in his email, waiting to be read.

"I need access to my email."

"Mat, it's Sunday night. Nothing we do tonight, or even likely tomorrow, will change anything. Let them think they've gotten away with it. Let them think for a few more days that we don't have a clue—which we kind of don't. In a couple of days we'll see how your body feels and go from there. Bombing a police car is a serious offense. The state investigators are doing their best."

One other thing had been nagging at Mat. "What about that camper?"

Niall frowned. "Camper?"

"The RV you were all hot about, the one out behind Chester's. It's a long shot, but what if the owner is our arsonist?"

Mat was looking at Niall—it was something he liked to do; Niall was ruggedly handsome, and Mat wanted to memorize everything about him. So he didn't miss the half-wary, half-guilty expression that crossed his face. "Have you talked to Marshal? I thought he stopped by this morning."

"He stopped by and introduced me to another doctor who apparently assisted with my surgery."

Niall leaned back, his head banging against the front window. "That asshole."

"Niall, what does Marshal have to do with the camper?"

He held up a hand. "Just listen, okay?"

Mat nodded.

"I was right, and wrong, about the RV. I was right, the driver was acting shifty, but I had the why all wrong. It turns out he was hiding from someone, but not the law. Marshal asked me to see if there was any way to get Trevor's ex-father-in-law off his back. First he asked me to make sure Collier was legit, not a scam artist or on the run, and now he's asked me to look into the father-in-law."

Mat let that sink in for a minute. He was certain there was either something Niall wasn't telling him or information Marshal hadn't given Niall.

"The doctor Marshal introduced me to this morning, Trevor Collier." He paused, but Niall did not rush to add anything, so Mat continued putting two and two together on his own. "He was living in that RV, and somehow or other, Marshal found him" —he remembered Collier saying his son had asked Marshal for help—"and took him and his son to his house." Mat didn't need to hear the rest of the story; he'd known Marshal for almost fifteen years. "Am I right?"

Niall nodded.

"I don't know why, but Marshal is a magnet for a good sob story."

"If it makes any difference, this guy seems legit."

"I can't believe he went behind my back. I can't believe you agreed to it."

"You're awfully protective of Soper."

Mat shifted far enough to stare at Niall. "Yeah, so? He's one of my oldest friends. He's a nice guy, and people think they can take advantage of him because he'd give you the coat off his back if you asked."

"He let me stay with him."

"And if I'd known that at the time, I probably would've argued with him about it. It's really not my story to tell, but after what Marshal's been through in his life, I'm surprised he trusts anyone. Sometimes I wonder if he brings strangers into his home as a sort of test."

"Huh."

"Yeah."

TWENTY-SEVEN
NIALL

Niall was surprised the household survived the next couple of days. Riley had certainly been introduced to some new words. When not being smothered by his family, Mat was stewing about the case, certain the bombing and the arsons were related, worrying over the details until he was completely intolerable. Even Fenrir took to hanging out upstairs with Riley when Mat was in a mood. The status of Duane Cooper ate at him. Mat went so far as to call Birdy Monday, making sure that there was surveillance on Cooper's house.

Niall only heard Mat's side of that conversation. The short answer must've been yes, but then Mat had gotten an earful about checking in when he was supposed to be recuperating. Niall hid his grin, listening to Birdy chew Mat out.

By Tuesday Mat still looked bad, covered with yellowing bruises, but he was able to walk without wincing, and he claimed his chest didn't hurt as much. Niall wasn't sure he believed him —actually, he didn't believe him at all—but also knew if he was in Mat's position he would be doing and saying the same things. Anything to get back to normal.

The mysterious fingerprints bugged Niall, and he was just as interested as Mat to see if the DA had been able to obtain the financial records for the marina and Cooper.

What was the motive, though? Why set fire to the marina? Why try to kill Mat unless he'd been getting close? But Mat swore he had no idea.

Maybe they were looking at this from the wrong direction?

They were sitting outside on the front porch again, the day nice enough that Niall didn't need a coat. Even though they'd reviewed the facts what seemed like a million times, Mat wanted to go over what they knew again.

"Okay," Niall said, "start from the beginning, like—just stream of consciousness."

Mat took a deep breath before he began. "The fires started after the holidays, right around the first of the year. Devon and I think, or thought, they were set by some of our local troublemakers. Small fires set in empty structures—garages and a public restroom. Then there was your place. I'm including it because we only have Jackson's word that Sean set it. Sean was my brother, and he was a bully and a jerk, but I have to say, the idea of him turning to arson just doesn't sit well.

"The next fire was the one out at the Wainwrights'. Which aligns more with the fire at your place than the others. And then of course the marina. All started by gasoline, which is impossible to trace. The Wainwrights' barn is where we, Devon, found the gas can."

"There has to be something, something that was a trigger for all this." Niall was trying to think how to ask his questions, the right way to help Mat's process. "I had only been back on the island for a few days when my place was torched. I suppose, if it wasn't Sean, that the perpetrator might have thought it was abandoned? And therefore it would fit in with the garages a bit more... except my tent was right there, and I'd been working on the roof. I tend to think Sean really did set fire to the cabin. The Wainwright barn wasn't in use, you said."

Mat nodded, staring out over the yard at nothing, thinking. "I wasn't actively investigating the fires until the barn. Devon is good at what he does, he doesn't usually need my help. The Wainwrights had been planning on converting the barn into a bed and breakfast—burning it down before the remodel wouldn't bring them any money."

"No," Niall said. "No one except you, Devon, and Birdy knew about the gas can?"

"Nope."

"What got you concentrating on Duane Cooper?"

"Nothing to do with arson. But now that the marina's gone and that fancy boat along with it, it seems mighty convenient. But he had no connection with you or the Wainwrights, and now we'll never see the records he had stored in the office. I went over there to see if he needed help pulling together the files for the county. The documents he did provide us don't make much sense and he was a terrible record keeper. Birdy thought maybe he was fudging numbers, but we don't have enough information to know for sure."

"You were at the marina? I'd forgotten that."

"To take a look at a new boat Birdy saw when she was out there. I spoke with both Sharleen and Duane for a few minutes." He shrugged and winced.

Niall watched as a single Steller's jay swooped down from one of the evergreens along the perimeter of the property. It hopped along the lawn, pecked at something, and glanced furtively around before fluttering away again.

"We need those financial records," Mat said again. His original request had been lost in the system, he'd been informed. They'd had to start the process over again.

"The fingerprint wasn't Cooper's," Niall said. The fact that the prints weren't in the system ruled out both anyone in law enforcement and the perennial lawbreakers on the island. And, while the accelerant in each fire was gasoline, there wasn't much else to connect them. The homemade bomb was unique but relatively easy to make, though whether it could have been placed under Mat's cruiser before he'd parked at the station—or if someone had been brazen enough to do the deed right there—he still wasn't sure.

Was there a copycat arsonist on the island? Maybe the first few had been set by kids, and then someone else decided to take the opportunity to set their own.

"If we don't focus on Cooper, who would you have on your list?"

"Sharleen Dixon had access as well, of course, except I can't see how this fire would benefit her," Mat said. "She's lost her only source of income at this point. The marina was her bread and butter… but we'll still need to rule her out."

"What about some of the earlier fires, anyone there?"

"Devon Flynn doesn't think so."

How Niall found himself at Sharleen Dixon's house, with Mat in the passenger seat, he was never going to be able to explain. If, or rather *when*, Mat's family discovered Niall had allowed Mat to talk him into stopping at Sharleen's on the way to a follow-up appointment at the hospital, they were going to flay him. One hundred percent dead.

"Turn here." Mat directed Niall to a driveway marked by a mailbox painted with colorful wildflowers.

"Nice house," he commented when the two-story log home came into view.

"It sure is."

"Tell me again why we're here? Because I want to be able to tell Alyson before she cuts off my balls."

"It's on the way to my appointment. It makes sense to stop and check in with her. She's the only witness we have. The only one we know for sure was at the marina the day of the fire, and maybe she's remembered something."

"Isn't this part of Flynn's job? Aren't you impressed with how she's managing while you're... on... sick... leave... *because you were nearly killed?*"

"Park by her truck." Mat ignored Niall's words, pointing toward the only visible vehicle, a banged-up four-wheel-drive truck perfect for pulling boats, although it seemed a bit much for Sharleen. "Here's the thing. Birdy is friends with Sharleen. They may even be related, second cousins or something—I'm not sure on that. Birdy is on her way to becoming a very good officer, but you and I keep coming back to Duane and Sharleen. We can't find Duane, so I want to talk to Sharleen again. We'll just keep going down the list. The Wainwrights are next."

Niall set the parking brake and unclipped his seat belt, watching as Mat did the same and keeping an eye out for any sign he was in pain. If he was, he was doing a very good job of hiding it.

"And we both know the longer all of this goes unsolved, the less likely we are to catch the arsonist—and the bomber," Mat added.

"If they're related."

"Christ, Niall. For now, as sheriff, I'm assuming the Wainwrights' barn, your place, the marina, and the bombing are all one suspect, or suspects."

Niall flicked the locks open. Mat was right, and he wanted the fucker caught as much as Mat did, but he wanted Mat to stay at home and heal and let *him* catch this fucker.

"You have your weapon, right?" Mat asked.

"How—" Niall didn't finish the sentence. He didn't want to know how Mat had figured out Niall had put on his shoulder holster and tucked his Ruger inside. This whole fucking expedition was fucking stupid; Niall figured at least one of them should be armed. Wait...

He turned his head, eyeing Mat. "Where is it?"

Mat grinned. "Tucked into my waistband. Hopefully I won't need it, because it took me ten painful minutes to get it there. I'd be like that sloth in *Zootopia*. Riley loves that damn movie."

Niall had no idea what Mat was talking about, as he hadn't had any kids in his life before. He scowled, hoping to get his point across.

Mat rolled his eyes. "Just in case, okay? I'm just going to ask Sharleen some questions and then we'll head to my appointment. If nothing else, maybe we'll learn something that will point us in the right direction."

"Someone knows we're here," Niall said. A curtain in one of the front windows had twitched.

"I'll ask the questions. You just, I don't know, be observant."

The door opened as soon as they reached the top of the stairs. An older woman waited on the other side.

"Good morning, Sheriff."

"Good morning, Sharleen. I have some follow-up questions about the fire. Do you have time?"

Some sort of internal battle was waged. Sharleen clearly did not want to answer any more questions. Niall thought she almost protested.

"I answered your questions before. And I've been over and over it with the state investigators."

"I appreciate that, but I want to go over things a bit differently this time. I know"—Mat smiled apologetically—"it's inconvenient. But I'm sure you want to do everything you can to find whoever did this to the marina. Can we come inside? It's still a lot for me to stand."

"I suppose," she said, grudgingly opening the door wider so they could enter.

Sharleen Dixon was tall and lean; she'd been a smoker once, if she wasn't still. There were telltale lines around her mouth, and the inside of her house was infused with the odor of stale cigarette smoke. The scent was slightly nauseating.

She led them through a mudroom and hallway, past a door he thought probably led to the upstairs and into a great room divided into a living and dining room. It was a lot of house for one person.

"Have a seat." Sharleen sat at the big dining room table, which, Niall noted, had a view down a sloping lawn to the water below. Instead of sitting, he walked over and looked out the window. In the water he spotted the edge of a dock with what appeared to be an upside-down rowboat on top of it. There was a small boathouse or shed perched on the bank.

"Niall's just giving me a ride to the doctor after this. You don't mind if he's here, do you? It seemed mean to make him stay in the car since he's being nice enough to drive."

Niall glanced over his shoulder, catching Sharleen's gaze. She did not want him to stay—she did not want either one of them to be in her house—but Mat was doing his "I'm harmless, the injured sheriff just trying to do his job" impression so well that there was no way for her to object without being very rude.

He turned his attention back to the view. The sun hadn't quite cleared the tree line yet, so much of the yard was in shadow. Even in the minute he stood looking out the window, the yard and water brightened as sunlight finally made it over the evergreens.

The yard was well maintained. Here and there were flower beds jammed full of colorful blooms. Horticulture was not Niall's strong suit, but his grandmother had done her best to educate him. She'd taken him on long walks around the island, teaching him about the flora native to Piedras. It had been, he realized now, a way for her to help Niall calm his mind. She'd given him an anchor to the land.

Niall recognized the easy plants like bluebells, rhododendrons, and late-blooming tulips. Along the edge, the grassy lawn gave way to native grasses harboring little oases of native plants. From where he was positioned, he identified early-blooming camas, shooting star, and the dainty white of the woodland star. The wet winter and now-warming days must've been perfect for them. Maybe when he got started on rebuilding the cabin, he'd restore the flower beds too and grow roses like some sort of Agatha Christie character.

Behind him, Mat began speaking. "I want to take you through the day of the fire again, but this time let's start a few days earlier."

"I feel like I've been over this."

Mat went on as if he hadn't heard her. "Tell me about the days before the fire. What were they like? Were you busy? Did anything strike you as odd?"

"Well, everything's so jumbled."

Niall wandered away from the window, half listening. It was habit for him to see what people read. Like the house itself, Sharleen's bookcase was handmade, and it was jam-packed with books of all sorts. On the wall nearby hung an oil painting. It was beautiful, capturing the delicate, swirling palette of colors that bloomed on Piedras in late spring—nothing like the paintings at Lulu's restaurant. But it wasn't the books or the painting that caught his attention. It was the pair of men's work boots tucked between the couch and the bookshelf—much too large for Sharleen, even if she was a tall woman.

"Your friend is making me uncomfortable."

"My apologies," Mat said. "Niall, do you mind?"

"Sorry, it's habit. You've got a great collection of books. Do you mind if I take a look?"

Now he was doing his best impression of a bumbling Columbo. Randomly he picked a book and tugged it off the shelf. It was a like-new copy of *A Taste for Death* by PD James. He flipped it open and saw that it was signed.

"I'm a Rankin fan myself." He spoke randomly as he tucked

the book back into its spot on the shelf. He wanted a closer look at those boots. "You two go ahead and talk. Don't let me bother you."

Mat had to think he was out of his mind, but those boots were not Sharleen's, and Mat had said she was long divorced. That of course didn't mean she couldn't have a boyfriend, but Sharleen's body language was telling Niall something was off. She didn't want either of them in the house, and Niall wasn't falling for the "I don't remember" ploy. The woman was smart; her bookshelf proved it.

"How about the day before the fire?" Mat pressed on.

Niall took another book from the shelf, a copy of *The Concrete Blonde* by Michael Connelly. He pretended to be reading the title page while he eased down onto the couch. This was also a first edition. Niall knew less about the value of books than he did about plants, but he found it more than a little odd that a dockmaster was able to afford this big house, a newer truck, a collection of hardcover books, and original artwork.

"Sharleen?" Mat prompted.

Niall glanced up, catching Sharleen's wary gaze on him; she returned her attention to Mat.

"Oh, um, the day before. I was at the marina most of the day. Was that the day you stopped to visit? No, you were there earlier in the week." She tapped the table. "The weather was bad, I remember. I get cold a lot easier these days. Anyway, I try to be at the office nine to five during the week in case anyone needs my help or needs me to unlock the boatyard so they can get inside. But because of the rain it wasn't busy. I worked, came home at five and, you know, just the normal."

"And you didn't see Duane?"

"I don't think so."

"Last time I asked, you said he might be doing something for his ex-wife. We can't locate Duane, and when Deputy Flynn talked to his ex, she said she hasn't seen or talked to Duane in years. Do you know why Duane might say he was visiting her?"

Out of the corner of his eye, Niall watched Sharleen shake her head.

"No. Maybe I just thought he did?"

Niall stood. "Mind if I use your bathroom?"

"What? Oh, um, sure. There's one—just go through that door there and then the one opposite."

What Niall really wanted to do was take a look through the entire house. He pushed through the door into the hallway on the other side. For the sake of believability, he opened and shut the bathroom door before turning down the hallway toward the stairs. He didn't know what he would find. Maybe nothing. Regardless, he'd veered so far off their script that he might as well snoop around and see if someone—Duane Cooper?—was hiding upstairs. He hoped Mat trusted him enough to keep Sharleen occupied.

Slowly he crept up the stairs, doing his best to keep his movements quiet. He hoped any creaks would be explained away by the wind.

The upper floor was three-quarters of the lower. The door of the room directly across was shut, and he opened it to see an office furnished with a desk and more packed bookshelves but otherwise empty.

The hallway turned the other direction, opening to a landing with more doors, one of which was open. He headed that way. The feeling that he needed to hurry and get back downstairs pressed on him.

A quick look revealed nothing in the larger bedroom. The bed was tidily made, and he didn't have time to open closet doors. The upstairs felt empty. As silently as possible, he made his way back down the stairs and opened and shut the bathroom door loudly before heading back into the great room. "Sorry about that." He grimaced.

"We should get going. I'm going to be late for my appointment."

Niall frowned but played along. Mat was in no hurry to have Dr. Soper look him over.

They said their goodbyes to Sharleen, and Niall couldn't help but notice the look of relief on her face as they turned away.

In the car, Niall asked, "What was that all about?"

"I got a text from Birdy. Did you find anything?"

"Not really. A large pair of work boots tucked between her couch and bookshelf was about it."

Mat grinned, "Ah, Sherlock. And the mud on the sole of the boot is a kind only found on the rocky shores of eastern Piedras Island?"

Niall made a face. "Nooo, but they are too big for Sharleen. She's not our Cinderella. I'd say Cinderella is a man."

"Take me to the station. We need to talk to Birdy."

"After your appointment," Niall said. He couldn't allow Mat to weasel out of it.

Mat groaned. "Niall."

"After."

"Sir, it's wonderful to see you up and about." Birdy stepped toward him as if to hug him before thinking better of it.

Mat took a deep breath, enjoying the stale air of the station in a way he never had before. He'd missed it here. "It's great to be back."

"What did the doctor say?"

"I'm healing well and will be able to be back on desk duty soon. Thank you for asking." He was fudging about *soon*, but ten days wasn't soon enough. Birdy was doing a great job, but she just wasn't experienced enough yet. "What do you have?"

He'd finally made it to his desk and eased himself down into the chair. Birdy half perched on her desk, facing him. "This is rumor, but you know how the island is."

Yes, Mat did. If something was rumor, there was a high chance of some sort of truth behind it. No matter how twisted, there would be a kernel of truth. "Hit me with it."

"Merle Wainwright and Sharleen Dixon were, or maybe still are, having an affair."

"Okaaay. How does this fit in with arson?" Other than the fact that they had both been hit hardest.

"It doesn't much, not at first glance. But, sir, if the rumor has come all the way around to me, then Joella surely knows about it too. Since I've been on the force, I'm a little less likely to hear the same kind of gossip I did a few years ago."

"And..."

"I'm not sure how to say this."

"Just say it, Flynn. Police work is not polite business."

She took a breath. "Joella is not a nice person. Gracie knew her, of course. She knows everyone. They were in school at the same time. Joella... doesn't like to share. She was mean in high school, the one who would ruin things if she'd been left out."

The back of Mat's neck began to prickle. He recalled offhand comments his mom had made over the years about Joella Wainwright always needing to be "queen bee" or something like that. He looked up at Niall, who appeared to be leaning casually against Mat's desk, his attention fully on Birdy, but was in fact coiled like a... panther... about to spring.

"And?" Niall prodded.

"And, Merle and Sharleen were a thing in high school. From what Gracie says, Joella decided she wanted Merle and made it her mission to break them up. They've been married since they were in their early twenties."

"Keep going. There must be more."

Birdy rolled her eyes. "This is secondhand and speculation from Gracie, but... there've been whispers for a while, I guess, that Merle and Sharleen have been seeing each other. I'm friendly enough with Sharleen, and she never said anything to me, but..." She shrugged. "Also, Gracie said that she heard Merle wanted a divorce. This was a few years ago, I guess."

The bullpen was quiet while Niall and Mat processed the information. Somewhere over their heads a fan whirred.

Niall broke the silence first. "That would explain the boots. They could be Merle's, not Duane's."

Mat asked, "Birdy, do you think Joella set fire to the marina to try to kill Sharleen? Was the barn fire part of a sort of shell game to confuse us, or was Merle the intended victim? And how does this fit in with the car bomb?"

"The bomb doesn't fit in, sir. I decided to leave that out. In my opinion, that was Duane Cooper."

"How long have they been…" Mat twirled his finger.

Birdy shrugged. "I don't know, sir. I just learned about the alleged affair."

"Murder by arson seems… unlikely."

"Well, it didn't work, did it? Maybe it's just a warning? Maybe Joella is trying to get Sharleen to leave the island. Joella isn't the type for divorce, and if she was, she'd do the divorcing, not the other way around. She'd want to control the whole thing. Maybe Merle asked her, and she said no. Maybe she's trying to intimidate him? We never did learn who killed those sheep in February, maybe it was Joella. I'm sure she's a decent shot."

"What's that movie?" Mat asked. "The one where she boils a bunny?"

"*Fatal Attraction*," Niall responded.

"Right. Let me just put all this together. Merle Wainwright and Sharleen Dixon are having an affair—"

"Allegedly," Birdy interjected.

"Allegedly having an affair. Joella Wainwright finds out and is pissed off, or maybe Merle asks for a divorce, but she doesn't want one. To try to get her husband to stop seeing Sharleen, she possibly kills several expensive sheep, sets fire to the barn they were going to remodel, and when that doesn't work, she decides the marina needs to go. It's possible, in a crazed Glenn Close way. I wish we had her fingerprints." He was thinking about the unidentified print found on the gas can.

"I could go and talk to her? She'd probably offer something to drink, and I can, maybe, take the glass?"

"Save me from Miss Marple," said Niall, shaking his head.

"Have you spoken with Merle?" Mat asked.

Birdy shook her head.

"Let's start with him."

"One more thing," Birdy said, standing and moving around to the front of her desk. "Cathy DeWitt delivered this yesterday. She apologized for the delay." She handed Mat a thick legal-sized envelope with *Sheriff Mat Dempsey* written clearly in block print across the back.

"Cathy DeWitt is in the DA's office," Mat explained to Niall. "I requested financial records for Cooper, the marina, and Sharleen."

The atmosphere in the room turned electric as Mat fumbled with the brass brad holding the envelope closed and let the paperwork slide out onto his desk. He flipped through until he found Sharleen's name and quickly scanned the pages. It only took a few minutes to find the information he was looking for. "Well, look at that. Merle's been giving Sharleen money," he said. He handed the record to Birdy, who began to read it.

After a few minutes, she said, "It looks like it's been going on for a while. Those records go back over five years."

"That seems like it would make Joella very angry." Niall sounded as if he had his prey in his sights.

"We need to pay the Wainwrights a visit," Mat said.

Niall's gaze swung around to land heavily on him, his green eyes boring into Mat. "You will let Birdy and me handle anything physical. Deputize me."

"What?"

"Make me a temporary deputy."

Mat recognized the tingle in his gut. They were on the right track. And Niall had a point about needing authority. To be honest, Mat didn't know if he could make Niall a temporary deputy at the drop of a hat, but he figured he'd ask forgiveness later.

Birdy had done a great job. The detail about the Wainwrights' history with Sharleen was the kind of information Mat didn't have easy access to. It fit in an odd sort of way; he and Devon had never been able to reconcile the garage fires with the others. He wondered if Niall's cabin was part of the scheme or if Trey Jackson had been right and Sean had set that blaze.

They took two cars to the Wainwrights'. Birdy drove her cruiser, and Niall and Mat took his car.

"It's really uncool to take a, what, twenty-plus-year-old Subaru to question a suspect," Mat complained.

"It's a perfectly good, running vehicle, asshole. And since you blew up your last vehicle, this is what you get."

Deputy Radden was on patrol, and Birdy had sent Deputy Holstrom to Orcas to help fill in their gaps. The young father had finally recovered from the plague his young children had brought home.

As Niall negotiated a curve that swept past Marshal Soper's house, Mat made a mental note to call his friend and find out what the hell was going on. Marshal had managed to avoid any personal conversation while Mat was in the hospital, and at today's appointment Mat had seen a different doctor. It made sense—Marshal was needed in the ER—but it still irritated Mat.

The Wainwrights' place came into view on Mat's right. They had a lovely east-facing parcel of land that dropped down to the road and continued to the water on the other side. Niall turned in. It was about fifty yards from the road to the house.

The farmhouse, which was light gray with sage green trim, was one of the oldest remaining houses on the island, dating from the early 1900s. The Wainwrights had spent quite a bit of money over the years bringing the structure up to date. The original carriage house had been converted to a garage, and one of the outbuildings beyond that housed the creamery.

Niall parked next to Birdy. Mat had the door open and one foot out before Niall could make it around to his side.

"I can do it," Mat snapped. He was tired of being handled with kid gloves. Niall had been sleeping on the living room couch since Mat got out of the hospital, lending a helping hand every time Mat so much as wiggled a toe, and Mat had had enough.

"I know you can do it. I just—fine." Niall stepped back and let Mat heave himself out of the car. Side by side, they mounted the stairs to the Wainwrights' front door. If Mat was a little slow, out of breath, and possibly in pain, at least Niall didn't comment.

The door opened without them knocking.

"Hello, Sheriff, and—well, hello, what brings you all here today?"

Joella Wainwright reminded Mat of a squirrel or chipmunk. She peered at them, her dark eyes skittering back and forth. She was holding a rag of some sort in both hands, as if she'd been busy dusting.

"Good afternoon, Mrs. Wainwright," Mat said. "We'd just like to ask a few questions. This is my chief deputy, Birdy Flynn, and my newest deputy, Niall Hamarsson. May we come in?"

Her eyes grew wide. "Now?" she squeaked, reinforcing Mat's impression of her as a chipmunk.

"We have a few questions about the barn fire. Is Merle around?"

"Merle? Oh, yes, Merle. Um, no. No, he's not."

"That's fine," Birdy assured her. "We can ask you the same questions. Do you mind? Sheriff Dempsey is still recovering from his injuries."

That seemed to startle Joella into action. "Oh, of course, silly me. Come in." Joella attempted to smile, but it didn't reach her eyes. Opening the door, she backed up so the three of them could troop inside. "Please have a seat."

She waved toward a set of floral couches set in an L shape, one in front of a window and the other against a wall. On the wall was a painting depicting island meadows in full bloom, the purples and blues of the native wildflowers a smear of color. The most striking aspect, though, were the clouds. The artist managed to make them seem alive, swirling in the wind above the meadow.

"Would anyone like something to drink? I can make coffee or…" Her voice trailed off.

"Water sounds great. Let me help you. I'm sure Sheriff Dempsey would like coffee." Birdy followed Joella across the room into what must be the kitchen.

"Tell me she isn't going to steal a glass," Niall said.

Mat sat down on the couch against the wall. From there he had a view of the backyard and what he thought was the back of the carriage house. It was a beautiful building; they'd done a lovely job. He thought his mother had told him that even the windows had been refurbished. "She's going to do *something*," he replied.

Niall was pacing the room, peering at objects sitting on a side table and then out the window before coming to stand by the couch. "I recognize that painting. I mean—isn't that by the same artist as the one in Sharleen's living room?"

Mat took a second look. He hadn't been focused on the art at Sharleen's, but now that Niall mentioned it… "Yeah, you're right. I think it's, they're, by Daisy Karrass. She's local."

"So this wouldn't be an expensive piece, then?"

"No, it would, unless they bought it when she was first starting out. Daisy made it big. Her stuff is pricey."

"Huh."

A crash sounded from the kitchen, followed by Birdy's apology for being clumsy and Joella assuring her it was an old cup, one she didn't care about.

Slowly Niall looked downward, his gaze meeting Mat's. "Are you kidding me?" he whispered.

Mat just shook his head. He didn't want to know what Birdy was up to.

TWENTY-NINE
NIALL

Niall was certain Joella would not be pleased that Sharleen had a painting by the same artist she did—especially if Merle had gifted the piece to Sharleen and Joella found out about it. "Where do you think Merle is?" he asked quietly. The two women were still in the kitchen.

Mat shrugged. "I didn't see his truck. When they get back, say you left something in the car and take a look around."

"Will do, Sheriff." Niall touched his forehead with his index finger.

"Screw off, *Deputy*," Mat muttered. "Remind me to fire you when we get back to the station."

Niall wandered back over to the front window that looked across the front porch and east. In the distance he could see a few sheep wandering around. Closer were the remains of the barn that had burned. Orange tape wrapped around it fluttered in the breeze, reminding people it was a crime scene and the barn was the victim.

Joella, followed by Birdy, came back into the room. She placed a tray with four cups on it on the coffee table in front of the couch. "There's sugar and cream if you need it."

Niall patted his chest and then his back pocket. "I'll be right back. I left my phone in the car." He felt like a fool, but without making eye contact with Mat, Birdy, or Joella, he plastered an apologetic grin on his face and eased his way out the front door.

The farm was beautiful. Niall stood on the top step for a moment, taking in the view. Every vista was unique, and he would never tire of any of them. He trotted down the steps to his car and opened and shut the door, feeling like he was the side bit in a poorly acted junior high school play.

The evening was calm and almost warm. Birds of various types chirped, called, and cawed. Feeling even more foolish, Niall put his phone to his ear, pretending he had a call, and began to wander away from his car toward the other two buildings next to the farmhouse.

One was obviously an old carriage house that had been remodeled to fit modern cars. Next to it was a smaller building, its door slightly ajar. Niall decided to peek in there first. Mat had told him that the Wainwrights mostly had sheep, but they also kept four cows on the property; their handcrafted cheeses were in high demand both on Piedras and on the mainland.

He stuck his head around the door. No one appeared to be inside, and he wandered in, taking in the stainless steel tables and small vats that must be used to process and store the milk and cream or... whatever. The building had a musty, grassy smell to it. He did not find any sign of Merle Wainwright.

Back outside, Niall gave up pretending he was on the phone and began to walk back toward the house. The wind had died down almost to nothing, and during a lull in the chatter of the birds, he heard a faint rumble coming from the carriage house. The interior of the structure was dark; through a small window, Niall could see two vague car-like shapes inside.

Motion to his right caught his attention. Niall looked over, realizing a window that must be in the kitchen looked right down on him and Joella Wainwright was staring at him. The expression on her odd, scrunched face was both horrified and gleeful, if that was possible. There was something about the garage she didn't want him to find out, but she also thought it was too late.

Niall panicked. Joella was a trapped animal, and thus dangerous—who knew what she might do. Mat was in the house, where Niall couldn't protect him. Joella must have seen the emotion on his face. She disappeared from view.

Niall's heart raced. He knew Mat would never forgive him if Merle Wainwright could've been saved and Niall went for Mat instead. "Fucking fuck."

The large double doors were closed and locked. Niall ran around to the side of the small building, looking for another way to get inside. At the back he found a single door. He grabbed the handle, turning it, but it was also locked. He glared at it and raised a foot to kick it in. If he was wrong, Mat was going to have a lot of explaining to do.

The door frame splintered under the force of his kick. He shoved the door open and, holding his breath, entered the structure, quickly taking in the scene. Before he did anything else, he turned off the engine of the older sedan with the hose stretching from the tailpipe to the mostly closed car window and opened the big garage doors. Then he turned back to the body in the car. He couldn't think about what might be happening in the house right now. Wainwright needed his help.

Carefully, Niall dragged the man out of the car and lay him flat on the ground. His face was cherry red, a sign of carbon monoxide poisoning. Niall knelt down next to him, placing a hand on his chest and an ear to his face. The man was still breathing, at least. Merle was big, and unconscious he was difficult to move, but Niall managed to get him outside to the driveway and fresh air. Pulling his phone out of his pocket, Niall called 911. Dispatch assured him the ambulance was on its way.

Birdy burst out of the house. "Call 9-1-1!"

Niall felt the ground move underneath him. He stumbled forward to clutch at the bottom railing of the porch.

"Not for Sheriff Dempsey, sir—he's okay. It's Joella. She tried to kill herself."

Niall gulped in air and tried to slow his pounding heart. "Christ, the man is going to be the death of me," he muttered.

He looked over his shoulder. Wainwright lay still, but his color looked slightly better. Far away, Niall heard the shrill call of the ambulance as it raced to the farm.

"What happened?" he asked.

"Kitchen knife. Sheriff Dempsey is with her."

The ripples from Joella and Merle Wainwright and Sharleen Dixon's love triangle were going to be felt on Piedras for months, if not years, Niall reflected.

They were all finally back at the sheriff's office, after following the two ambulances to the hospital from the Wainwrights' farm. Merle had been whisked away and put on oxygen. Joella was in emergency surgery for the knife wound to her chest; there was a wound on her wrist too, as if she'd tried there first.

Mat, Birdy, and Niall had waited at the hospital long enough to question Merle Wainwright when he regained consciousness, and he'd confirmed what they'd speculated: Merle and Sharleen were having an affair, and it had been going on for several years.

Merle *had* asked Joella for a divorce at least once, but she'd gone into a rage, threatening to kill herself. She'd made Merle promise he would stop seeing Sharleen. He hadn't, although he'd tried to make sure Joella didn't find out—which meant a lot of sneaking around, and he obviously hadn't managed to fool his wife. Yes, Merle had been giving Sharleen money on a regular basis, from his business account into her business account.

"WoodlandStar LLC?" asked Birdy.

Merle nodded, the oxygen hose bouncing.

"Did you give Sharleen the painting by Daisy Karrass?" Niall asked.

The man nodded again.

"What about the Whaler?" Birdy interjected. She turned to Mat. "Remember? It was registered to that LLC."

Another nod. The oxygen mask over Merle's face made it difficult for him to speak, and Niall could tell he didn't want to answer any more questions.

The attending doctor intervened at that point, insisting they needed to let Merle rest. They could return to the hospital later on or, better, the next day if they had further questions, he told them.

"And"—Dr. King raised an eyebrow, his knowing gaze running up and down Mat's body as he stood awkwardly, using the side of Wainwright's hospital bed to support himself—"Sheriff Dempsey, I believe you are still recovering from your injuries. Please go sit down before you fall down and end up back here again."

They were just leaving the hospital when Sharleen rushed in from the parking lot. In the short time since Niall and Mat had seen her, it seemed she'd shrunk several inches. Her face was ashen, and there was evidence of tears on her cheeks.

Seeing the three of them standing there, she came to an abrupt halt, her eyes wild. "Sheriff, is he going to be okay?" she demanded.

"I think so. Did he call you?"

"One of the nurses. He asked them to."

Birdy said, "Sharleen, we need to ask you a few more questions. Do you have any reason to believe that Joella Wainwright may have set the marina fire?"

Mat thought she'd set the barn fire first to remove suspicion and then torched the marina.

"Of course I suspected that bitch! She threatened me to my face! She threatened Merle!" Tears welled in her eyes.

"Why didn't you say anything?" Birdy asked, moving closer and putting an arm around the older woman's shoulders.

Sharleen wrapped her arms around herself, leaning into Birdy. "I didn't know what to do. Merle asked me to be quiet. He was going to try one more time to reason with her. He should know by now, Joella's never been reasonable. If she saw something she wanted, even if it belonged to someone else, she figured a way out to make it hers. She stole Merle from me years ago, and now she was trying to do it again."

She covered her face, her shoulders shaking as she sobbed. Niall met Birdy's glance and nodded. He and Mat headed to the cruiser while Birdy escorted Sharleen inside to the waiting area. A few minutes later, Birdy reemerged and met them at the car.

Niall watched as Mat eased gently onto his chair. He had to ache all over and certainly was in more pain than he would admit to, but he'd insisted on coming to the station instead of heading home right away. Niall understood, even if all he really wanted to do was to take Mat home, put him to bed, crawl in next to him, and hold him in his arms. Niall needed to reassure himself Mat was alive. He wanted to hear Mat's heartbeat and feel the warmth of Mat's skin against his own.

When Birdy had yelled for 911, Niall's life had flashed before his eyes as if he were the one in peril. A flashback to the crushing loss he'd experienced the night of the bombing had swept over him again, making him feel faint. Even after Birdy had clarified the ambulance was for Joella, he'd still had to bend over and rest his forearms on his thighs for a moment while he pulled himself together.

If this was what it was like to need someone—well, it was too late now. There was no going back. If he was going to do this thing, be *with* Mat Dempsey, it was all or nothing, and Mat was just going to have to get used to it.

Once Mat seemed comfortable, Birdy sat at her desk. Niall continued to stand, choosing to lean one hip lightly against Mat's desk with his arms crossed over his chest.

Mat said, "So, Merle and Sharleen. I wonder what possessed him to buy her that boat?"

Niall shrugged. "We'll find out eventually."

"And none of this has to do with Duane Cooper," Mat added.

They were quiet for a minute, the only sounds coming from the air cleaning system or the street outside.

"Joella's fingerprint will match the one on that gas can Devon found," Birdy said.

They all nodded. Niall was reasonably sure they were all trying to process Joella Wainwright's toxic need to *possess* her husband: if she couldn't have him, no one could have him. How did that even happen? What had set her on this path of destruction and attempted murder? Niall didn't want to possess Mat, he wanted to be *with* Mat.

"Dollars to doughnuts, Duane Cooper was responsible for the IED, though," Mat ground out.

Duane hadn't been seen since before the marina fire, but Mat had already confided in Niall that he was sure Duane was behind the bombing.

"I agree, sir, but why?" asked Birdy.

"Damned if I know. But he would've known how to make one. He served in the first Iraq War as an ordnance disposal specialist."

They fell quiet again, thinking, Niall was sure, about why someone, seemingly an old friend—at least an acquaintance— would want to kill the sheriff. And why would he resort to a bomb? So many whys.

Out of the corner of his eye, Niall saw Mat trying to find a comfortable position on his chair. The mystery of Duane Cooper and the IED would have to wait for another day.

"There's nothing else we can do today. If you don't mind,

Deputy Flynn, I'm going to take the sheriff home and put him to bed. Even though he hasn't said anything, I have a feeling he feels like he's been hit by a truck—again."

Niall knew he was right, because Mat didn't even attempt to protest.

"Good evening, sirs."

"Good evening."

Mat grumbled all the way out to the parking lot with Niall hovering by his side. "I can walk on my own, for fuck's sake."

"If your niece hears that, Ella is going to wash your mouth out with soap regardless of your injuries," Niall commented, leaving Mat to get in the car on his own.

"Fine." Mat slumped against the seat.

Niall had to pinch his lips together to keep from laughing as he backed out of his parking spot and began to head toward the Dempsey household.

After half a mile or so, Mat commented, "I know you think this is amusing."

"I really don't. Ella scares me."

She did kind of intimidate Niall. Ella was a fierce protector when it came to her daughter, and her brother too. He didn't want to do anything that put him on her bad side.

Mat let out a big sigh. "Me too."

Niall had to ask. "Are you worried about Cooper?"

"No," Mat replied. "I probably should be, but by tomorrow everyone on and off the islands will be keeping their eyes and ears open for him. I don't think he has anywhere to go. Wherever he's hiding… he's stuck there for now."

"Maybe he did drown."

Mat shook his head. "He's alive. And I'm going to bring him in."

THIRTY

NIALL

As he drove past the sheriff's office in Hidden Harbor on his way to the ferry terminal, Niall winced. Mat would be expecting him this morning. Mat was back at work on light duty, and thank fuck for that. Niall knew what an ass *he* was, but Mat was giving him a run for his money. They'd fallen into a habit of Niall stopping by the station with fresh coffee and a pastry for his... partner— there, he'd allowed the thought to spill into his head—and checking in to make sure he wasn't overdoing things, but today he had an errand.

Niall would see Mat, but only after he'd sorted out the yurt. He rolled his eyes. He felt like an old-fashioned suitor needing to be completely prepared before he knocked at Mat's door asking him if he wanted to go on a date.

Lopez Island was mostly flat, or at most rolling hills, a favorite place for bicyclists and sheep farmers. Now that spring had finally arrived, the landscape was dotted with community-planted daffodils and the grasses had turned from brown to green. He'd forgotten how different Lopez was from Piedras, though just as beautiful.

Island Yurt was located in Lopez Village alongside what Niall knew to be an incredible bakery. Even midweek, people were packed inside, waiting to order their favorite pastries. On weekends there would be a line out the door. Maybe he'd stop on the way home and pick up a few things. Niall didn't have much of a sweet tooth, but Mat did. It gave him a little thrill to be thinking about getting Mat a damn doughnut.

Ian Dennis seemed legitimately excited to meet Niall and talk yurts. He looked a lot like his grandfather. They had the same eyes, which sparkled a bit wickedly when Ian and Stu were excited.

Since it was a slow time of year, Ian was certain they could get Niall situated relatively quickly provided Niall didn't pick out a complicated design. They kept some stock of their yurt kits on hand, and Ian had a crew he could call. If Niall was willing to pay a little extra for labor, the yurt would only take a few days, maybe a week to build.

"At the worst it will take us two weeks. Between-island transportation is much easier," Ian said. "Less traffic, and it's locals getting the work early in the season. A win-win situation."

Niall pulled out his wallet and handed over his credit card.

The yurt took the check from the insurance company as well as a chunk of his savings, though he hoped to beef up the latter again when the condo sold. After looking at several models on the lot, he'd chosen a fancier one with a wraparound porch, four windows, and more floor space. He would be able to customize the inside as he wanted, even install a kitchen and bath. After the past winter's weather, he also went for the extra wind and snow options.

Ian grinned, handing Niall a copy of the signed contract. It was clear he loved what he did and was good at it. "If you decide to make it permanent, we can do that too. Give me a day or so to round everyone up. I'll be in touch. I'll need to come and see the space to get a good idea of the land. This one may take a day or two longer, but soon enough you'll be sleeping in your own yurt."

. . .

Niall left Island Yurt feeling as hopeful as he had in days and even managed to catch the eleven o'clock inter-island ferry run back to Hidden Harbor. He'd be back on Piedras by noon at the latest, and he hoped his string of good luck would keep going. The yurt was a surprise, somewhere they could be alone sooner rather than later. As much as Niall enjoyed Mat's family, he needed alone time, time to stare out at the water.

Niall recognized the buzzing feeling in his gut as excitement. Anticipation. It used to be something he felt only when he was close to solving a case, when he'd just put his finger on the key piece of evidence or testimony. The yurt was the right choice. As much as he loved Alyson, Riley, and Ella, he wanted to visit them, not be in the same house every morning. He needed privacy and coffee by himself—or with Mat. Mat hated the exercises he had to do for his shoulder—understandable, since they seemed to be about as enjoyable as undergoing enhanced interrogation—and somehow the situation had devolved into Niall bribing him with sex. And trying to have sex with a nearly-seven-year-old in the house was… impossible.

They'd see Mat's family almost every day anyway, because Fenrir and Riley had an unholy alliance. Niall couldn't say when Fenrir's allegiance had shifted, ever so slightly, to the youngest Dempsey, but Niall knew the dog would guard Riley with his life if it ever came to that.

That Mat would stay with Niall frequently and eventually move in with him—maybe when they decided whether the yurt would be permanent or whether they were going to build a whole new structure—Niall had no doubt. And that felt good. He kept revisiting their relationship in his head, turning it over and over, but since the day he'd nearly lost Mat, nothing had changed about Niall's feelings. He'd recognized and accepted them for what they were: permanent.

Niall and Mat waited together on the porch of the yurt, sprawled out on a double chaise lounge, looking out over the water while listening for the spitting sound of tires on gravel signaling their guests' arrival. Shay Delacombe and his great-aunt would be arriving any minute. The rest of the family—Alyson, Ella, and Riley—as well as Marshal, Trevor, and Caleb, would be arriving later. It was going to be perfect weather for a barbecue.

Family. Such an odd word in his mind, but one Niall was learning to savor.

Over the past couple of months, Niall and Shay had been meeting whenever Shay was on the island visiting Claribel. Niall had come to the conclusion that Shay wasn't actually intolerable. In fact, Shay reminded Niall a bit of himself. Shay had no patience for idiots; he was driven almost to the exclusion of anything else —except he seemed to have a soft spot for his great-aunt.

When Niall had first responded to Shay's note, they'd emailed back and forth for a couple of weeks before Shay suggested they meet for coffee one Saturday morning. Niall had hesitated. He still hadn't told Mat he was in contact with Shay. Besides, meeting Shay meant talking about feelings and relationships, and if there was one thing Niall was really bad at, it was *that*.

So, feeling like the blade of a guillotine was slicing the tiny hairs on the back of his neck, he'd broached the subject one Saturday morning when they were lying in bed.

"If I had a chance to find out who my father was, do you think I should do it?" Niall asked, staring at the ceiling.

Mat rolled over to peer at him, the midnight blue of his eyes blazing with a million questions. "Why wouldn't you?"

Niall smiled. "Answering a question with a question. Is this one of the hazards of a relationship where both people are in law enforcement?"

Mat sat up, disturbing the covers and allowing cool air to rush in underneath them. Niall let himself be distracted for a moment by his broad chest, wanting to trace the mass of scars from the bombing. Mat was self-conscious about the scars, but to Niall they meant Mat was alive.

"Why are you worried about it?" Mat asked. "Whatever you decide, it's up to you, not me or anyone else, right?"

Niall took a deep breath before blazing forward. "If it means Shay Delacombe and I are half brothers? Would that bother you?"

Practically, Niall knew Mat wouldn't be bothered. Mat was his and he was Mat's.

Mat gaped at him and then managed to sputter, "Were you ever going to tell me?"

"I just did," Niall pointed out.

Mat widened his eyes and raised his eyebrows. "You know what I mean!"

Niall hid a grin. He did know what Mat meant, but he still enjoyed riling Mat up. And if Niall had disliked Shay in the past, Mat had despised him.

"Of all the people on the island you could possibly be related to, it has to be Shay Delacombe?"

With everything that had happened, Niall had forgotten about the film he'd sent off to Seattle for developing. The thick envelope had been returned quickly enough but had sat at the Orca Motel until Ricky remembered to tell him they were waiting there for him.

The previously undeveloped photos had been more of the same: a young, happy Ana Hamarsson together with Shay's father, David. It made Niall curious about what had happened to them. David had been at least fifteen years older and married, but after a lifetime of reading people's expressions, Niall believed David Delacombe had been in love with his mother. The emotion he saw on the man's face was genuine.

"Would it be that bad if Shay and I are half brothers? Are you going to change your mind about shacking up with me?" Niall had teased.

Mat let out a big sigh. "No, dammit. I'll like him if it kills me."

"I'd appreciate it if you stayed alive."

After meeting a few more times with Shay, they'd decided to go ahead with the testing. That had been over a month ago, and the results had just come back. Niall and Shay were both fairly certain what the test would reveal.

Then somehow it had seemed easier to Niall for him and Shay to meet on his own turf and read the results together. So he figured he'd invite him to the barbecue... and if he was inviting Shay, he might as well invite Claribel too, because Alyson seemed to like her more these days and was worried about the Delacombe matriarch.

"It's time we set aside these old feuds," Alyson had commented one evening when Mat and Niall were over for dinner.

Since Niall had never been involved in any feud, he had no problem with it.

. . .

Niall reread the contents of the letter in his hand. Even though the results were exactly what he expected, seeing the words typed out made him feel weightless. He and Shay Delacombe shared enough DNA that they likely had the same father: a 99 percent probability.

"Well, I guess it's official," Shay said, tossing his results onto the picnic table. "My reputation is ruined."

"What about mine?" Niall asked.

Mat added, "And mine. I'm more worried about mine."

"Boys," Claribel said, her eyes a little teary, "I know you don't care about an old lady's opinion, but I'm glad Shay finally sent you the box. It's been in my care for ages. David left it to me, and damn if I knew what to do with it. I thought about throwing it away, but when you came back to Piedras, Niall, it seemed better to let you and Shay decide."

Niall wanted to know what had happened to David and Ana, but that was a story for another day. Today was a day for stories with happier endings—a day to celebrate the family Niall still had, a patchwork of people who'd snuck into his heart.

Fenrir woofed, recognizing the sound of Alyson's car, and bounded off to greet the rest of the guests. Mat hadn't officially moved in with Niall yet, but it was only semantics at this point, seeing as he spent every night there. It was only his possessions that hadn't migrated over yet; Niall had his heart.

By the end of the day, Niall fully intended for their relationship to be official. He wasn't sure what had come over him, but one day a few weeks ago he'd been walking with Fenrir while Mat was on duty, and they'd passed Piedras Island Jewelry. It was a little store tucked in next to Harbor Barber where Niall got his hair cut. The sunshine had hit the plate glass window just so, and Niall had seen a display of wedding rings. Being married was never something he'd considered before; it hadn't even been a legal option until he was almost thirty-two, at which point he'd been with someone he didn't love.

Inside the quiet of the store, Niall had asked to see the rings. There were several styles to choose from, one with diamonds set inside the band, another with rainbow stones. In the end he chose two plain bands crafted from platinum.

"These are lovely, some of my favorites. Would you like to have anything inscribed on the inside?"

The damn rings were burning a hole in the pocket of his shorts. Since the day he'd picked them up, Niall had second-guessed himself, and now here he was, about to make a declaration in front of everyone he could call family. He was way out of his league. Grand gestures were not something he'd ever done, but... he knew asking Mat to marry him was important. Mat had never said anything, not even hinted at it—but still, Niall knew.

"What are you thinking about?" Shay asked. "Not regretting the test results already, are you?"

Niall hadn't noticed Shay approaching. Last Niall had known, Shay was down at the beach talking with Marshal and Trevor while Riley and Caleb waded in the water and Fenrir chastised them for being *in* the waves.

"Huh? No." Niall shook his head, looking over to where Mat was having a heated conversation with Ella and Alyson about whether or not Riley should be allowed a puppy. He didn't know why Ella was arguing; she was going to lose. Claribel seemed amused by the conversation. His hand strayed to his pocket, where he fiddled with the box for the hundredth time.

"You might as well do it and get it over with, otherwise Mat is going to think something's wrong. You've been avoiding him since everyone got here." Shay looked pointedly at Niall's pocket.

Just as Shay said that, Mat glanced over. Niall saw he was frowning and there was worry in his eyes.

"Well, fuck. How'd you know, anyway?"

"Just go do it." Shay made a shooing motion with his hands.

Niall tried his best to look nonchalant as he walked over to where Mat was sitting with the women. "Heya. Can I talk to you for a second?"

"Not like that, you bozo. Christ." Shay's voice came from behind him. Maybe *Niall* was regretting the results, if it meant Shay would be interfering every time he turned around.

"What?" Mat asked, glancing from Niall to Shay and back again.

"Now he's going to think he's done something wrong, or worse."

Niall swung around to his half brother. "Did I ask for your help?"

"No, but apparently you need it."

Mat came and stood beside Niall. "What's the matter?" he asked.

"I'm trying to ask you to marry me, but Shay keeps butting in," Niall spat out.

And suddenly, except for the people down at the beach, everything was silent.

Mat peered at him, his blue gaze uncertain. "Um, what was that?"

A hand gripped Niall's shoulder, pressing down. Getting the hint, Niall dropped to one knee. "Mat Dempsey"—he dug in his pocket for the rings—"would you do me the honor of marrying me?" He opened the box. The two rings gleamed in the early summer sunshine.

The inscription inside Mat's band read, *I'll always come home.*

"You are saying yes, right?" Shay prompted Mat.

This was not going at all as Niall had envisioned.

"Yes! Yes, I am saying yes. What I mean to say is, yes, Niall Hamarsson, I will marry you." Mat sounded a little breathless.

"Hold out your hand."

Mat held out his hand, and Niall thumbed one of the rings out of its snug spot and slipped it onto Mat's finger. It seemed a bit large.

"We can get it sized," Niall said gruffly.

Mat tugged on his biceps. "It's perfect. Get up here so I can kiss you."

Thankfully, Shay finally left them alone, wandering over to where his great-aunt waited.

"I can't believe you proposed," Mat whispered.

"I'm not sure I did. It might have been Shay," Niall groused.

"I love you, Niall."

"I love you too," Niall whispered into the shell of Mat's ear.

Unsurprisingly, Shay ended up being in charge of the barbecue.

2/4: Grab **Black Moon** *from your favorite retailer, or ElleKeatonAuthor, and begin reading right away!*

One corpse, two corpses, old corpse, new corpse.

Summer is crashing into fall, Mat and Niall have a wedding to overthink.

ABOUT ELLE

Elle's characters are snarky, a tad damaged, and definitely have minds of their own, but the mystery is always solved and hearts crossed. Currently, there are over forty Elle Keaton books available for you to read and many have been produced into audiobooks.

Romantic Suspense and Mystery Romance by Elle Keaton
Shielded Hearts
Veiled Intentions
West Coast Forensics
Reclaimed Hearts
Subtle Deceptions

For more information, to purchase signed paperbacks or audiobooks — or another ebook, please visit my website:
ElleKeatonAuthor

Thank you for supporting this indie author!

AFTERWORD

This is a work of fiction, created without use of AI technology. Any names, characters, places or incidents are products of the author's imagination and used in a fictitious manner. Any resemblance to actual people, places, or events is purely coincidental or fictional.

Elle Keaton's creative body of work cannot be used in any manner for the purpose of training AI.

The author, Elle Keaton, supports the right of humans to control their artistic works. **No part of this book has been created using AI-generated images or narrative, as known by the author.** The primary style sources used in the writing of this book are the online versions of the Merriam-Webster Dictionary and The Chicago Manual of Style. Due to their inherent limitations for fiction-writing and the author's personal style choices, there are instances where other style guide rules have been consistently applied. Region-based idioms, age- or era-appropriate slang, UK spelling and style rules, and other deviations based on specific dialects may inform some of these choices. Should you have questions, please contact the author at: dirtydog press@gmail.com

ACKNOWLEDGMENTS

I wish to acknowledge the following entities, copyrighted names that do not belong to me, corporations, and real people: I thank you in advance for letting my characters use them/you in my story.

Agatha Christie, I could only aspire to Miss Marple.

Boston Whaler, sorry I burned your boat.

Peter Falk and the character he created, *Columbo*

Kirk Cobain (RIP) and Nirvana for the song, *Come As You Are* from the album *Nevermind*

The **Disney** corporation for *Escape to Witch Mountain and Zootopia*

Indiana Jones and the Raiders of the Lost Ark, **LucasFilmLDT**

Jack Daniel's Tennessee Whiskey

Mack truck company, sorry. You sure do get blamed for a lot but we know it wasn't you.

Fatal Attraction, **Jaffe/Lansing productions and Paramount Pictures** (and Glen Close she was a bad ass)

Subaru, thank you for being so reliable and for letting Niall drive one of your cars.

Sincerely,

Elle Keaton